HER LAWLESS PRINCE

QURILIXEN LORDS: A QURILIXEN WORLD NOVEL

MICHELLE M. PILLOW

MICHELLEPILLOW.COM

This fearless cat-shifter never imagined she'd become the prey.

From NY Times & USA TODAY Bestselling Author, Michelle M. Pillow, a fantasy science fiction romance!

Cat-shifter Payton refuses to be tamed by any man.

Being the adult daughter of the fiercest shifter commander on the planet does NOT have its perks. Add to that the fact that she's also a princess, and Payton has spent most of her life besting the over-protective palace guards to enjoy moments of wild freedom.

She never imagined she'd need those skills to escape with her life.

When a mysterious stranger arrives spouting conspiracies about her people's future, she's sure he needs a one-way trip to medical supervision. But the infuriatingly seductive outlaw knows things about her he shouldn't–intimate things, embarrassing things. And when one of his warnings turns real and takes them captive, Payton is made a believer. She only hopes it's not too late to save her people from extinction.

A Qurilixen World Novel

The Playful Prince
The Bound Prince
The Rogue Prince
The Pirate Prince

Qurilixen Lords

Dragon Prince

Marked Prince

Feral Prince

Fire Prince

Her Lawless Prince

Poisoned Prince

Cursed Dragon

Captured by a Dragon-Shifter Series

Determined Prince

Rebellious Prince

Stranded with the Cajun

Hunted by the Dragon

Mischievous Prince

Headstrong Prince

Space Lords Series

His Frost Maiden

His Fire Maiden

His Metal Maiden

His Earth Maiden

His Woodland Maiden

Dynasty Lords Series

Seduction of the Phoenix

Temptation of the Butterfly

To learn more about the Qurilixen World series of books and to stay up to date on the latest book list visit www.MichellePillow.com

To my husband, John, and the adventure we are on every day.

VAR TERRITORY, PLANET OF QURILIXEN

Princess Payton of the Var had spent a lifetime escaping her cage. The wild inside her would build until it exploded if she hadn't.

Princess. The title represented so many contradictions.

Authority behind gilded cages.

Freedom on a schedule.

Power that must be tempered and controlled.

None of those restraints came naturally to a cat-shifter.

Since the moment she'd been born, Payton felt the wild inside her growling to get out. How could she not? Her mother was a space pirate. Well, her mother said *captain,* but since *Captain* Sam had kidnapped Payton's father in his white tiger form and tried to sell him on the Torgan Black Market, she could read between those big bold lines.

Her father, Prince Falke, was the Var commander. *The.* As in, the commander of all commanders. The top-ranking officer in the cat-shifter military who had control over soldiers and palace guards. He'd held the position for centuries. Perhaps it was his rigid control that caused her to rebel. She inherited his white tiger and understood how difficult that self-restraint had to be for him.

Payton had never met her grandfather, the late King Attor, but by all accounts, the man had been a hard disciplinarian who left more than a few scars on his five sons. Her grandmother had been one of Attor's many wives.

Payton's need to run free was why she now sprinted through the thick trees to escape the palace guards tracking her. Her parents wanted her in the safety of the palace when the Federation ships arrived. No one knew when they'd come, only that they would. After the shifters forced their soldiers off the planet in what amounted to a rebellion, the Federation would be forced to react.

Blast the Federation. She hoped their ships flew

into the deepest, darkest, nastiest black hole in all the universes.

Payton wanted all thoughts and worries to blow from her mind. Her heart pounded violent and strong. She let her body half shift with the form of a white tiger, so she stayed upright as the power of the cat entered her legs. White fur covered her skin, and claws extended from her nail beds. If she fully shifted, she would have to lose her clothing, and she didn't want to arrive naked at the settlement.

She heard the guards losing ground behind her, and a smile crossed her features. They could never catch her. She once hid alone in the forest for months with twenty men searching for her because she'd wanted to avoid visiting dignitaries.

Payton vaulted over obstacles in the thick underbrush and leaped to swing from branches. Her lungs burned, and her muscles strained. She had run the distance between the palace and the alien settlement of Shelter City so many times that she could travel the route with her eyes closed.

The euphoria that came from these fleeting moments of pure freedom was like a drug, and she was an addict. She wanted more. She wanted to keep running wild.

All too soon, the distant sound of metal clanging

on metal drew her back to reality. The sad beacon rang out over Shelter City as constant as canvas flapping in the breeze. Many shifters hated the settlement. Payton hated what it represented—the oppression of the Cysgodian people by the Federation and the Federation's attempt to establish permanence on her homeworld.

A virus had overrun the planet of Cysgod, and the Cysgodians had been desperate for a place to go. When the Federation brought their plight to the shifter royals on Qurilixen, how could they refuse them sanctuary? Qurilixen had three suns, two yellow and one blue. The blue's radiation had healing properties that could help the alien visitors. And it worked. In time they had healed.

Unfortunately, saving the Cysgodians came at a cost. The Federation used it as an excuse to set up a temporary base on Payton's homeworld as they claimed domain over the settlement. The Cysgodians lived but, in return, had been subjected to thirty years of the dysfunction that was the Federation's dictatorship over them.

The shifters were changing that. They'd chased the Federation away and were helping the Cysgodians build an independent life for themselves.

Payton grabbed a branch and launched herself

between two trees to land in a clearing. She automatically pulled the tiger back inside, alighted on the ground, and crouched in her human form.

"Oh!"

The soft word took her by surprise. She spun toward the sound, arms lifted and ready to fight. She'd been so focused on listening to the chase and enjoying the run that she hadn't paid attention to what might be in her path.

A man raised his arms to the side and took a step back. Dark brown eyes met hers, framed by strands of long black hair that escaped the tie at the nape of his neck. "Not a threat."

He wore what looked to be Cysgodian clothing, but they were a little too neat as if the holes had been sanded into newer material rather than by natural deterioration. She tilted her head to look at his temple. The slight discoloration of his black marking indicated he was indeed Cysgodian. All Cysgodians had the genetic trait, although in various colors, and it made it easy to pick them out of a crowd.

Payton lowered her hands and relaxed her stance. Though there was something familiar about the man, she was sure she'd remember seeing him in the alien settlement. She'd been sneaking into

Shelter City since its inception, and it could be assumed she had come across everyone more than once.

But not him.

His stoic expression and brooding face would have stood out. And those haunted eyes. His gaze didn't hold the usual blend of anger and resignation. It seemed troubled, searching. He didn't glance away from her in deference, knowing she was a shifter.

Cysgodians tended to fear shifters. For thirty years, both sides had watched each other from afar. Trust took time to build.

"You shouldn't be in the forest. It's not safe. You could get lost and starve," Payton said. "Go back to the city."

Lack of food wasn't the most dangerous threat. Some in the shifter community believed they'd done their duty by the Cysgodians and that it was time to send them on their way. Those factions were not opposed to forcibly escorting the aliens off-world to be done with it all. And, though Payton hated to admit it, a few feral cat-shifters would rather throw all aliens in a deep grave and bury them.

"Come with me," she instructed. "I'll escort you back to the city."

"You're her, aren't you?" The man studied her.

Payton arched a brow.

"You're the Var princess," he insisted. "Payton."

Payton nodded. She wasn't surprised that he recognized her. She and several of the other royals had been making their presence seen in the city since taking over from the Federation.

The man continued to stare at her, and she wasn't sure what to make of his forthright gaze.

"Yes," she answered when he didn't say anything else. "I'm Princess Payton."

His attention remained steady. He stepped closer, and she stepped back to keep the same distance between them. Intensity radiated from him as if his very existence depended on taking in every detail of her face. The focus made her nervous.

She listened to the forest to see if they were alone. Her cousin, Roderic, and one of the dragon princes had been attacked a few months earlier by a Cysgodian faction that wanted to drink shifter blood under a misguided attempt at immortality.

Is that why she didn't recognize him? Did he normally skulk around the city in a hooded cloak mumbling about blood magic and shifter oppression?

"Misplace your cloak?" she asked, half expecting

Blood Fanatics to jump out of the trees even though she didn't detect them.

He glanced down at his clothes and appeared confused.

"Never mind. Do you know where you are?" she asked.

"A forest?"

"The city is this way." Payton motioned that he should walk with her. "I'll show you back."

"I'm not lost," he said, moving to join her.

"Then what are you doing out here?"

"At the moment?" He gave a small laugh. "Walking with a princess."

The man made her nervous. Payton didn't fear for her physical safety. One swipe of her hand and she could claw him open. Instinct told her not to trust him, that he was not as he seemed.

"What is your name?" She became keenly aware of how close he walked as he matched his stride to hers. Her hand tingled, and she felt claws trying to extend from her fingers.

Why was the cat trying to come out now?

"Nyle." His eyes stayed intently focused on her. "May I ask you something?"

"No, it doesn't hurt to shift," Payton answered

before he could finish his thought. "Just as it does not hurt to breathe."

It wasn't exactly true. Yes, the shift was uncomfortable, but it was an old bone-cracking pain that she was used to. Non-shifters always wanted to know.

"That is not what I was going to ask," Nyle said.

"No, I will not shift for you." She wasn't some kind of genetic oddity made for entertainment. "I'm sure you've seen us shifted in the city already."

"Not that either."

Payton stopped walking. "Ask."

Nyle continued to study her. The intensity of it became unnerving. "Is it true your mother is a Ticaron princess? I look at you, but I'm not seeing it."

"She's half Ticaron." Payton frowned. "How do you know about that?"

"And your father, the cat-shifter commander of the royal armies, is half Roane on his mother's side, right?" he continued.

This time Payton didn't answer. How could he even know that? Though it wasn't exactly a secret, neither was it a well-known fact. Her family didn't talk about their lineage with outsiders.

Payton's mother, Princess Samantha, didn't

enjoy speaking of her Ticaron father. The man had tried to brainwash his daughter into complete obedience, and he'd poisoned her cat-shifter mate for not being worthy of joining the Ticaron family.

Not that Payton's paternal grandfather was much better. King Attor of the Var had been a calculating man who raised his sons to believe true love didn't exist, only loyalty. He'd started a war with the other race of shifters on the planet, the dragons, that lasted for centuries during his rule.

"You don't appear submissive like most Ticaron women, and most Roanes have very, uh..." Nyle let his words trail off, and he gave a light cough.

Payton's expression fell by small degrees into a frown as he spoke. What he probably wanted to say was that the Roane were renowned for their insatiable sexual appetites. They literally took energy from their sexual partners...not that the partners complained.

Was he trying to offer sex to her?

The thought took her by surprise. Sure, there had been a few visiting alien lovers, but their appeal rested in the fact they wouldn't be around too long to annoy her.

"You're one-fourth human, one-fourth Roane, one-fourth Ticaron, and—"

"I am Var," she stated firmly. Her hand balled into a fist.

"Yes, but I mean you're not just a Var. There are a lot of conflicting alien predispositions inside of you," Nyle insisted. "I find it fascinating. So, my question is, which one is dominant—"

"I do not want to punch you because I fear it will kill you," she managed through tight lips. "You are being overly familiar and will stop speaking to me now."

His mouth opened, and he looked surprised. He closed it and nodded once, not talking.

Payton walked faster. She'd interacted with several Cysgodians and still maintained that this man was off. She felt his eyes on her but didn't look in his direction to encourage conversation.

She took the easiest route through the trees to get to the top of the cliff that overlooked the city. The ugly stone structure of the Federation's stronghold stretched along the topside and stood dominant over the ravine. Metal arches crisscrossed over the roof, amplifying their signals into space. The whole structure lacked craftsmanship and imagination.

Halfway down the cliff on a wide ledge were the barracks that once housed the soldiers. The evenly spaced buildings had been built with military precision, each identical to the next and looking exactly as they had since the Federation put them up thirty years earlier. They now acted as apartments for Shelter City's citizens.

Payton finally looked at her traveling companion and asked, "Have you moved into the barracks, or are you still in the city?"

Not everyone had wanted to relocate from their homes.

Nyle eyed the top stronghold. Payton pointed down to the barracks. His gaze shifted downward.

"I don't live there," he said. It appeared as if he kept his gaze purposefully from her.

Payton found herself staring at his neck. Tiny dark strands clung to his flesh. The thought that all was not right tickled her mind, but she dismissed it as irritation after his rude questions about her family. "I think you can find your way to the city from here."

Nyle began to answer. "Thank—"

Payton strode away from him, cutting off his words. She went along the tree line toward the cliff-side path that would take her down to the city. Ignoring the gentle slope of the beginning, she hopped down from the top of the cliff and dropped several feet to the path. She breathed a little easier knowing his eyes were off her.

The man lingered in her thoughts as she rushed down the path. She paused as she reached a large misshapen tree that allowed privacy from those below and above. This was the only spot on the path that was secluded. It grew along the cliff's side, surviving both time and precipice.

Payton could identify with that tree. Strong roots held it firmly in a place it didn't belong. It would never move, never stop being a tree. Just as she would never leave the palace or stop being a princess. Her feet were rooted in duty and honor and all the things it meant to be a Var royal. Those brief moments of freedom were all she had to look forward to. Like when the wind blew through the tree's branches and delighted its leaves.

Hearing footsteps, she continued on her way, not wanting to be stopped in conversation.

The more she thought about it, the less she doubted Nyle had been offering sex when he brought up her Roane heritage. She refused to feel any kind of disappointment in the realization. She'd seen handsome men before and wasn't one to be swayed by a pretty face. Being involved with someone from the city was a mistake.

She'd never tell her cousin Roderic that. He'd married a Cysgodian woman. But really, that relationship was proof enough. The couple had a rough go of it, and Justina's people still looked at her funny.

Why was she even thinking about all of this? She didn't have time for relationships.

The city seemed oddly barren now that most of the population had moved to the barracks. Rusted metal ship parts helped create walls. They butted against stone and anything solid the Cysgodians had been able to scavenge. It was all strung together with chains and rope. Canvas hung between them to give shade, a necessity on a planet cast in constant daylight, but for the one night a year that all three suns set simultaneously.

Cysgodians lurked along the edges of the marketplace like the remaining ghosts of a dead town. They walked over the shadowed sidewalks of which the pieces of metal and warped boards were glued down by dried mud.

Payton couldn't blame them for not wanting to move to the barracks, even though they were nicer. This town had been the only one the alien visitors had known on Qurilixen. Given a choice, she'd probably pick the city over the barracks. She liked the open air more than the sterile interior walls.

When she focused her hearing, she detected the sound of teenagers running through a distant street. They still came down from the cliffside to roam their childhood playgrounds and camp in abandoned homes.

Gone were the days when she had to hide her identity from the crowd with layers of mud and costumes. She made her way quickly through the streets, turning down familiar alleys, before finally crossing a street to slip between two metal buildings.

The narrow opening was a close fit and not any path one would normally take, as it looked like a dead end. She turned sideways and slid down to the end before rounding a corner. A thick metal sheet overhead blocked the sunlight. As a shifter, her eyesight easily cut through the darkness. She turned another corner and stepped up before reaching a hidden door.

"Yevgen," she called softly as she pushed open the door without knocking. The cyborg had an irrational fear of the radiation from the blue sun, or so he claimed. She felt it had less to do with fear and more to do with the fact that he liked being stowed away in his secret dark lair.

A blue glow came from a wall of monitors. Payton had scavenged some of them for Yevgen. He used them to watch the city, something that had gotten less interesting without the people living in it.

The home had been constructed between the exterior walls of the surrounding buildings. The paint didn't match, and the walls cut in at uneven angles. His usual sling chair hung empty from the ceiling. Since the cyborg had not come to the planet with legs, he normally needed the chair to move around.

Payton's picture appeared on the center monitor. It had been taken probably twenty years ago while she'd snuck through an alleyway. A heart burst over her face and twinkled before disappearing. Yevgen had been the first to discover her identity in the city and had followed her with his nearly invisible cameras for years before she'd detected them. They'd formed a strange friendship.

She smiled at the screen and suppressed a laugh. "Come out of hiding. I'm alone."

The soft whirl preceded the thumps of mechanical feet as Yevgen slowly walked from behind the monitors. She had brought him the new legs. They'd been scavenged from another cyborg she'd defeated in a fight. The translucent skin showed the tubing and mechanics under-neath. He'd fashioned a pair of short pants over them. The dark material hung unevenly over his thighs.

"Welcome, Princess. It has been one hundred eighty-six hours since I have last seen you, but your beauty has not diminished a second."

"They increased the number of guards at the palace. It took longer for me to get away."

"I have not detected the Federation ships. You are safe with me, my princess." Yevgen had infil-trated the stronghold's computer system thanks to Payton sneaking him access.

"You've finally got them calibrated." Payton nodded in approval at the legs. His height matched hers as he took stunted steps toward her. "Well done."

Mechanical irises focused on her, and she knew her image would be reflected on the monitors, showing her what he saw.

"I have had extra time now that the city is empty," Yevgen answered, turning to the screens.

Various images of the city showed on them, some grainy, several flickering. Payton's eyes went to the Federation stronghold at the top of the cliff. Nyle wasn't there.

"No one has come for trades. It is very quiet," Yevgen said. "I miss the chaos."

A group of teenagers appeared. One swung a metal pipe at a wall as others watched in boredom. They sat against a building in the shade.

"Are you ready to move to the stronghold?" she asked. "We can keep you out of the sunlight."

He glanced away. The screens flickered with images of the past when the streets had been filled, as if to express his longing for the city to return to the way it had been when he could watch over it and log the many activities.

Payton again looked at the screen with the stronghold. "Yevgen, did you tell anyone about my grandparents? About who they were?"

"Do you mean King Attor? I discussed him with your cousin, Roderic. The old king had one hundred and sixty-three half mates, all off-worlders. He believed in emotional detachment and that life mates were the lot of lower society, for those who could not afford more than one wife or had no opportunity to negotiate with aliens for them." Yevgen smiled. "Are you saying you are ready for me to be your half mate?"

The cyborg wanted very much to love her. It had become a bit of an obsession. He brushed his fingers against her cheek. They felt like the flesh of a man, but underneath moved a metal skeleton.

"You are of a higher society and can have emotional detachment while I will love you," he insisted logically.

"Not King Attor. The others. Did you tell anyone about—?"

Yevgen's eyes flashed red, cutting off her words. Payton tensed as she listened for what had set off Yevgen's alarm. The monitors dimmed, casting the home into darkness.

2

NYLE GLANCED AT HIS WRIST, TRYING TO BLEND into his surroundings as he followed the signal on his wristband. It wasn't too difficult in the near-empty streets. He kept his head down and his path steady. No one appeared to care.

The city air smelled of rust and rotting wood. He imagined it to be an archeological site from some ancient civilization left to rot, only to be rediscovered centuries later by historians eager to peel away the secrets of who had once lived there.

However, this city was only thirty years old.

The shocking contrast of Shelter City compared to Cysgod caused guilt to rattle around inside of him. Cysgod had prided itself on clean living. Buildings were constantly washed and polished until they took on the sheen of wet glass. The air had been filtered, probably too much in hindsight. Natural immunities had diminished over the generations to be replaced by artificial ones.

More than the physical difference between pristine and wreckage was the feeling radiating from the Cysgodian people. There used to be so much pride that it crossed over into arrogance. Now defeat and bitterness lingered in their expressions.

Nyle's tracker led him to a large building. Someone had placed a rock in front of the door since the latch looked as if it had been struck by a heavy object. He kicked the rock aside and slipped into the dimly lit interior. He let the door swing closed behind him.

Light beams streamed through holes in the ceiling and walls to illuminate an eclectic collection of old engine parts and salvage scrap. Jagged pieces of metal had been cut from some of them, but the layer of dust said they hadn't been touched in many years.

More recent were the footprints in the dirt that tracked like children playing, as were the occasional handprints climbing up the side of scrap. Nyle tried not to think of the carefully manicured parks and gardens on Cysgod.

This was not how Cysgodian life was supposed to be.

Tiny particles of dust stirred as he dragged his fingers over the top of a disassembled engine. He followed the tracker to the side of the building and frowned as he reached the wall. The tracker indicated he needed to be on the other side, but he was close.

Nyle pressed his ear against the wall and heard a muffled voice, "...Attor. The others. Did you tell anyone about—?"

The sound stopped. Nyle ran his hand over the metal barrier, pressing at it to test its strength. When he checked along the wall, he couldn't find a door.

Taking the tracker from his wrist, he placed it against the wall and held down a button to activate a cutting laser. The device had originally been designed to help agents escape unfriendly situations and make their way back to a rendezvous point. Nyle had made a few modifications.

When he'd cut an opening large enough to fit through, he pushed at the wall to bend the metal back and slipped inside.

Nyle felt something press against his temple, and he stopped midway.

"What do you want?"

Though the tone was low, he recognized her voice. "Princess Payton?"

She snatched the tracker from his hand.

"Up. Slowly." She pulled whatever weapon she threatened him with from his head and took a step back.

His eyes instantly went to her as he obeyed. Though he'd seen images of her, he never imagined he'd run across her on this trip. She pointed a blaster pistol at his chest. He watched to see if her hand wavered, but she held steady. This woman would have no problem shooting him.

Not surprisingly, that only added to her attractiveness. Nyle had a weakness for unpredictable women. The moment he'd seen her leaping onto the path ahead of him, he'd been struck by her wild beauty. The flush to her cheeks as her lungs contracted and expanded filled him with desire. The feeling had rocketed through him, making words tumble out of his mouth.

Blue lights flickered and outlined monitors, the backs of which faced him to create a partition. The space had been built out of exterior walls, which explained why he'd had to cut his way inside.

"Interesting hideout you have here," Nyle

stated. He lifted his arms to the side to show he meant no harm.

"I like it. It suits me," Payton answered. "Or it did before you sliced a hole in my wall."

Nyle smiled and glanced around. "Sorry, Princess, but I wasn't talking to you, and this isn't exactly your wall."

He found it fascinating that this is where Yevgen's programming had led him. When he'd smuggled the cyborg onto the Federation ship, Nyle had never imagined the device would cobble together such an impressive command center hidden in the heart of the city. It would be a shame to have to destroy it all.

"Is it, Yevgen?" Nyle called out.

The soft whirl of mechanical limbs revealed where the cyborg hid on the other side of the partition. Nyle gestured around the monitors to indicate his intent before stepping in that direction to face Yevgen.

"Stop," Payton ordered. "I didn't invite you in."

"You live here, too?" Nyle glanced around in surprise.

Payton shrugged. "Consider it my second palace. What do you want?"

"To plug a hole," Nyle answered. "Reverse time. Fix a mistake that cannot be fixed."

Payton's gun lowered, and she frowned. He realized she wasn't serious about shooting him.

"Are you...unwell in the mind? Perhaps you are in need of medical supervision?"

"I feel like a man who's traveled a long way for a short conversation."

Payton re-aimed her weapon. "Who are you?"

"Cysgodian Nyle, bastard son of an unknown off-worlder and Diana," Yevgen answered. The cyborg finally showed himself.

Nyle flinched at the formal Cysgodian descriptor. It had been a long time since he'd heard it. "I prefer Nyle."

"You do not belong here," Yevgen answered. "You are supposed to be dead. Shoot him, my love. Set the universe to right. He is a traitor."

Nyle gently waved his hand to stop Payton but was distracted by Yevgen's words. He wasn't worried as he studied the cyborg. Yevgen didn't have it in his programming to attack. "My love? You think you love her? Do you think she can love you? A machine?"

Payton made a small noise. "He's not just a machine."

"I assure you, he mostly is." Nyle had built that machine. "The rest is just blood and tissue."

Yevgen furrowed his brow. "This is her palace. She is my wife, and so I declare it out loud by Var half-mating tradition as taught to me by Prince Roderic of the Var during our information exchanges. The data says she is for me, and we are well suited."

Payton gasped and started to speak. "Whoa—"

Love? Nyle couldn't help his burst of laughter as he cut her off.

"What happened to your wiring since you left the quarantine lab?" Nyle asked. "It's fascinating. You were supposed to monitor these people, not declare love for the natives."

Yevgen's irises contracted, and his eyes flashed with blue light. His head lowered, and his mechanical legs shifted back and forth in agitation.

"Hey!" Payton demanded, stepping toward the cyborg as if to physically protect him from the ridicule. "Don't laugh at him. He's a hero. He's helped save this city more times than I can count. And so what if he's my half mate? What do you care? You better get on your knees and bow to the Prince of Shelter City before I have you thrown into a prison ward for trespassing on Qurilixen, you traitorous pile of prongin droppings."

Nyle wasn't sure what a prongin was, but it didn't sound flattering.

"He's not capable of..." Nyle let his words trail off at Payton's expression. Though her words had been forceful and angry, they did not match her eyes. Her gaze begged him to stop talking.

His tracker gave a low, long tone, and he instantly reached for his wrist, only to realize Payton still had it.

"You need to hand that to me—" Nyle ordered.

"You heard my wife." Yevgen suddenly charged forward, swinging his arm. "On your knees."

Nyle lifted his hands in surprise to defend himself, but the cyborg struck him on the side of the head. As he crumpled to the ground, all he could think was that the attack should not have been possible.

3

"Yevgen, what have you done?" Payton shoved the blaster to Yevgen and kneeled by Nyle to check his pulse. "He's alive. Get me the handheld medic."

"He is not supposed to be alive." Yevgen didn't move. The light from the monitors flashed behind him.

Payton frowned, not understanding all that was happening. Yevgen had never seemed the murderous type. Nyle was Cysgodian, but not from Shelter City. That shouldn't have been possible. They'd been told all the others were dead. Maybe a few had been off-world when the Cysgod outbreak happened? It's not like there had been time to do a proper census when trying to evacuate an entire planet.

"We cannot be seen abusing Cysgodians when we just ran off the Federation for that exact transgression." The device in her hand gave another low tone. She handed it to Yevgen. "Deal with this thing."

"He is breathing," Yevgen stated. "My preliminary analysis of the situation states that it would be best if he stopped."

"What is wrong with you?" Payton muttered as she moved to retrieve the handheld unit for herself. She went around the partition to search by the monitors. Finding it shoved on the side of Yevgen's sling chair, she grabbed it.

The image of a much younger Nyle on the screen caught her attention. His hair was shorter, and he stood rigid, posing for a photo amongst a group of Cysgodian scientists. She recognized no one else.

Payton leaned closer. "Yevgen, what is this?"

As if in answer, the image disappeared to be replaced by bodies lining a street. A fire burned in the background as two men in black jumpsuits carried a corpse toward it. More photos of death followed, which were bad on their own, but it was the people who had still been alive that made Payton want to look away. Their raw grief and suffering went beyond anything imaginable. Sickness had taken hold in them, and they knew they were destined for the funeral pyres.

Payton had heard stories and saw a few pictures the Federation provided when they were pleading with the shifter royals to allow the survivors safe harbor.

"Are these from Cysgod? Where did you get these?" Payton asked. An alien language appeared on the screen next to the photos. "I can't read it."

The image flickered, and the words were translated into the Old Star Language so she could understand them.

"All survivors to receive medical screening before boarding the Federation ships for quarantine ride to a new location. General Sten assures the population that all will be cared for with the highest standard possible," Payton read aloud, only to mumble, "well, Sten's a blasted liar."

Nyle's group photo reappeared.

"Virus transmission linked to scientific laboratories." Payton frowned. *"Citizen evacuations started this morning with several non-medically cleared people left to die without medical staff to tend to the*

sick. Though I had no symptoms, I was denied entry and escorted to Central Hospital. Within our numbers, Ranald, a technician with Yeven Genetic Cyborgtronics Laboratories, claims that the virus originated in a cyborg tissue-growing facility where he was employed. The goal had been to create superior organs to prolong cyborg lifecycles.

"Though he was unable in his last breaths to give me a full breakdown of the science, he supplied me with this photograph of the lab superiors in charge of the project so that they may be identified amongst any chosen survivors and properly questioned. Also, Ranald gave me a warning. The formulas remain in lockdown at Yeven Genetic.

"Several of us will attempt to destroy the facility so that no other people will be exposed to this virus. With luck, this, my last newspaper chip article, will be sent in time to be within transmission range of the ships. To those who have gone ahead, we who have been left behind wish you peace. May all the Federation's promises come to fruition. Remember us. Remember us all, and the deaths that did not need to—"

The low tone of the device sounded again, interrupting her.

"Yevgen, where did you find this virus data?

Why haven't we seen it before?" Payton glanced around the partition at him. He wore the wrist device and walked back and forth in the small space, watching the screen.

Nyle still lay unconscious on the ground. Had he been responsible for the virus? Why was he here now? Did he work with the Federation?

Payton carried the handheld toward the unconscious man. She kneeled on the ground and lifted the medic unit next to his temple, only to hesitate. His lids were partially opened. She remembered the feel of those eyes staring at her as they walked the forest path to the city. Instinct had told her things were not right with him and not to fear him. Had it been wrong? At the time, she'd thought he was lost.

"Nova traded her father's old newspaper chip for information," Yevgen said as he continued to pace. "It was not a priority as I was instructed to gather information about Federation wrongdoing in Shelter City before their ships arrived."

Payton pressed the handheld to Nyle's temple to scan for injury but didn't wake him up.

Yevgen was right. The Federation's impending visit was a top priority on the planet. Solving the old mystery of the virus was important, but thirty years' worth of damage had already been done. Knowing which laboratory to blame didn't help the shifters keep the Federation from trying to stake claim to Qurilixen territory. Still, they would want Nyle alive for questioning about it.

One problem at a time.

The Federation would want answers as to why the shifters had expelled General Sten and his men off the Qurilixen base—a station that was meant to be temporary. The soldiers had overstayed their welcome, but that was a moot point in the scheme of intergalactic politics. They had claimed the right as guardians to the Cysgodian refugees. Without reason, to kick them off-world sooner would have been an act of war. Now the shifters needed to justify their actions to prevent that war.

The low tone sounded, again interrupting her thoughts.

"What is that thing?" Payton asked. The hand-held medical unit indicated that Nyle had a bruise inside his head and that pressure rendered him unconscious. The cyborg had whacked him good.

"It appears to be tracking me," Yevgen answered, holding the device out and turning in a circle. "I am a red light."

"I think it found you. Maybe shut off the noise." Payton again hesitated, not pushing the button that would inject the medicine needed to wake Nyle up. "He knows how to find this place. What are we going to do with him?"

"He is not supposed to be alive. You have my logical vote." Yevgen reached for the blaster pistol she'd dropped and handed it to her. The low tone sounded again.

Payton closed her eyes in annoyance and took a deep breath. "What the hell did this guy do to you? I've never seen you act like this. Did he make you in that Yev-whatever-cyborg lab?"

Yevgen tilted his head in thought. His eyes flashed an array of different colors. "Yes. I suppose this is my creator. I believe he put his blood inside me to make me."

"Well, put away your thoughts of patricide," Payton ordered. "We're not killing him. We're going to ask him questions. We need to know why he's here. Why now? Did the Federation send him to stop you from helping us collect evidence?"

She pressed the button and let the handheld inject Nyle. Within seconds, he was blinking. He flung his arms up in defense and wriggled on the ground before settling when he realized the attack had ended. His eyes went from Payton to Yevgen and then back again.

"We have to run," Nyle said.

The low tone sounded.

Nyle pushed up from the ground and held out his hand for the tracker. Yevgen pulled his wrist away, clearly not parting with his new toy.

"Hold your finger over the screen and press down hard," Nyle said.

Yevgen frowned but obeyed.

Payton gestured the pistol at Nyle. "This better not hurt him."

"Lift it," Nyle said, again reaching as if he could will Yevgen to give the device to him.

Yevgen lifted his finger. "I am gone. There are blue dots."

"Blast it!" Nyle swore under his breath. "Where? How many?" He looked at Payton, not waiting for an answer. "You need to hide. Or run. Run and hide. Just get out of here."

Payton had no intention of doing any such thing. "Who is it?"

Yevgen moved around to the front of the monitors.

"They're people you don't want anything to do with," Nyle answered. "Give me the blaster."

"I see them," Yevgen said. "Three men, two women, humanoid, heavily armed."

Payton pointed the weapon at him instead of handing it over. She gestured for him to go around to the front so she could see what Yevgen had found.

"Only five?" Nyle frowned.

"Who are they?" Payton again asked. Five figures in matching burgundy uniforms made their way across the screen. "They're dressed more like a space crew than military. How are you all sneaking on-world? Our communications towers should have picked up your signatures."

"We have to destroy this console." Nyle lunged for Payton's hand and swung the blaster toward the monitors. He squeezed her finger, forcing her to fire the weapon. She jerked back, and the blaster flew from her hand.

Sparks erupted over the displays as they fizzled and died.

"No!" Yevgen reached for the monitors as if he could save them.

"Hey!" Payton grunted in protest as she pushed Nyle away. Fur sprouted over her skin, and claws erupted from her fingertips.

"They can't have access to this information portal," Nyle said. "We need to run."

He began leading the way toward the opening he'd cut.

"They are coming that way," Yevgen said, pulling Payton in the opposite direction toward the door. "You go this way, my princess."

"Yev, you're coming with me," Payton said.

Yevgen shook his head. "I will remain here with my equipment. A space captain must go down with his ship."

"Because he has no choice," she muttered. "He's in deep space without a pod."

She used to think that a lack of reactive fear was a great cyborg trait. Now, not so much.

Payton didn't have time to argue. "You declared that you are my half mate. It's your job to protect me. So, protect me."

He considered her statement and then nodded. "Of course, my wife. I'm recalibrating my priorities."

A loud pop sounded overhead. Yevgen wrapped his arms around her like a shield. Debris rained down on them. Yevgen grunted and fell back. She saw the blue light of his eyes flash and go dark.

Light streamed from above. Nyle appeared from behind the partition. He started to run toward her but smoke billowed from the ground, hiding him. Payton reached for Yevgen's arm, hoping to get him out the door, but with one smoky breath, she was on her knees.

Nyle's hand reached from the smoke toward her, across Yevgen's body. His fingers curled before his hand dropped.

"Which ones do we take?" a man asked.

"The console is dead," another added. Sparks punctuated his words, lighting the smoke.

Payton tried to push up from the ground, but her arms shook.

"All of them," a woman answered. "We need to get them out of here before our ship is detected, and we don't need this shifter sounding an alert to her people. We'll sort it later and jettison whomever we don't need into the deep black once we're far away from this infected hellhole."

A foot pressed into Payton's back harder than was necessary, forcing her to the ground.

"Easy, sweetheart, go to sleep now." The man's gruff voice wasn't exactly soothing.

Payton tried to growl, but the only thing that came out was a gurgle as she fell into complete darkness.

4

Payton felt as if a vise pressed against her back and chest, locking her into place. Each breath was hard won, like drawing air through a tiny hole. The urge to shift and fight became strong, but something kept her body from expanding into cat form. Trying was painful.

"Oh, hey, easy," a soft voice soothed. Someone held her head and petted her hair away from her face. "I'm sorry you got caught up in this. I'm going to figure a way out of here."

Out of...?

Payton pushed away from the voice and scrambled to find her bearings. Her body tingled, again wanting to shift protectively, but she couldn't complete the transition. Her vision remained blurry, and she felt as if lights came at her. She swiped her hand, only finding air.

She tried to gulp for breath, but her lungs wouldn't fill. Payton grabbed at her chest. Her fingers glided over the slick material.

"Easy, princess. You are unharmed. Don't be frightened."

Payton blinked several times before being able to focus. She touched her hair where he'd been stroking her, scratching to erase the lingering sensation of his hand.

Nyle crouched on the floor, reaching for her. She looked at his fingers, remembering them coming from smoke.

"Where...?" She glanced at the silver walls and ceiling. Cold metal pressed into her bare feet. Thin rows of light crossed at the seams in the metal panels. The room was empty but for a large rectangular platform next to the wall and a mat on the floor where she'd been sleeping. The platform was empty. "Spaceship?"

Were they in space?

How in all the black holes were they in space? How long had she been out?

Payton had been on a few spaceship flights with her mother's old shipmates. Rick was one heck of a pilot and liked to give them thrills by spinning through the skies and pretending the controls weren't working. All the Var royal children had to go up as part of their training. If forced, Payton could probably fly a small ship—with some trial-and-error judgment. Her mother had insisted they learn. Unlike her brother, she didn't yearn for space travel, at least not anymore. She used to want to stow away on the ships, but now she found them to be too confining, like being locked in a building surrounded by blackness and death. She loved the forest, the fresh air, and the ability to run free.

Payton pulled at her tight shirt. When it didn't loosen, she extended her claws and tried to cut it. As she slashed through the material, she scratched her flesh. The material instantly sealed back together.

"It's a constriction suit," Nyle explained. "Fetish wear. The nanotech keeps the wearer from breaking free. You need a device to deactivate the cloth."

Payton tried to cut through faster and pulled it apart, but the material moved over her fingers like water and reformed. "Why am I in fetish wear?"

If their captors thought she was going to serve

any fetishes, they better think again. She'd rip the manhood of any slargnot who tried to come at her.

When she glanced up at Nyle, his eyes were on her chest, watching. "My guess is they realized it could keep shifters and other alien species who swell their forms from expanding."

Payton grimaced. "They apparently don't want us breathing either."

"You are less scared than I thought you'd be." Nyle leaned his head back against a wall and shut his eyes. He looked as if he had been awake for a long time. Had he been watching over her? Why?

Payton stopped pulling at her clothing and studied him. "Fear doesn't serve me now."

That didn't mean the feeling wasn't there but dwelling on it wouldn't change the fact that she was far from home. What had her father always said?

"When battles seem to be at their lowest and most dire, focusing forward is the only way through."

"Who are they? What do they want with us?" She didn't think it was a coincidence that their kidnappers appeared moments after Nyle. "What do they want with *you?*"

Nyle opened his eyes to look at her. "What makes you think they are after me?"

"Because I didn't do anything." Payton pushed

up from the floor and took several deep breaths. Her thinking cleared by small degrees. "And if they wanted to kidnap and drug a member of the royal family, there are easier targets than—"

Payton stiffened.

"What?" he asked.

"Where's Yevgen?" she asked. "I saw the light go out in his eyes. Did they take him too?"

Nyle pointed behind her.

Payton turned and moved toward the platform. Behind it, shoved in a corner, was Yevgen. His cyborg eyes didn't glow with power. Blood stained the side of his shirt. She wasn't sure how much blood a cyborg carried, but it looked like he'd lost a lot by the breadth of the dried crimson. How had she not smelled it earlier? Now the unmistakable scent filled her head, and she could smell nothing else.

Payton fell to her knees next to him and gave his body a light shake. She put her hand on his chest, trying to feel a heartbeat but finding cold flesh over his metal frame instead.

He was dead.

"Oh, no, Yev." Tears filled her eyes. "No. No. No. Yevgen."

She gave him another shake. The cyborg didn't

respond. The pain of grief rolled through her at the loss of a friend. She'd never worried about his mortality, always assuming he'd survive well past her hundreds of natural years.

"I'm sorry about your...uh, husband-mate," Nyle said. He didn't sound as if he meant it.

"Don't you care at all? You created him," Payton insisted.

"I have a creator's fondness and a scientist's curiosity, perhaps," Nyle said.

"You're his father."

"I wouldn't go that far." He shook his head. "It's like a pilot has a fondness for his restored ship, or a chef for his favorite electric knives. They're objects. Not people."

"Knives don't talk back." Payton wasn't sure why she wanted to argue with this man, only that she wanted to invoke compassion in him for her friend.

"They're all tools built to aid in a function. Computers talk, but we don't miss them when they're gone. Yevgen's function is to process and communicate information. He was built to help the Cysgodian people. From what I gathered from his little secret fort, he's been doing that. Though, I will say, those legs are a surprise. It would appear something in his programming has encouraged self-improvements. If he hadn't become so dangerous, I'd find it fascinating."

She wanted him to stop talking about her friend like he was simply a computer. "Yevgen has... He's... He was..."

"What? Alive?" Nyle chuckled.

"Yes." Payton nodded.

"I suppose I could thank you for the compliment, but facial patterns and human mannerisms weren't my departments."

"He was alive. He felt things." Payton took a deep breath, trying to pull her grief back into the realm of realism. "Or he tried to feel things. I can think of nothing more human than persevering in the face of failure. Who are you to say he wasn't?"

When she glanced back at him, Nyle looked as if he felt sorry for her. "As I said before, he was built to help process and communicate information. His directive was to take care of the Cysgodians. That is what you witnessed."

Payton felt irritation bubbling inside of her. She didn't want his pity. "I think it's time you told me exactly what is going on. And we're not talking about anything else until I know the truth. Why are they doing this?"

"Yevgen somehow gained access to information he shouldn't have. He also managed to hack into the Federation database. I'm not sure how he accomplished it, but clearly, his artificial intelligence grew beyond normal parameters. Though to be honest, our initial intellect projections didn't go out thirty years." Nyle appeared next to them. "It's the same reason I came to find him and shut down his operation."

Payton had been the one to give Yevgen access to the database so that he could help them collate data evidence to keep the Federation Military off their planet. Her people still needed that information. Without it, what was to keep the Federation from deleting their wrongdoing, blaming everything that couldn't be erased on a rogue general, and invading Qurilixen anyway? "What did he find?"

"Nothing that should concern a princess from Qurilixen," Nyle tried to dismiss.

"I'm not having the best of days. Now, I never thought of myself as a violent person, but something about you makes me want to hit you. Hard." Payton steadied her gaze. "Want to try that answer again? Maybe a little less patronizing?"

"I might have to disagree. The first time we met, you threatened me. The second, I ended up unconscious. And now, the third, I'm again being threatened. You may be more forceful than you think." He locked his gaze on hers. "Can I ask you something? Because I'm exceedingly curious to know the answer. What is it about this cyborg that made you marry him?"

"Yevgen knocked you unconscious, not me. Stop trying to change the subject. This mission of yours wouldn't have anything to do with that newspaper chip picture of you that he uncovered, would it? Maybe you're only here to make sure your secret doesn't get out."

"Answer my question, and I'll answer yours."

Payton sighed. This man was exasperating. "Yevgen is a hero. He saved many lives, including mine. Many times. I saw no reason not to give him what he wanted. It's not like I plan on finding a life mate. Now your turn."

"No."

That was it. She was going to hit him. And no one could say he didn't deserve it.

He glanced at her balled fist. "The answer is no. This isn't about the newspaper chip picture he uncovered."

"But the article connects you to the virus," Payton argued. What else could it be?

Payton lightly touched her friend's cheek, willing a spark of life into his eyes. Nothing happened.

"You know he's a machine."

"We've established that fact. But what I think you mean to say is that he doesn't love me back." Payton let loose a long sigh. Her feelings were clearly beyond Nyle's understanding. How could she make someone understand loyalty and friendship if they didn't already know it? "It doesn't matter to me that he's a cyborg. I'm not a machine. He's my friend. All he wants is to understand love. Sometimes the yearning for something is enough."

"No." Nyle shook his head and knocked his fist on Yevgen's metal chest plate. "I mean, he's a machine. I can try to reboot him. If there isn't too much damage, he'll be mostly the same."

Payton placed her hand over Nyle's to stop the knocking. A tiny shock of awareness went up her arm, and she quickly drew away. That feeling had nothing to do with the desire to hit him. She flexed her fingers and stood, needing to put distance between them. The sensation had been unexpected.

"You can fix him?" Payton asked.

The room felt too small. The tight compression of the suit left her light-headed. It also made her very aware of every nerve and muscle in her body. She sat on the rectangular platform.

"Not without tools," Nyle answered, even as he lifted Yevgen's bloody shirt to check the tubing along his side. "And an infusion."

"What information did he find?" Payton tried not to stare at Nyle's hands as he worked.

"I'm not sure what our kidnappers think he knows," Nyle said. "He probably hacked several things he shouldn't have when in the Federation database."

"Do you know who has us?"

"Mercenaries for hire. I thought I had a bigger head start and would be off the planet before they arrived. I managed to tag them with my locator while we were all on Torgan. Rumors of Yevgen's breach had made their way onto the black market. I was there to erase the intel of his location, but I wasn't fast enough. Luckily, not many people cared to pay for the information before I arrived. Of the handful who did find out, few people want to fly out to the X Quadrant to fetch an outdated cyborg.

Qurilixen isn't exactly on any main flight routes. But I'm guessing our mercenaries have Federation contacts or plan on blackmailing them. Either way, these are not people we want to be stuck on a ship with."

The thought gave no comfort, not that he had meant it to. Payton wondered if her family knew she was gone by now. Probably not. If their communication towers didn't see this ship land (something that was troubling in and of itself), they might not start looking for her for weeks. After slipping the palace guards again, they would think she was roaming the forest. Her best chance was if one of her cousins went to check in with Yevgen and found the cyborg missing and signs of a skirmish.

"What information did he find that you are after?" she asked.

"Clues to a scientific formula that was meant to be lost." Nyle pulled down the shirt and started twisting Yevgen's head. "It needs to stay lost."

Payton had to look away. Cyborg or not, she couldn't watch Nyle decapitate her friend. "Tell me about the formula."

The sound of twisting stopped. Yevgen's head remained attached.

"It's the kind you don't want out in the universes," Nyle said.

Payton gave an exasperated sigh. Whatever they used to knock her out had left her with a slight headache. "Your non-answer answers are annoying. We're trapped in space, presumably because of this information, and you want to talk to me in riddles?"

His eyes met hers, and he struggled to answer.

Payton felt her claws extending from her fingers. She wanted to punch something until all her aggravation was spent. This metal box of a room was not good for her mental health. "When I was losing consciousness, I heard a woman say something about jettisoning us into the deep black. I'd like to know why I'm dying."

"The virus," he whispered, the sound so faint she barely heard it even with her shifter hearing.

"You mean—?"

His look cut her off, and he nodded. He came to sit next to her. Leaning close, his mouth came close to her cheek. Her breath caught as his heat radiated onto her skin.

He whispered into her ear, "I was able to scan the room for cameras with the tracking device Yevgen took from me. We're not being watched, and I don't think they're listening, but this is a ship, and I believe we should err on the side of caution. If they don't know about it, I don't want to give them the idea to look for it. Right now, they're most likely tasked with collecting Yevgen. My best guess is they don't know what he knows, only that he knows something."

Payton tried to lean back to look at his face, but he moved with her, keeping his cheek close to hers. His hand touched her hip, holding her next to him. She remembered the newspaper chip article from Cysgod's last days.

Ranald gave me a warning. The formulas remain in lockdown at Yeven Genetic. Several of us will attempt to destroy the facility so that no other people will be exposed to this virus.

"Your cyborg friend should never have been in that database. Not only did he have access to the Federation's secrets, but he also opened a portal that let them peek into his. I don't know if they looked, but if they found it, they could know everything *he* knows."

She felt Nyle breathing. It tickled her skin, and she heard each slow intake and release of air. She couldn't help but wonder if worrying about someone listening was an excuse not to have to answer her questions about the virus. Was he being paranoid? Cautious? Evasive?

"Please, stop asking questions," he insisted. "Think of the kind of person who would buy a planet killer. We can't let that happen."

Payton nodded.

"I'm sorry you were dragged into this, Princess."

"You can back away now," she said, all too aware of him.

The hand on her hip instantly lifted, and he pulled away.

Now was not the time to entertain inappropriate thoughts with a man she shouldn't trust. Payton needed Nyle on her side. One, they were kidnapped together so they both wanted to escape. Two, she needed him to repair Yevgen. That second need was complicated. She wasn't sure if it was in Nyle's best interest to reactivate the cyborg. He might fry Yevgen and make sure all his secrets remained erased.

"I know you don't trust me," he said as if reading her thoughts.

"I didn't say that."

"Your expression did. You're not one to hide your feelings, are you?"

To her surprise, she gave a small laugh. "So I've been told."

"I like that about—" Nyle's words were cut off by the sound of the door sliding open.

Payton stood, claws extended and ready to fight. Nyle tried to step in front of her like a shield.

One of the burgundy-clad mercenaries stood in the entrance, filling it with his large size. Payton stepped to the side to better watch their captor. The tips of his brown hair had been colored with silver, not exactly military standard. He had been one of the mercenaries on Yevgen's surveillance.

"You need to let us go," Payton demanded. "Now."

"Stow it," the man ordered. She recognized his voice as the one who had stepped on her back unnecessarily hard in Yevgen's home. He held an injector in one of his hands.

"Leave her alone. She doesn't need to keep sleeping," Nyle said. "We'll behave."

Payton frowned. She had no intention of behaving.

"What do you want with us?" Nyle asked. "You've had us in here for days."

Days? Payton took a deep breath. There went any hope of being close to home. If they managed to take control of the ship, how difficult would it be to fly back to Qurilixen? Sure, she might be able to figure out *how* to fly it, but to navigate using an alien computer system? She had to pray to the gods that the computer database used the Old Star language so she could at least understand it. The universes were vast, and finding Qurilixen might prove impossible without help.

It looked like she had no choice. Yet again, she needed Nyle. Trusting him would still prove to be difficult, but she couldn't get out of this on her own. He was the only one who could fix Yevgen and possibly find her homeworld.

"Well?" Nyle insisted.

"You're going to repair the cyborg," the man stated. He retracted the injector without coming after her with it.

Nyle tried to move in front of her. "Why would I do that?"

Payton again stepped in the opposite direction to watch their captor.

"I assume you want to eat sometime soon," the mercenary stated.

"Nah, I've been looking for an excuse to diet," Payton quipped. If she had gone days without food, that would explain the pain in her head.

The man glanced over her as if she were nothing and then said to Nyle, "Do it or we launch your woman into the black, after we have a bit of fun with her first."

"Touch me, and you will have the full force of the Qurilixen army on your ass," Payton warned.

"Right," the man drawled sarcastically. "Because I'm worried about a bunch of kittens attacking in deep space. No one knows where you are. Help is not coming."

Anger won.

Payton let claws sprout from her hand, and she started toward him. "You should—"

The man lifted his hand. The shirt around her chest tightened, cutting off her words. He pointed a device at her.

"Stop!" Nyle ordered.

"Blast...you...to..." Payton gasped. She fell to her knees and clawed at her chest, fighting for each tiny breath.

"Release her." Nyle charged the man and swung. He landed a blow across the mercenary's cheek. The compression garment's control fell to the floor as the mercenary shoved Nyle across the room. Nyle pushed off the wall and went right back into the fray.

Payton crawled for the remote and slapped her hand desperately against it. The garment tightened. She heard the men fighting. She hit it again.

Suddenly, the nanotech released, showering down around her in tiny pieces like sand.

Kitten this, slargnot!

Payton inhaled deeply. Her body instantly shifted into full cat form, and she pounced. Her shoulder nudged Nyle aside as she landed on their captor's chest. The momentum slid them out of the holding cell into the corridor. She roared as she pressed her claws to his neck.

A blaster shot past her head.

"Back off," a woman yelled. She was the same one who'd ordered all three of them to be taken prisoner from Yevgen's home. Slicked, short black hair gave her angular face a severe expression, made more so by the piercing glare of her green eyes. A smudge of black had been smeared beneath her right eye.

Payton roared. The woman kept one pistol aimed at Payton and pulled another from the holster at her waist to point at their holding cell.

"I said back off," the woman warned. "Or I'll shoot both of you and find someone else to repair the cyborg."

Payton felt her claw snag flesh. One slash and the mercenary wouldn't be rejoining his crew.

The woman fired. Nyle grunted in pain.

Payton lifted her paw. The mercenary shoved at her chest. She let him push her aside but kept her movements slow so that he knew it was her choice to let him live.

"Fuse, get your ass off that floor," the woman ordered. "I told you not to play with the prisoners. If you're so bored, go fetch them something from the food simulator before I let her eat your worthless hide."

The large mercenary obeyed, grumbling, "Yes, Captain Rita."

The woman didn't have Fuse's respect, but she clearly inspired his fear. Fuse marched down the corridor almost like a pouting child simmering with rage.

Payton growled low in the back of her throat.

Rita motioned with the weapons. "Get back in there, beast. You'll return to the compression suit if you know what is good for you. Otherwise, we might begin to think you're more trouble than you're worth."

Payton remained shifted as she kept her gaze on the captain. When she finally moved, she kept each step measured to convey that she was in complete control. These captors needed to know she wasn't scared of them.

She detected the smell of Nyle's blood but heard his steady breathing and knew he wasn't in danger of dying from the wound.

"Get me a list of what you need to repair the cyborg, Dr. Nyle," Rita said when Payton had returned to the room.

"I'm not a doctor," he answered. "What makes you think I can fix him?"

"If you insist, Cysgodian Nyle, bastard son of an unknown off-worlder and Diana. We know you built him, and we know you can repair him," Rita said. "Get me the list of what you need. I don't want to kill the shifter, but if you force my hand I will, and it will not be pleasant. All we want is the cyborg."

Payton gave another low growl, still not shifting back to her human form. The animal inside her was too agitated and did not want to give up control.

"Before you get any more ideas, there are only two ways off this ship," Rita continued. "One is with my permission. The second is to eject yourself into the deep black."

Payton and Nyle didn't move.

Rita pointed along the wall. "Decontaminator is in that corner. Use it. You both smell of squalor."

The captain stepped back and waved her hand over the wall scanner. The door slid shut, locking them inside.

"I think that escape plan went well," Nyle muttered sarcastically.

Payton forced her body to shift back to human form. Staring at the door, she swore, "I'm going to throw that woman out into the deep black before this is all over."

Nyle cleared his throat.

Payton turned her attention toward him. He glanced down her body before averting his gaze. Realizing she was naked without the compression outfit, she held out her hand. "Give me your shirt. I'm not putting that monstrosity back on."

Nyle sneaked another peek before again turning his eyes to the far end of the room. He did as she said, pulling his shirt over his head. Blood trailed down his arm from the blaster shot, but the graze looked superficial.

Payton chuckled as she took the shirt from him. As a shifter, she was used to nudity. It's not like their clothing magically morphed forms with them or absorbed into the skin. Sure, with a half shift they still were upright, and Var clothing made allowances. Shifting into full cats left them naked. A forest full of lost clothing outside the palace proved that point.

"You're looking a little flushed." She pulled on the shirt. It was infused with the heat and scent from his body. A shiver rolled over her. "Is it the arm?"

He glanced in her direction. "I'm a man, and you're beautiful naked. I'm lucky all you notice is *flushed*."

The honest answer took her by surprise.

He ignored his wound as he stood and moved toward Yevgen in the corner.

"You can't give them what he knows," Payton said. "You can't reboot him here."

The shifters needed the evidence Yevgen had found, especially if the information wasn't recoverable from the cyborg's damaged console. She couldn't let their captors access it, and she couldn't allow Nyle to erase him.

"I have to look like I'm trying until we come up with a plan to get all of us out of here." He pulled down Yevgen's short pants to expose his hip. "I think the first step will be to remove these legs and make him more portable. If we must run, we'll need to carry him."

Payton wanted to protest. Yevgen loved his new legs. But Nyle was right. This was about survival.

She sat back on the platform to watch and let her bare feet dangle over the side. Without the compression, her stomach felt the emptiness from not eating. Closing her eyes, she listened to Nyle's movements. "Let me know if I can be of help."

NYLE TRIED TO KEEP HIS EYES OFF THE VAR princess. Mapping Yevgen's new wiring to the legs gave his hands something to do, but his mind strayed back to the image of the sexy woman standing naked before him. How was a man supposed to concentrate with that on his mind?

It wasn't like he hadn't seen naked women. In fact, back in his laboratory days, he'd helped build several female models before settling on Yevgen.

What didn't help was that he'd developed a small fascination with the princess while watching Yevgen's feeds before arriving on Qurilixen. Solo space travel could be very, *very* lonely. Fantasies of the princess had proven to be a more enjoyable way to pass the hours.

Now she was here in the flesh.

"How did you know?"

Nyle stopped studying the tubing in Yevgen's hip and glanced at her. The nanomaterial from her previous outfit remained scattered over the floor. His shirt hung over her like a short dress to reveal the long length of her legs. She leaned on the platform, resting her shoulders and neck against the wall. The position left her in half-repose. The image did nothing to calm the thoughts swirling in his brain.

"How did you know that Yevgen was in the Federation database?" she clarified when he didn't answer.

Nyle paused to check his wristband for any new signals. When he was reasonably sure no one was listening, he answered, "I've always known what he was doing. When I stowed him on the Federation ship, I made sure I had a link to him. I piggybacked off the—"

"Piggy-what?"

"I hid a signal in the Federation's inventory report transmissions," he explained. "Whenever they sent in their reports, I received information from Yevgen. It was the only system I had time to infiltrate while the Federation loaded citizens."

Nyle liked that he didn't have to guess what she

was thinking. Everything was right there in her expression—suspicion, determination, exasperation, slight annoyance, and judgment, but also curiosity. What he didn't see was fear.

Yevgen's recordings of her had given Nyle insight. Though outspoken, she was also tender. She cared deeply for her people, for the Cysgodians, for her family. Any decision she made would be in the best interest of others.

But why half mate to a cyborg?

"Then?" she prompted.

"When the footage in those transmissions became much clearer, I realized those files were no longer compressed and tied to harmless inventory reports. Yevgen had gotten into secure channels and the directive automatically reprogrammed to an optimized route. Not surprising, since he's always improving his processes. I knew it would only be a matter of time before he was discovered. That discovery would lead them to me. I had planned on shutting down my surveillance, but then one of the last transmissions I received had the last Cysgod newspaper chip publication in it. That changed everything."

"You were worried that someone would go after the..." Payton kept her gaze steadily on him, refusing to say the word virus. "Did you make it? Was it yours?"

Nyle hated that she felt the need to ask. But she didn't know him. He couldn't blame her for her questions.

Nyle again checked the wristband, making sure they weren't being listened to. He lifted it to show her. "All clear. They didn't appear to know what we talked about before they checked on us."

Payton nodded that she saw it. "Was it yours?"

"No. It came from the organ-growth lab of one of the senior project leaders. I worked more with programming." Nyle had spent years trying to forget those days. "But it *is* my fault. And my responsibility to make sure it never gets out."

She sat forward, eyes sharp. "You released it?"

"It was my organs they were cloning and putting into the new cyborgs. Something about my parents' genetic mixture made my tissue optimal for accelerated growth. They quickly had a surplus and began experimenting with resistant alien viruses." Nyle's hands shook as the echoing cries from the past filtered through his brain. If he closed his eyes, he'd be tortured with the agony of bloody memories. The nightmares had never really gone away.

"Why would they do that?"

"Money. Cysgod wanted dominance over the cyborg technology market. We were competing with Galaxy Playmates."

"The sex dolls?" Payton arched a brow skeptically at Yevgen.

"We had to scrap the female models because the buyers kept wanting those functions. The amount of processing power needed for a pleasure droid's various skills worked against what we were trying to accomplish. We were more interested in creating intelligent servants—pilots unafraid to fly dangerous missions while passing as humanoids, soldiers who could pass bio scans, ash minors who could withstand the temperatures on Bravon, and eventually doctors we could deploy to dangerous regions of the galaxy. Live carriers for organs and antibodies. The possibilities were endless. We could save lives by not having to risk them in the first place."

"How does that explain the virus testing?" Her attention stayed focused on him.

He hated that she knew the truth, that he'd had a part in what had happened on Cysgod.

He hated more that he was the one to tell her that truth. But he couldn't lie.

Nyle stood to stretch and directed his attention back to Yevgen. "The thing that gives a cyborg an advantage also gives them a very humanoid disadvantage."

"Living tissue can still get sick," Payton concluded. "But you didn't get ill? You put Yevgen on the Federation transport, so you were there during the height of the outbreak."

He went to pick up the compression suit controller and swept the scattered nanomaterial toward Yevgen's injured side with his foot. "This will stop more fluid loss when we move him."

"And give me a reason not to be wearing it when they return," Payton said. "Not that I would be."

"Our first defiance didn't turn out so well." He calibrated the controls and then directed the compression material to wrap around Yevgen. It didn't look quite as fetching on the machine. "Captain Rita wasn't lying. Unless you know where you are and how to fly an escape pod to the nearest port, there's no escaping a spaceship."

"They have to fuel sometime," Payton said. "And I'm confident I can figure out how to fly a pod if I have to."

"If they don't shoot us out of the sky," he said.

"They won't. Not if we have Yevgen with—"

The door slid open. Fuse stood holding a tray with one hand and a blaster with the other. Glaring at Payton, he put the tray on the floor and kicked it lightly with the tip of his boot. Two bowls filled with what looked to be foam slid toward her.

Payton grimaced. "What the blasted spaceport is that?"

Fuse gave her a superior grin. He touched the cut on his neck where Payton had clawed him. "She said I had to feed you. She didn't say you had to like the menu."

Fuse gave a dark laugh as the door slid closed.

"Wait!" Nyle called to stop him. "I need tools."

The door reopened.

"Lasers, wrenches, medical supplies—" Nyle began.

"I'll let the captain know." Fuse again shut the door.

"I'd like to eject him into the deep black as well," Payton muttered. She gave a small shiver of disgust. "I'm not eating this bile."

Nyle reached for a bowl and sniffed before licking the foam.

Payton's nose wrinkled, and she leaned away from him.

"It's an aerated nutrient paste," he said. "You should eat it. I won't be able to carry both of you if you lose your strength."

"It's probably poisoned." She shook her head.

"They won't kill us. Yet. They need us. Besides, poison is too passive for a brute like Fuse."

"You. They need you," she corrected. Payton picked up a bowl and studied it. "But I see your point." She tried it and frowned. "It tastes like dirty leaves."

"We're lucky Fuse lacks imagination. It could have been so much worse. I once spent a day on a fuel port that only served elteeb stew." The food had been swimming in the broth. He'd preferred to starve on that layover.

Nyle quickly ate the foam and returned the empty bowl to the tray.

"I don't suppose you can build a blaster with all those tools they're bringing you," Payton mused. "Maybe ask for a laser with enough jolt to stun them into submission."

"I have a feeling I'll be supervised during repairs."

"If it's Fuse, I'm pretty sure that slargnot doesn't know a blaster from his forefinger." Payton gave a little grin and placed the bowl back on the tray. She hadn't finished her meal.

The overhead lights began to dim. The ship's

environmental controls were warning them of the upcoming sleep cycle.

Payton glanced at the ceiling as she moved toward the wall opposite Yevgen. She ran her hands over the metal panels. "I will never understand why they feel the need to hide controls."

"A designer thought it was more aesthetically pleasing," he answered.

"The children born in Shelter City didn't understand wall sensors when we first moved them into the barracks after evicting the Federation. Most of them had never seen them work or been inside a building like that, though they'd spent their entire lives living underneath it." Her hand found the hidden scanner inside one of the beams of light, and the corner rotated to reveal a small decontamination chamber. Without the captain pointing it out, there would have been no way of knowing it was there.

The lights dimmed a little more. Payton stepped inside, triggering green lasers to begin dancing over her body. She pulled his shirt over her head and stood naked in the unit as the light bathed her.

Nyle knew he should look away but couldn't. The room lights continued to darken as the green glow of the lasers cast over her.

Did she know how torturous she was being?

The thin trails moved over her hip. His hand flexed in response as if he could feel the curve of it beneath his fingers. One zigzagged up her thigh, and he wished that were his tongue as it concentrated along the apex. When she lifted her hands to her hair, letting the waves fall through her fingers, he couldn't breathe. The lights danced over her breasts and along her stomach.

He'd had so many fantasies of her, an alien princess, but none of them compared to this reality. Before, she'd been like an intergalactic celebrity created just for him—a familiar image that his mind could play with. But now she was flesh and bone, a woman within crawling distance.

His mind could not control her actions. He couldn't make her look at him, beckoning him to join her in the small space—a space so narrow they'd be forced to touch. He couldn't make her whisper how much she needed him. And he found he didn't want to. Yes, he wanted *her*, but he didn't want to control her like a fantasy.

She picked up the shirt from the floor and held it in front of the lights to clean it. The lasers concentrated on the tear where the blaster had hit his arm to remove the blood.

When the lasers shut off, it cast them into a dim

light. The ship's environment had changed to mimic nighttime darkness.

"It's like a cave in here," she observed as she held the shirt in her hands. "I'm tempted to sleep shifted. It will be more comfortable."

Nyle tried to speak, but no words formed a response.

Payton chuckled. She tossed his shirt onto the platform. "Don't worry. I won't eat you."

He watched as white fur rippled over her body. He heard the soft crack of bones as she fell forward to her hands and knees. Her body expanded beyond the confines of her human form. Claws clanked softly on the metal floor. His heartbeat quickened to be in a room with what looked to be a wild beast.

Payton's fanged mouth opened wide as she yawned. The low rumble of her voice crackled. Nyle would have preferred to sleep next to a human woman rather than a cat, but it was probably for the best. After what he had witnessed in the decontaminator, he wasn't sure he could keep his hands to himself all night. There was only so much space in the small room to lie down, and knowing she was close would surely mess with his dreams.

Payton leaped onto the hard platform, walked in a circle, and then settled on her bed for the night. It seemed she did not intend to rest next to him on the floor mats.

Nyle watched her for a moment before going toward the decontaminator to bathe. Her head did not turn in his direction.

He knew he had no right to feel disappointed. It wasn't like he could act on his attraction. She was a princess. He was the last living person who could be held accountable for the tragedy on Cysgod. In no universe would they end up together.

6

Nyle's presumption had been correct. Their mercenary captors didn't trust him unsupervised with tools. They also didn't trust Payton within ten feet of them. After the first night, they forced Nyle to carry Yevgen to another part of the ship, leaving her alone, locked inside the small room.

The fear had been easier to manage when Nyle was trapped with her. He gave her something to focus on outside of herself.

Payton longed for the fresh air, the feeling of dirt under her feet, and the sound of the wind crashing through the leaves overhead. The rows of lights did not change. The air did not move. She had run her hands over the walls, looking for secret compartments. There were none.

The metal walls, ceilings, and floors created an oppressive prison cell, and she felt the panels pressing in on her. It made it difficult to breathe. She even left the corner decontamination booth open for the few extra feet that it allowed and the variance in the horizontal patterns.

Payton tried to tell herself to focus on the future, on the next task that needed to be done. Only, in a cell, that meant one thing—don't lose her mind. Without a sky, there was no counting the minutes ticking past. She closed her eyes and tried to picture herself running through the forest. It worked for a moment, but then she'd come up against a large tree and would be unable to pass as it grew around her like the cell walls.

She thought of her parents, of those moments when the days she'd been missing became months and then years. Her father would tear up the entire planet looking for her. Her mother would tear up the high skies. That search would become their lives.

Would they blame the Federation?

Would they blame the Draig and start the old wars against the dragons?

Would they blame her?

Would they blame themselves?

Her stomach growled in protest, and she frowned. She should've eaten the dirty leaf foam.

Payton saw the fear in their captors' eyes when they looked at her. Would they starve her in this cage instead of facing her claws again?

What if Nyle didn't return? What if Yevgen turned on and gave away his secrets? What if Yevgen never turned on again?

Payton had spent plenty of time alone, but never like this. She paced in endless circles, trapped with her thoughts. This could not be how her life ended. She wasn't prepared for it. She should have at least five hundred more years before she had to think about dying.

The sound of the door sliding open caused her to jolt in alarm. She swung around to face whoever intruded upon her mounting panic.

Nyle balanced a tray on one hand and carried a bundle in the other as he walked in. He wore a burgundy shirt similar to the crewmen. "They let me use the food simulator. I wasn't sure what you liked so I guessed, but it's not foam."

The door slid shut behind him.

"What took so long? I thought I was going to die in here." Payton automatically went toward him. Her hand lifted to hover over his arm, and she stopped herself short of touching him. She remembered all too well the awareness that took over her body whenever they made physical contact.

"I've been gone five hours." He started to smile but then stopped as he saw her face. "Are you all right?"

His gaze captured hers, and she felt herself leaning closer. Payton forced herself to look at the tray he carried. Two rounded lumps of bread sat on plates.

"Five hours?" She couldn't believe it had only been that long. Hearing his voice did something to soothe her cagey nerves. "It felt like five years. There is no air in here. It's too quiet. Too..." Her frown deepened. "*Metal.*"

"You're not all right." He placed the tray on the platform and returned to her. "I'm sorry. I would have demanded to come back sooner had I known you were claustrophobic."

"I'm not. I mean, I don't think I am." Payton took a deep breath, calming herself. "It's this ship, knowing that the unbreathable blackness surrounds us. I started to worry they'd just leave me in here."

"I won't let that happen." Nyle reached for her but stopped himself.

Payton felt drawn to him. She wanted him to

touch her, to feel a connection to another living creature. She told herself it was simply a reaction to being alone, but the feelings she experienced whenever they touched stirred deep within her.

"What's happening?" she asked, ignoring the chemistry bubbling between them. "Is Yevgen...?"

Nyle studied his wristband to check the room, before speaking, "I repaired the hole to stop any more fluid loss, and I'm now removing one of his legs. I told them it would conserve his resources for the repair. I'm working slowly to buy us time."

"Time to do what?"

"I'm still working on that part. I've seen a total of seven different crew members. I'm sure there are more. They took me to a storage closet where they kept a food simulator and to a laboratory to work. Other than that, it's been corridors and armed guards."

She liked focusing on the sound of his voice. It reached out to her like a lifeline, pulling her from the darkness of her mind and refocusing her attention on making a plan. "What else did you find out?"

"We're in deep space. What glimpses I saw of the outside were nothing but stars and blackness. An escape pod would not be advisable." He lifted the bundle gripped in his fist. "I brought you clothes. It's not a compression suit."

She took the clothing and placed them next to the tray. Payton remained in his shirt. "What else?"

"I've been thinking about everything that's happened." He stayed close to her, his voice soft as if whispering secrets. "Captain Rita knows my Cysgodian title and that I helped create Yevgen. Even if they read the newspaper chip article, it wouldn't have told them about Yevgen or my full name. All the article had was that old picture of me, and that the formula remained behind. No one has called me the bastard son of an unknown off-worlder and Diana since I left Cysgod."

"Yevgen did. When you broke into his home."

Nyle frowned. "He was the first in a long time. I can't say that I've missed the reminder."

"You didn't know your father?"

"My mother wouldn't name him. Her parents were strict, and she was young when she had me. By the time I was about ten years old, I realized the stories she told me of him were made up. Sometimes he was an intergalactic celebrity. Other times he was a space pirate, or a spy, or a warrior who had to go home to save his planet. I've come to the conclusion that he was a mediocre man who either ran away from his responsibilities or had disappeared before those responsibilities arose."

"Who do you think told the mercenaries your full name?"

"The Federation would have it in the Cysgodian census records, which would have listed my employment at Yeven Genetic. However, they weren't told the source of the virus. No one wanted to take credit for that. When it first started, the company tried to deny it. My best guess is that the Federation hired Captain Rita and her mercenaries to retrieve Yevgen. They could have put most of the pieces together if they read that article. I still can't believe he found that after all these years."

Payton nodded. The assumption made sense. "We've been waiting for the Federation to return to Qurilixen in response to our arresting General Sten and ejecting them from the base. We couldn't figure out why they were taking so long to respond. Maybe they wanted our attention diverted to possible retaliation while they sent in their mercenaries. Yevgen found evidence that General Sten thought to claim Cysgod for the Federation once the virus had passed. If no Cysgodians were left to protest, he would have been able to."

Her stomach made a small grumbling noise,

reminding her of her hunger.

"Perhaps." Nyle gestured at the food. "You should eat. I'm told it's better warm."

"How did you land on my planet? We were watching the skies."

"Parasite ship." Nyle reached for a plate and held it out to her. "I believe this should taste close to your planet's blue bread."

"Parasite ship?" Payton took the plate and held it, not eating.

"It's like an escape pod that the main ship doesn't know is there." He sat on the platform and lifted the bread from his plate. "I hitched a ride with Syog traders. I detached as they were landing. I imagine it is the same way the mercenaries got on-world. Turn off the controls, free fall a little, and a ship is ignored as an atmospheric disturbance."

"It sounds as if we need to update our planetary defenses." Payton watched him try the food. Her eyes lingered on his mouth. "Why do you think they let you keep the wristband?"

"They don't know what it is. To them it probably looks like clothing." He showed her where he had taken the bite. Something had been baked into the bread. "You need to eat. They're traveler pouches."

She arched a brow.

"I learned about them from a New Earth woman I met in my travels," he continued. "She would make it for her family for their holidays. It's stuffed with meat and other things. Easy to carry."

At his insistent look, Payton took a small bite. "It's good."

A loud bang sounded on the door.

Nyle frowned. "They want me back."

"Why are they knocking? It's not like we expect courtesy from them." Payton gave a rueful laugh.

"They want my assurance that you're in human form," he said. "They've been told you almost ripped out Fuse's throat."

"If I wanted him dead, he would be," Payton said. "Will you be close to a food simulator?"

He nodded. "Do you have a request?"

Payton took his food pouch from him, claiming it for her own. "Next time bring more. I'm not one of those delicate aliens who consumes tiny portions. Shifting burns energy."

"Noted." Nyle took a step toward the door and hesitated. He pointed at the clothes. "Put those on and come with me. I don't want to leave you in here again."

"They won't like it." Payton took a bigger bite

before setting the pouches down. She grabbed the pants and shook them out before slipping them on. Var clothing had laces up the sides for easy removal, which also made them adjustable. These pants, not so much. They fit a little too snugly at the hips, and she wiggled back and forth trying to stretch them out.

Nyle turned his back when she pulled his shirt over her head. Payton suppressed her laugh. The sheer undershirt did little to hide her nudity, but the snug fit was a lot more comfortable. The vest zipped shut along the side and had a large brass buckle that strapped along her chest. The long, sheer sleeves were left to show.

"Much better than the compression suit, but still not optimal for shifting," she said, tugging on boots.

He glanced over his shoulder. "I think that's why they let me bring it."

"Thank you for getting it for me." She folded his shirt and placed it on the platform.

Nyle went to the door and lifted his hand. Payton went after him and caught it, stopping him before he could knock on the metal. Her fingers wrapped around his. Energy vibrated down her hand, a complete awareness of their touch.

"We can fight them," she whispered.

"No. I've never flown a ship like this."

"Yevgen can if you repair him. He can learn anything."

"What if I can't repair him?"

"This ship could remain on life support long enough to call for help. You know communications and such. We can find my brother. He's with my mother's old crew. Or we can notify the palace. They will come for us." She didn't let go of him.

He shook his head in denial. "No."

"Yes," she countered. His look didn't change. "Why not?"

"These are trained fighters. There are too many of them. They have weapons. We're in deep space. They might have friends close by. The Federation probably knows they have us." The reasons rolled out of him.

"It's better than being trapped and waiting. I need you to promise me that you'll get Yevgen and his information back to my people if something happens to me. They need the evidence against General Sten to keep him off the planet and to free the Cysgodians from Federation rule."

"I don't want you hurt." He guided her hand to his chest and held it against him. She felt the beat of his heart under her palm. The rhythm drummed faster than it should have.

"This isn't about me. It's not about you. What we want doesn't matter. What we *do* matters. It's about saving the people on Qurilixen." She took a deep breath, staring at their intertwined hands. "It's about ensuring no one goes looking for that virus. For all we know, it could still be there in the lab."

When she glanced up, it was to find him watching her mouth. His lips parted, and he slowly leaned toward her. The moment felt inevitable as if it should have already happened between them, as if it had been building to this since the very beginning.

"If I find an opening, I'm going to take it," she whispered.

"As will I." His voice was just as soft. He leaned in for the kiss. Their lips brushed, and every part of her concentrated on the contact.

Another loud bang sounded on the door, reverberating over them. Payton instantly pulled away. Nyle took a deep breath.

"To be continued." Payton patted his chest. She went to grab the food pouches and took a bite before nodding toward the door. "The future is waiting for our actions."

7

Nyle tried not to furrow his brow as he looked at Yevgen's leg. Payton stood across from him, paying more attention to their guards than the cyborg. He wished she'd stop glaring at their captors. They hadn't wanted to release her from the holding cell, and if she continued with her silent threats, they might change their mind about letting her out.

"You're supposed to be helping me," Nyle whispered.

Payton turned her attention to him. She glanced at his mouth. A tremor worked through him. He couldn't forget the brief press of her lips to his. Her nearness made it difficult to breathe.

"What do you need me to do?" She turned her attention to Yevgen's face and then away.

Nyle eyed the guards. "Did someone mess with the unit while I was gone?"

The two mercenaries stared at him and didn't answer. They sat across the room, observing. Sandon and Thane were slender compared to Fuse and appeared of higher intelligence. Sandon spoke very little, but when Nyle asked for complex scientific equipment, the man knew what he was talking about. Thane had been chatty before Payton's arrival, speaking with an almost bored need to fill the work hours. His conversation didn't have much in the way of purpose but seemed designed to showcase his trivial knowledge.

"Look at this," he whispered, pointing at the leg. "Someone reconnected all of this wiring."

"Who would do that?" Payton asked before seeming to answer her own question by turning her sharp attention toward Yevgen's face.

"No," Nyle said.

"Yevgen?" She leaned close to study the cyborg's eyes. "Are you in there, my friend?"

"Speak up," Thane ordered. "No secrets."

"He's not activated," Nyle stated. He tapped the metal tip of a wrench to create noise as he whispered to Payton, "Maybe we have an ally aboard this ship?"

"Why would an ally reattach his leg? To what purpose?" Payton countered.

"I don't know. All I know is he couldn't have done it himself." Nyle kept his tone soft.

Thane came closer. "Is he ready?"

"No," Payton and Nyle answered in unison.

"Then get back to work," Sandon ordered.

"You have one more day," Thane added.

The timeline was news to Nyle.

"What happens in a day?" Payton asked.

Thane started to answer, but Sandon's hard look cut him off.

"Less whispering, more work," Sandon said.

Thane moved back to his chair and settled back. Nyle could tell the men didn't perceive much of a threat with the distance between them. Close up, they kept a wary eye on Payton in case she tried to shift.

"Hold this wire," Nyle instructed Payton. He didn't need the extra set of hands for a cyborg limb removal, but he wanted her to look busy.

Nyle had seen the look on her face when he brought her food. She'd been about ready to claw through the walls. He wouldn't be leaving her alone on the ship again if he could help it.

Payton held the wire as Nyle went in to cut it.

Yevgen's fingers lifted slightly to tap Nyle's arm, causing him to miss. The cyborg should not have been able to move while powered down.

Payton and Nyle glanced at their guards to see if the men noticed. They hadn't.

"Faulty wiring must be causing a glitch," Nyle explained, not understanding what was going on with the unit. He'd worked on thousands of them in his lifetime.

Nyle moved to cut the wire. Yevgen smacked him again.

Nyle shared a look with Payton.

"Maybe we start the next plan," she whispered. "He wants to keep his leg."

Nyle studied Yevgen. "I suppose..."

The next plan would be a blood transfusion to replace the cyborg's lost fluid.

Nyle turned to tell the guards, "I'm going to need a medical kit that has a transfuser and—"

"Are those parasites?" Payton interrupted loudly, pointing at Yevgen. She took a fearful step back. "We've got to get out of here. They'll eat through the ship's hull!"

"What?" Nyle turned to look at the cyborg's chest in confusion. He didn't see anything.

Thane and Sandon stepped forward to look for

themselves. Sandon pulled his blaster pistol from its holster.

Nyle watched Payton's expression change from fear to bemusement. Fur sprouted over her features as clawed hands grabbed the guards by their heads and slammed them together. Thane fell across Yevgen, unconscious. Sandon swayed but quickly caught himself. A rogue shot zipped past Nyle, causing him to jump back.

Sandon turned to fight. He lifted his weapon to aim it at Payton. Nyle didn't hesitate as he lunged at the guard's back. Leaping onto the man wasn't the most elegant fighting tactic, as they both fell toward the metal floor grates, but it served its purpose. The weapon slid away from them. Sandon grunted as Nyle pressed on top of him.

Payton grabbed the pistol and ordered Nyle, "Move."

Nyle rolled to the side just as Payton shot Sandon. The man grunted and then stopped moving.

"What did you do?" Nyle demanded, looking at the fallen guards. She hadn't left them with much of a choice. Either they waited for punishment, or they tried to overtake the ship. Neither prospect seemed ideal.

"I started the next plan," Payton said as the fur retracted into her skin. "I can't believe the parasite thing worked. My uncle Rick told us that joke when we were children."

"This was the next plan?" He pointed at Sandon. "Killing a guard?"

Payton nudged him with her foot. "He's not dead." She showed the blaster grip where the controls were embedded in the weapon. "I stunned him. In case we need prisoners."

Her explanation was better. Barely.

"*This* was the next plan?" Nyle repeated. "Overtaking our guards in the middle of deep space on a ship full of mercenaries?"

Payton actually looked bemused. "We talked about this. I said if I found an opening, I'd take it. And just now you agreed to the next plan."

"I thought you meant the next plan on repairing Yevgen," he countered.

"Why would I mean that? He's fine." Payton frowned. "We discussed this."

"No. We..." Nyle started to take a mental tally of their surroundings. The guards had two blasters between them. A few of the lasers could cut through metal, and he might be able to break into a wall panel to find the controls to open the door. That was if the ship's computer system didn't detect him fumbling around inside the walls.

"You weren't talking in code?" Payton asked.

"What code?"

"Faulty wiring." She frowned. "Huh. I really thought we were communicating on another level. Guess not."

"How is faulty wiring code?" he argued.

"Because he's clearly telling you not to take his leg," she shot back, irritated. Heat flushed her features. "He loves that leg."

"He doesn't love." Nyle had tried to tell himself that her delusion wasn't as deep as it sounded. His tone came out harsh. "He's a machine. A tool. A fancy, programmable tool. If anything, he tapped into his self-improvement directives to give himself mobility to make his job of protecting the Cysgodian people easier."

"Why are you yelling at me?" she asked. "This was the plan. We're going to escape. They can't have Yevgen. You heard them. We have one day before... whatever they plan."

"Stop saying this is our plan." Nyle wasn't sure what he wanted to do to the woman more: yell at her or kiss her. Either way, he knew he needed to protect her, and they currently weren't in a position for him to do that adequately. "We're in deep space. The plan was to buy time until we could remove Yevgen's legs for easy transport. Then when we landed at a fuel port, we could try to escape when our odds were better."

"What if the next port is a Federation docking ship?" Payton countered, her eyes flashing with the threat of a shift. She lifted Thane off Yevgen and laid the unconscious man on the floor. Looking at the cyborg, she asked, "Can you walk?"

Nyle didn't know how many times he needed to explain how machines worked.

"As long as you stop trying to take off my legs," Yevgen answered. His eyes lit up as he moved to sit. The mechanisms in his chest sounded a little rough. "How would you like it if I removed your legs?"

Nyle stared at the cyborg in surprise. "You're deactivated."

"Reality says differently." Yevgen moved to stand and swayed a little. He eyed Nyle. "I require blood."

Payton hugged Yevgen. "I'm so glad you're awake."

Nyle felt an unreasonable pang of jealousy.

"As am I, my wife," Yevgen answered. "Do not

fear. You are in good hands now. I will save you. I am not afraid of these mercenaries."

"Can you fly this ship?" Payton asked him. "We need to get somewhere safe where I can contact my mother's old crew to come and get us."

"I am not at optimal functionality." He looked at Nyle.

Payton turned her attention to him. "Well?"

"What?" Nyle eyed the pair.

"He needs blood," she said.

"So do I," Nyle answered dryly.

"You'll make more." Yevgen lifted a cutting laser.

Nyle instantly backed away from him.

The cyborg ignored him and walked along the wall. He ran his hand over the panels before rubbing his face against the metal surface.

Payton glanced around. "How do we do it?"

"We need a medical unit and a transfuser." Nyle did not like the feeling that Yevgen was suddenly calling the shots or that the cyborg was about to play the hero. He frowned as Yevgen spread his arms and placed his chest flat against the wall. "I think your husband is cheating on you with the ship."

Payton glanced at Yevgen and shrugged.

"Here we are." Yevgen took the cutting laser to

the wall and began slicing his way through the metal. He made a heart shape in the metal and then turned to wink at Payton before reaching into the ship's wall. He yanked wires and connectors from within before pulling them apart to attach the ship to the back of his hand and arm.

Nyle went to Thane and took the man's blaster pistol. He handed it to Payton. "Yevgen, see if the space pods are able to reach a safe port."

"Do you wish to eject our captors from the ship?" he asked.

"I wish not to risk fighting an unknown number of captors if there is a safer way off this ship," Nyle explained.

Payton clearly wasn't afraid of a fight, but he was afraid *for* her. In hand-to-hand combat, she could claw her way to victory. But against a pistol? Even the toughest aliens went down when shot. Their captors hadn't given any indication they cared if Payton survived this trip.

Yevgen's eyes flashed red, then blue. "There are thirteen crew members on this ship. Two incapacitated."

Nyle studied Thane and Sandon, watching to see if they were starting to wake up.

"Three in the cockpit," Yevgen continued. "Four

in a sleep cycle. One in the corridors. Three in the mess hall."

"That's doable," Payton stated. "I can handle eleven."

"Would you like me to alter their breathing environments?" Yevgen asked. "There are tamper locks in place, but I can expel the oxygen completely."

"We're not murdering an entire crew," Nyle stated. "And I quite enjoy being able to breathe. I vote we keep the oxygen where it is."

"Is it murder if we're in battle?" Yevgen asked Payton.

"Honor dictates that we must spare a life if it's in our ability to do so," Payton said.

"Everyone made their choices," Yevgen countered. "They chose to kidnap us."

Payton considered his words. "Some people are driven to difficult choices by—"

"Can we not have a philosophical debate right now?" Nyle interjected. They both looked at him like he was overreacting. "You realize we're not exactly on a leisurely space cruise, and those aren't the spa directors napping on the floor."

"He's downloading how to fly the ship," Payton said. "We're just making conversation."

"I'll lock the sleepers in their quarters," Yevgen stated.

Payton nodded. "Lock the mess hall too. Shut off their communicators so they can't alert the others. That'll leave the cockpit and the corridor. Can you fly the ship?"

"Yes, my wife." Yevgen nodded. "Flying is easy."

Another pang of jealousy filled Nyle. He envied their closeness.

No, envy wasn't a strong enough word for what he felt.

He resented a freaking cyborg. A machine. A tool he'd helped to build.

Nyle found himself staring at Payton's mouth, remembering her standing next to him, those beautiful eyes of hers inviting him closer. He wanted her to look at him, but she stayed focused on Yevgen.

"Know that if I do not make it, my love for you will never die," Yevgen stated.

Bloody space balls.

Nyle grunted and lifted his blaster as he moved toward the door. "Are we escaping or what?"

Thane groaned.

Payton shot, blasting the side of the guard's leg to stun him. Thane fell unconscious once more.

"Take this." Payton handed the blaster to Yevgen. "And grab my clothes."

Nyle automatically averted his gaze as Payton pulled off her shirt. He noticed Yevgen openly watched her disrobe. He stared at the cyborg, willing the machine to look away.

A soft tapping noise and light growl turned his attention downward. Payton had completely shifted and waited on all fours. In many ways, it was hard to imagine this fierce creature coming out of the beautiful princess.

When Nyle turned his attention back to Yevgen, the cyborg frowned at him.

"She is my wife," Yevgen stated as if claiming possession.

Nyle grimaced. "We need to look at your programming. It's glitching."

"My self-diagnostics indicate I need blood. Otherwise, I am fully operational." Yevgen's eyes appeared to zoom in on Nyle. "I do not think you can say the same."

"You're right. I'm already fully operational. I have enough blood."

"Perhaps you should follow behind us so we can protect you." Yevgen pulled the ship's wires from his arm.

"I'll be fine. Try not to get yourself deactivated." Nyle held his blaster at the ready and made his way toward the door. "She needs that information stored in your head."

"Shows what you know. My information is not kept in my head. My storage is—"

"I know where it is," Nyle quipped. "I helped design you. Now be quiet and concentrate on what we're doing."

8

Payton listened to Yevgen and Nyle bickering. She growled low in her throat to shut them up before pawing at the door. She was a lady of action, and this standing around didn't suit her. She needed them to keep moving forward. The more she thought about panicking in the holding cell, the more ashamed she became. What kind of Var warrior was she? Five hours locked in isolation, and she allowed her emotions to be blown away like a scrap of linen in the wind.

Nyle's leg brushed her side as he ordered, "Open it."

"I only take orders from my wife," Yevgen stated.

Payton would have laughed if they weren't in

the middle of a serious situation. She looked at Yevgen and snorted.

"As you wish, my love," Yevgen answered. "It will take but a moment."

If she didn't know better, she would have thought Yevgen purposefully tried to irritate Nyle.

Payton didn't want to stop and think about the bizarre triangle she was starting with Yevgen and Nyle. Yevgen was her friend and, sure, technically her half mate because she'd not cared enough to naysay his claim at the time. She trusted him, and he'd saved hundreds of lives.

Nyle was her... Well, he wasn't exactly a friend. She guessed he could be called more of a fellow prisoner. She thought about what it felt like to kiss him. Even now, she was drawn to be closer to him. But his former workplace was responsible for endangering an entire planet.

No. Endangering was too nice of a word. Cysgod was uninhabitable thanks to the virus.

But was that Nyle's fault? He blamed himself, that much was clear. He'd also programmed Yevgen to be the Cysgodians' protector and snuck him onto the Federation evacuation ship. He'd monitored the cyborg's activity from space and arrived on Quril-ixen to stop Yevgen's information from being stolen.

Those were not the actions of a coldhearted planet destroyer. If anything, she got the impression that he had imprisoned himself in guilt since it happened.

"Left," Yevgen stated before the door slid open.

The sound of gliding metal jolted Payton into action. All thoughts cleared from her mind as she became singularly focused on stalking her prey. Her paws moved silently, following the grated lines of the ship's corridor. Her heart beat hard and steady. The hunt was easier to face than sitting in a cell waiting for the future to happen.

Payton listened past the sound of Yevgen and Nyle's feet. A soft shuffling drew her attention, and she turned down another corridor. She lowered her head and lengthened her stride. The men's footsteps quickened to keep up with her.

The animal inside of her liked the hunt, needed anything that would get her mind out of the cage. She kept her breathing even. The footfalls came closer.

Payton charged around the corner, ready to fight. She lifted a paw.

"Payton, no!" Nyle jumped in front of her.

Payton watched him sweep a humanoid child into his arms. She instantly retracted her claws.

The boy cried out and began kicking and throwing his arms wildly. "Let. Me. Go!"

The boy's heel smashed into Nyle's thigh. Nyle grunted in pain and fell against the wall.

"Yevgen, open that door," Nyle ordered.

Yevgen tapped on the hand scanner. The door to the sleeping quarters opened.

Nyle pushed the squirming kid inside. "Stay."

Yevgen closed the child inside. The sound of fists could be heard banging from within.

Nyle turned on Yevgen. He lifted his blaster as if he wanted nothing more than to shoot the cyborg. "You could have told us the person roaming the corridors was a child!"

Yevgen tilted his head and frowned. "You did not ask for biological information."

Nyle stared down at Payton. "This is my point exactly. He's a machine. Any reasonable being would know that detail was important enough to share. What if you hadn't stopped your attack?"

Payton grunted softly at the thought. She would never have clawed a child, but Nyle had a point. Yevgen should have told them.

"Who is he? I'm asking now," Nyle said.

"Captain Rita's son. His father is listed as unknown, but there have been secret communications about him with a Federation general. A wife is not supposed to know about the boy, which is the only reason Rita is given certain jobs. I did not have time to find out more."

"We're now holding a general's son hostage? Wonderful," Nyle drawled in anger. "This is why we need to think before we act.

"Cockpit is this way." Yevgen turned around and walked down the corridor.

Nyle lowered his weapon. Payton stared at Nyle a moment longer before moving to follow the cyborg.

"There aren't pregnant women or babies hanging in the cockpit, are there?" Nyle grumbled as he followed her.

"No." Yevgen's tone was matter of fact. "Biographical data indicates there are two males and a female. Humanoid. Adult. Medical logs reveal one of the males is polydactyly and a eunuch."

"That's incredibly helpful." Nyle shook his head. "Good to know we're dealing with an extra toe."

"I know," Yevgen stated. "You're welcome."

"I should have yanked his wires when I had the chance," Nyle muttered. "Blasted piece of broken-down space debris."

Payton wasn't sure if Nyle understood that cyborgs and shifters could easily hear his grumblings.

Payton heard muffled voices coming from the direction of the cockpit. She quickened her pace, ready to unleash her mounting energy and fight someone.

"You're sure someone was trying to hack into the bio controls?" Rita's muffled voice came through the door.

Payton's claws fully extended. Captain Rita was a worthy target of her anger.

"Fuse, check the payload," the captain continued. "Cage the princess and get her ready for Torgan's sale. Eject the scientist. If he's trying to bypass ship controls with Thane and Sandon breathing down his neck, he's too smart for his own good. This job is too big to mess around. We can replace him once we land."

Hearing the threat against Nyle, rage clouded Payton's reasoning. A door slid open, and she began to run. As a figure stepped out of the cockpit, she pounced.

She smelled Fuse before she focused on his face. The scent of his sweat was as good as a brand. Her claws dug into his chest as her paws shoved him back. She growled, wanting nothing more than to tear them all apart. The sound of Nyle's feet running behind her stopped the instinct. For some reason, she cared what he thought, and he did not wish to kill everyone on board. If she were thinking clearly, that is what she would want too.

But they'd planned to eject him from the ship. Not just threaten to do it to keep them in line. Rita had given an order.

Fuse slammed his fist into the side of her head, knocking her off his body. "I'll make you sorry, you little—"

"Stop her!" Rita yelled.

Payton felt heat graze her back but ignored it. In battle, she let the cat take over. The animal acted on pure instinct.

"Watch your aim. Stun her. Don't kill her," Rita ordered.

"You will not touch my wife," Yevgen cried. He started to charge, but Nyle shoved the cyborg aside before he could enter the cockpit as a blast ricocheted off the doorframe.

Nyle grunted in pain but kept coming forward. Payton saw the blur of his movements as she resumed her attack on Fuse. Rita charged Nyle, swinging her fists.

A third man held a blaster, erratically aiming back and forth between Payton and Nyle, as if trying to decide which should be his target.

Fuse punched her ribs. Payton roared and slashed his face. Fuse screamed in pain.

"Stop moving," Nyle ordered. "I don't want to hit you."

"Shoot him!" Rita yelled.

Payton left Fuse bleeding on the cockpit floor. She leaped onto the empty pilot's seat.

The cockpit was not designed for combat. Bulky chairs created obstacles in the small oval room. Seeing the blaster aimed toward Nyle and Rita wrestling on the floor, she instantly pounced on the man holding it. He panic-shot at Payton. She felt the graze of heat over her shoulder, but she was already in the air. Her body slammed into him, knocking him back. His cry was cut short as his head bounced off the metal edge of the console with an ugly *thunk*.

"Don't you dare touch my—" Yevgen appeared in the doorway. A grinding noise accompanied his sluggish movements. "Oh. Well done, love."

Payton turned, ready to devour Rita. Nyle had her restrained. One arm hooked her neck as she tried to kick.

"Stop," Nyle ordered. Rita kicked harder.

Payton forced the animal to retract into her body. The primal instincts were hard to control, especially when her heart was beating fast from the fight. The smell of blood came from Fuse, and he wasn't breathing. She had not intended to kill him.

Payton pushed to her feet as fur turned to flesh and asked, "Want some help?"

"Can you please stun her?" Nyle jerked as Rita fought him.

Payton crossed toward Yevgen and grabbed his blaster.

"Release her," Payton said.

Nyle let the captain go. Payton stunned her the moment Nyle was clear of the blast. Rita dropped to the floor, motionless.

"You're bleeding." Nyle moved toward Payton, stumbling around Rita to get to her.

"We need to secure the prisoners," Payton said. "They probably need a medic."

"I do not think that will bring the big one back to life." Yevgen leaned against the doorframe. "They can wait. I require blood."

She glanced down at Fuse. "I didn't mean to kill him."

"He chose his path," Yevgen dismissed. "I need blood."

"Your ribs," Nyle insisted, taking her wrist to lift her arm slowly out of the way. "Let me see."

Payton stood naked after her shift. She pulled her arm gently down as it hurt to move. "It's fine."

Even as she said it, she winced as she glanced down at the red splotch where Fuse had kicked her.

"That's not fine," Nyle said. "You need a medical booth."

"It *will* be fine." She ignored the pain. "Let's secure the prisoners and get this ship on a new course."

"What were you thinking? Charging in here like that?" Nyle demanded. "You could have been killed."

Payton frowned and didn't answer him as she looked around the cockpit. A long console lined with buttons, toggles, and blinking lights demanded attention. The wide viewing screen showed an expanse of stars, barely appearing to move as they dotted the blackness of the high skies. Their constellations meant nothing to her.

"You're reckless and dangerous," Nyle fumed, "and being around you is..."

"What?" She turned back to him and put her hands on her hips in defiance. Her glare dared him to go on. "Being around me is what?"

"Just..." He took a deep breath.

Payton cut him off before he had the chance to finish. "We don't have time for this. Yevgen, chart a course for someplace safe, then see if you can reach Rick Hayes or any of his crew."

"I need blood," Yevgen stated. When he walked, it sounded like gears grinding beneath his skin. "My organs are not doing well."

She stepped around Fuse to eye Rita and the third crewman. "We'll secure the prisoners and find a transfuser."

"The fallen one can go into the cargo hold. They have a coffin ejector for burial in space," Yevgen said.

"After you get into a medical booth," Nyle insisted.

Payton glanced down at her naked body. "Where are my clothes?"

"I dropped them in the corridor when Nyle attacked me," Yevgen said.

"I *saved* you," Nyle countered.

"Grab your lady friend. We'll put her with her son." Payton gestured at Rita, interrupting the bickering before they could get going again. "I'll carry the little guy."

Payton grabbed the man's arm and hefted him over her shoulder.

"Aren't you going to put your clothes on first?" Nyle asked.

"After everyone on the ship is secured." Her tone was purposefully flippant because she knew it would irritate him.

Nyle dragged Rita by her wrist out of the cockpit. He stopped to pick up Payton's clothing. She heard him muttering under his breath. "I don't know if I want to strangle you or kiss you. You are one frustrating woman, Princess."

9

Nyle watched as the device wrapped around his forearm turned red. The transfuser pulled the blood from his body and filtered it through a flat tube into Yevgen. His arm tingled beneath it, not painful but definitely noticeable. The cyborg made small noises of pleasure as Nyle's blood reached him.

"We can turn you off for this part of the process," Nyle offered.

"Then who would fly the ship?" Yevgen asked. "My wife needs me."

"Autopilot?" Nyle glanced at the controls. When they had returned to the cockpit, Yevgen had programmed a star route, and the ship flew itself.

Payton stood before the viewing screen. She

glanced back at them and smirked. The darkness of star-dotted space framed her, and for a moment, he could forget where they were.

Nyle had refused to give Yevgen blood until she went into a medical booth. The unit had fixed the worst of her injuries—two broken ribs and nasty blaster burns. After that, she'd thankfully dressed. Already every inch of her was emblazoned on his mind, which made it very hard to concentrate on the fact that they were in deep space on a stolen ship with a bunch of mercenary prisoners while on the run from the Federation.

"Where are you flying us?" Nyle asked, staring at the expanse of stars.

"Torgan airspace," Yevgen answered.

Payton again turned her attention toward them. "That's where they were taking us. They said they were going to cage me and sell me on Torgan."

"They would have made many space credits off of you." Yevgen glanced dismissingly at Nyle. "Not so much for you."

"How do you know that?" Nyle asked Payton.

"She's a shapeshifting princess. You're nobody," Yevgen answered.

"I overheard Captain Rita's orders as we were

approaching." Payton ignored the cyborg. "They said Yevgen was their payload. I was a payday."

"And me?" Nyle tried to meet her gaze. He was a little light-headed from all the blood Yevgen required.

Payton went to Yevgen and examined the transfuser on his arm. "They wanted to eject you into space and find someone else to repair Yev."

The cyborg laughed. "Payload, Payday, and Space Trash."

Nyle tapped the controller on the transfuser to stop the device.

"Hold on, I want more," Yevgen protested.

"You don't need more," Nyle dismissed.

Heat replaced the tingling as the transfuser healed the skin it had penetrated to retrieve his blood. He picked up the handheld medic they had found and pressed it to his neck. He felt it injecting him. The dizziness in his head eased.

"I don't think we should go to Torgan," Nyle said. The black market planet was a well-known haven for shady deals and even worse characters. Anything illegal could be bought and sold within the confines of the main complex. "That is where I was before I went to Qurilixen. They were about to have a Frendle's Chips competition. The market-place will be packed with outlaws."

Frendle's Chips was a strategic game of skill and a popular gambling sport in the universes. It also attracted many unsavorys who would shoot an alien on a dare.

"I don't think you are in a position to make those decisions." Yevgen pulled the transfuser off his arm and tossed it at Nyle.

"I don't think—"

"Enough of this," Payton interrupted, her voice raised. "What was mildly amusing is becoming tedious fast. I will not continue to listen to you bicker with each other over every little thing."

"Of course, my wife." Yevgen sounded contrite.

Nyle glared at him. "We should be flying away from the people who ordered our kidnapping. Not straight into their prison holds."

"Why Torgan?" Payton asked Yevgen.

"The Federation will notice if this ship changes course. Given my importance as the payload, it is reasonable to assume they will be tracking our progress. Also, Torgan is the closest port should we wish to use the escape pods. Seeing as our desired contacts, Rick Hayes and his crew, are space pirates, it is fair to assume we can locate them in Torgan's vicinity. I have been trying to contact them."

"Why not Torgan?" Payton turned her attention to Nyle.

"Your logic is faulty." Nyle stared at Yevgen, wanting to reprogram the smirk on his face. "Just because they're pirates, doesn't mean they'll be close to Torgan, even though pirates go there. We took over the ship, so we don't have to use the escape pods. We can just dock at the nearest fuel port and walk off. We can take plenty from this ship to barter for a ride. Stopping at a fuel dock is not suspicious if we are being tracked. By the time the Federation sends someone to check on why the ship isn't moving, we'll be on our way to Qurilixen." He turned to Payton. "Trust me. I've been avoiding people my entire life. I know how to disappear into deep space. Once we're on the run, they won't find us."

"I agree," Payton said. "Yev, find the closest fueling dock."

"I could, but it's not a viable plan. We should fly to Torgan." Yevgen stood and looked at the viewing screen. His eyes flashed as if recording the star's locations.

"Yev." Payton touched his arm. "We should go to the fuel dock."

"I can fly the ship." Yevgen placed his hand over Payton's. "Landing might prove difficult."

"Tell me you can land," Payton said.

"I will never lie to you, my wife. There are no instructions stored on this ship, and I do not recognize the layout of this antiquated alien console. Flying is easy. It was not favorable when I calculated the risk of trying to land. When we pass Torgan, we can eject the pods while the ship keeps moving."

Nyle stared at him in disbelief. "You said you could handle this ship."

Payton took a deep breath and stood quietly for a long moment. When she finally spoke, she said, "Get us to Torgan. Now that you have your blood, make sure you're protected from reverse hacks and access the ship's full database. Learn anything useful you can about the crew, their mission, whom they were supposed to meet."

"Yes, my love."

Payton grabbed one of the blasters off an empty chair. "Nyle and I are going to check the ship and see to it that the prisoners are fed."

Nyle was happy for any excuse to leave Yevgen's presence. When they were alone in the corridor, he said, "I never thought I'd side with all those techno-phobe groups who used to protest the cyborgtronics projects on New Earth when they first started, but..."

"Oh?"

"They were worried that cyborgs and other artificial intelligence would try to overtake humanity by wiping them all out or enslaving natural-born people." Nyle led the way down the corridor toward where they had taken him to use a food simulator earlier. "Scientists argued that their program guidelines would be strictly supervised and that they couldn't work past their protocols even if left on their own."

Payton sighed. "I know you think of him as some broken machine. Yes, he's eccentric, but I hardly think he wants to rule over humanoids. You said it yourself. He is programmed to help the Cysgodians, and he did that more times than I can count. He helped us remove the Federation's presence on our planet and exposed General Sten as a monster. He is loyal to the Qurilixen people, and I trust him."

"It's one thing to watch over people on-world, but we're in space, and his need to protect the Cysgodians doesn't include me. I monitored him the best I could from space, but clearly I missed glitches in his programming. It's not surprising. He's an old model who's been piecing himself together with spare parts. It didn't even register that he was still activated when we tried to remove his leg." Nyle paused by a hand scanner. "His only redeeming quality is that he is fixated on protecting his wife."

"Half mate," Payton corrected.

Nyle nodded, still trying to control his jealousy over that fact. "How could you marry him?"

"I didn't think it mattered." Her answer was so simple, so honest.

And he hated it.

"I can think of very little that matters more than our connections to other people." He would have given anything to have a woman like her by his side all those lonely years. Nyle put his hand against the scanner. It blinked red. Frowning, he gestured to Payton. "You try. Yevgen probably gave you clearance."

Payton pressed her hand to the scanner. The door to the small storage area slid open.

"The food simulator they let me use is in here." Nyle led the way inside. Lights sensed their presence and turned on. The simulator sat on a small table next to the supply drawers. "Those trapped in the sleeping chamber will have an emergency medic. It will keep them alive for a few weeks. We should at least feed that boy. What do you think he'd like?"

"Traveler pouches?" Payton shrugged. "Maybe just a variety of things. Too bad Rita is in there with him. I'd just as soon let her starve if not for the fact that she has a child. I feel bad for the boy. This doesn't seem like the ideal way to raise him."

"He appears healthy and cared for." Nyle began typing recipe codes into the simulator. He pulled out a traveler pouch and handed it to her. "Eat something. You said shifting takes a lot of energy."

Payton took his advice and bit into the pouch. He handed her a second one before starting a tray for the boy.

"You should eat too," she said. "You gave Yevgen a large volume of blood."

Nyle didn't feel like eating. "Yevgen doesn't deserve you. I'm not sure any man does."

She chuckled. "Because I'm frustrating, reckless, dangerous, and no man deserves to be trapped with that?"

"Yes, to frustrating, reckless, and dangerous." Nyle returned her smile. He felt like he knew her, probably more than he should have. He thought of those years watching her through Yevgen's feeds.

"And fascinating, brave, intelligent, stubborn, wild, beautiful."

She set her food down next to the simulator. "Go on."

"It doesn't seem real that we're here. Like this." He couldn't stop staring at her face.

Payton glanced around. "In a storage hold materializing food for prisoners?"

"Together." Nyle knew he wasn't making sense, at least not in the eloquent way he would hope to in such a situation. What was it about her that made all intelligent thoughts turn into a jumbled mess in his mind? "I've seen you before."

She didn't move as she stared at him.

Nyle closed his eyes. The mixture of smells surrounded them in the small room, coming from the tray of food he had materialized. He hadn't paid attention to what he'd prepared. All his attention was on her.

"I mean to say, I've seen you on Yevgen's video feeds that I watched before coming to Qurilixen." He opened his eyes to look into hers. "Something about you captivated me, and when I finally saw you, in real life, I was struck insensible."

"Why are you telling me this now?"

"I realize I might not have another chance."

Nyle lifted his hand, letting it hover in the air between them. He wanted to touch her, kiss her, hold her. He felt as if every inch of his body pulled into her gravity. "We could have died today."

Her lip curled slightly, but she didn't appear joyful. "We could die every day. That is why it is important to live a worthy life."

At that, he dropped his hand. "You're right, of course. I forgot who we were. Forgive me."

"And who are we?"

Was she toying with him? He took a deep breath and turned his attention back to the food simulator. He pushed random buttons. His hands shook as he was unable to concentrate.

"You are a princess," he answered. "I am the last man in the universe who can be held responsible for what happened on Cysgod. My life is not worthy of yours."

He had spent decades mentally churning over his past, every conversation he could remember, every project he worked on, and every passing inter-action he'd had with coworkers. He tortured himself with things he should have noticed, words he should have said, forms he should not have signed. He could have said no to them replicating his genetics. He could have followed up with the organics laboratory to see what they were doing with his cloned organs.

"Did you conspire to hurt the Cysgodians?" She touched his arm. The softness of her fingers caused a shiver to work over him.

"Ignorance is not an excuse. It is my body that made it possible for them—"

"So no," she interrupted. "You did not conspire to kill a planet. Did you choose your genetics, your parents?"

"Of course not."

"But you believe you need to be punished for those facts." She frowned, her eyes narrowing. "Are you doing everything within your power to ensure it never happens again? Have you spent a lifetime watching bootlegged streams—*what did you call it?* —piggybacked off of Federation inventory report transmissions? Did you program and smuggle a cyborg onto the rescue ships, a cyborg that was then able to protect the very people you programmed it to?"

"I..." He couldn't get his words past his throat.

"So yes." She squeezed his arm. "It's quite simple. There is only one direction we can go, Nyle. Forward. The Cysgodians need us to return the information inside Yevgen to Qurilixen."

"The way you see the world..."

Everything about this woman fascinated him.

"Not just the world," she whispered, leaning closer. "I see you too, Nyle."

There it was. Her gravity pulled him back in.

She kissed him, her soft mouth moving against his as if having a silent conversation. He knew no one would come by the opened door. Except for a malfunctioning cyborg flying the ship, they were for all intents and purposes entirely alone, surrounded by deep black, far from anyone who would know.

He followed her lead, leaning to deepen the kiss. Her hands ran up his arms and settled on his shoulders. No matter what else happened in his life, he would have this perfect moment.

10

PAYTON KNEW NYLE WOULDN'T MAKE THE FIRST move. The attraction boiled between them, and she saw the need in his eyes, but he held so much guilt he didn't think he deserved anything good.

She ran her fingers into the dark waves of his hair. His hands hesitated before gripping her waist to pull her against him. So much lay ahead of them and she wasn't sure when they would have another chance to be alone.

The Var were not modest when it came to sexuality. She knew what she wanted and wasn't ashamed to ask for it. Sex was as natural as the three suns in the Qurilixen sky.

Tiny vibrations seemed to pulsate through her body, extending from every point they made contact.

She stepped on the toe of her boot, jerking her foot free before doing the same with her other foot.

Payton was used to the animal lurking beneath her surface but wasn't ready for the thread of her Roane heritage to spark to life. The Roane attained vitality from sexual pleasures. She felt her body pulling at his energy, feeding on it like some hungry, desperate creature.

Their hips bumped the table with the food simulator. He held on to her as he stepped deeper into the storage room. The tall storage shelf rattled as he knocked into it, and it forced him to stop. She had him trapped against her. Her lips moved against his until she could hardly breathe.

"I want you," he moaned. "I've always wanted you. This has to be a dream."

Payton drew back long enough to pull her shirt over her head. The sexual energy that exploded inside of her was more primal than any animal shift had ever been. All thoughts left her as she sought to feel his skin against hers. She tugged at his clothing, ineloquently undressing him. He scrambled to help, and with jerking, desperate movements, he was finally naked. His shirt flew out of her hands into the corridor. His pants slid on the floor out of the way.

Payton took in every detail of his perfect face,

his neck, and chest. She touched the thick shaft of his arousal, unable to resist stroking the length.

Payton pushed at her waistband even as his arms wrapped around her. The full length of his warm, naked body fit against hers. She felt his arousal along her hip as she managed to wriggle free of her pants. The tight material dropped around her ankles, liberating her from their constriction.

"Princess," Nyle whispered. "Are you—?"

"Don't call me princess. I don't want to think about royal titles," Payton said, pressing her mouth back to his. She bit at his lip. "And please don't ask me if I'm sure about this. I'm the one attacking you. Maybe I should be asking if *you* want this."

Nyle glanced downward. His arousal pressed into her, completely ready. "I've wanted you longer than you could know, Payton."

"Good. Then that's settled." Payton ran her hands down his body, feeling strong muscles beneath the firm skin. They became a frenzy of movements. Her fingers wanted to play. Her mouth wanted to explore. Her eyes wanted to memorize every second. In the end, the need burning inside her overruled all.

Payton wanted to live in this moment but knew it was fleeting. She turned with him so that her back was to the shelves. Nyle cupped her breasts and kissed his way along her neck, nipping lightly beneath her ear.

She reached behind her head and rubbed her inner thigh against him. Nyle took the invitation, lifting her from the ground. He braced her hips as he drew his member along her sex. Energy pulsed through her like lightning striking her stomach. She cried out in surprise.

Nyle entered her slowly, and she couldn't remember wanting anything more in her life.

Mine, her thoughts whispered, as if staking claim.

The possessiveness didn't make sense, but neither did the intensity of her need. His dark eyes stared into hers, and she knew that they were meant to be.

His body rocked into hers, as hard and desperate as she felt. Her feet dangled behind him. He moaned softly against her neck.

Pleasure erupted, quaking through her like liquid heat. Her heart hammered so hard she felt it beating along the apex of her thighs and in her neck. Climax seized her, and for a moment, she couldn't move.

Nyle held her close. Her hands dropped from

the shelf onto his shoulders. His head remained buried against her neck.

"We should finish whatever it was we were doing," Payton whispered, unable to remember exactly what that had been. The lasting sensations of pleasure hummed inside her, giving her energy.

"I don't want to let you go," he answered, finally lowering her to her feet. "I don't want to leave this room."

"If I had the power to make the world melt away, I would." The metal grated floor against her bare feet hit like the cold sting of reality. "As much as we want to live in this moment, we must go forward."

She didn't need to remind him that there was too much at stake. He knew that as much as she did. She saw it in the way the invisible weight returned to his shoulders and the worry to his eyes.

"I want..." He struggled to finish his words.

Though she longed to hear what they would have been, she understood. "I know, Nyle. I want, too."

"My parents fell in love because of this planet." Payton stared at Torgan on the viewing screen. She'd seen pictures, but she never thought she'd travel here. Three rings spun at odd angles around a brown-gray planet. The view wasn't anything spectacular, the planet itself not particularly beautiful. Compared to other places, its drab desert landscapes could only be described as a sea of unforgiveness.

She was aware of Yevgen and Nyle on either side of her. If the cyborg knew about her making love to Nyle, he didn't say anything about it, and she didn't volunteer anything beyond stating they'd managed to slide a tray of food into Rita and her son. The captain was awake and spouting threats.

Payton felt strange standing between a half mate and a lover. This was not a position she had ever imagined herself in. Good thing they were in space and not the Var palace, and she didn't have to explain herself to anyone. What would she say? How would she introduce Nyle? Or Yevgen, for that matter? Telling the great Var commander that she married a cyborg wasn't exactly a conversation she looked forward to having.

Then again, that was hardly her biggest problem at the moment.

"I have not heard the story of your parents and their love in relation to Torgan," Yevgen said. "Please continue."

Payton gave a small smile as she thought of it. As a child, she found the adventure of it thrilling— pirates, poisons, betrayals, and danger around every corner. Payton and her brothers should never have been born if the stories were completely true and not embellished for entertainment's sake. The odds of surviving would not have been in her parents' favor.

"My mother was the captain of the crew that my uncle Rick now commands. He's not really an uncle, but he is like her brother so that's how we have always thought of him." She gave a small laugh. "My parents told us one version. Rick filled in a few details they probably wouldn't want us knowing about. Anyway, one night flying in deep space, the crew was playing a card game and drank too much Torganian rum, not realizing it was psychotropic."

"That was very foolish of them. The beverage is not recommended for humanoids," Yevgen lectured. "You must promise me, wife, that you will not partake of it while we are on-world. It is said to dull their thought patterns, give visions, and to cause them to act carelessly."

"I won't," Payton assured him.

Yevgen leaned back to say behind her toward Nyle. "You may partake. We don't need your mind. Just your blood supply."

"Yev, behave," Payton warned.

"Was there any permanent damage to the crew?" Nyle asked to keep the story moving.

"No. But they did end up hallucinating and running around Var territory, where they kidnapped my father in shifted form. My father will say it was fated by the gods. My mother will say she bested him."

Nyle leaned closer to her. She felt the heat from

his body. "So they fell in love because of the Torganian rum?"

"It is pronounced *roome-ah*." As if mimicking Nyle's movements, Yevgen also leaned closer. "Excellent story, my love."

Payton side-eyed them both before continuing, "It's not over. The crew was on a scavenger hunt hosted by Torgan's marketplace. It's a way for the market to get vendors with rare items to sell. They make a game of it. My mother and her crew needed a wild animal for their list and didn't realize that they'd kidnapped the Var commander in tiger form. By the time they understood their mistake, they were in deep space on their way to Torgan, and my father was in a cage."

Payton couldn't help thinking she had been destined for a cage on Torgan, too, if Captain Rita had her way.

Like father, like daughter.

"We should get into an escape pod soon," Yevgen said. "We do not want to miss our chance."

"Long story short," Payton concluded, "they made it to Torgan, fell in love, and have been together ever since. They are devoted to one another."

The back of Nyle's hand brushed against hers.

Tingles of awareness erupted where they made contact.

"Hailing *World Traveler*, this is Torgan Ground," a voice boomed from the console.

Payton gave a small jump of surprise.

"*World Traveler*, this is Torgan Ground. Please answer."

"I guess that's us," Payton said.

Yevgen glanced around at the buttons in front of them.

"*World Traveler*, this is Torgan Ground."

Yevgen pressed a button, then another, before making a small noise. Finally, he hit a series of toggles. "Torgan Ground, this is *World Traveler*."

They didn't answer.

Yevgen flipped another row of switches. "Torgan Ground, this is *World Traveler*."

"*World Traveler*, you are cleared for landing. Proceed directly to docking platform eight-eight-sixteen and report to Dock Master Wye."

Payton looked at Yevgen and shook her head in denial.

"Torgan Ground, this is a fly by." Nyle took over the conversation. "We're looking to drop off a single space pod for retrieval."

"Understood, *World Traveler*." The voice

paused. Payton looked at Nyle, who held up his hand for silence. "Pod may proceed directly to docking sandlot two-six-eleven to await manual retrieval."

"Thank you, Torgan Ground." Nyle reached to shut off the last switches Yevgen had turned on.

"What does that mean?" Payton asked.

"We aim for a sandlot outside of Madaga, where the main marketplace is located. Since they think we're having mechanical issues with our pod, they'll guide us in and give us wide berth to crash land. They'll send someone to pick us up. Since none of us are pilots, I figured that is our best bet."

"I can fly the pod," Yevgen stated.

"Yeah, like you could fly this ship," Nyle dismissed. "Come on, they'll be waiting for our launch."

"Yev, set a time release on the doors for after we leave?" Payton said. "Maybe two days. I don't want to starve the crew in deep space, but we need time to get away. Keep the autopilot on."

"Logically, it would be best if—"

"No," Payton cut the cyborg off. "We're not killers."

"Yes, my wife."

Nyle strode from the cockpit toward the storage

closet. He motioned toward the hand scanner, and Payton opened it for him.

"I'm going to grab something to barter." He took a bag from the wall and began loading it with supplies from the storage shelves. "We can sell the pod too. That should get us enough for a ride."

"I have the blasters," Payton said.

"Pod's ready!" Yevgen yelled, rushing past them. The clank of his footsteps echoed loudly. "All aboard!"

Payton waited until Nyle was ready before hurrying after the cyborg. The circular interior of the escape pod only had two seats facing each other and enough space on the floor to cram in a third. She motioned for Yevgen to take the floor. He obeyed, even though he looked as if he wanted to protest.

Nyle tossed a bag at Yevgen before crawling inside the tight space. As he buckled in, the cyborg pressed the bottom of his foot against the emergency launch button. The door closed, leaving them in darkness. Several clanks sounded, echoing loudly around them. She heard Nyle breathing and focused on it. Her shifter vision cut through the darkness enough so that she could see his face staring blindly in her direction.

Suddenly air hissed, and then warning tones

drowned out everything. Orange light illuminated their faces. None of them spoke as the pod jerked violently. They were ejected into the deep black. She felt them moving, but the metal walls blocked any view of the outside.

Fear tried to invade her senses as she thought of the airless space surrounding them. She searched the pod for any sign that they were not secure within the depths.

"Yevgen, are you flying us?" Payton asked, trying not to panic. She hated these confined spaces.

"No," Yevgen said. "I am sitting on the floor. The payload should have the chair."

Her heart beat faster. She had no time to deal with a cyborg's pouting.

"Payton," Nyle said, staring at her. "Look here."

She met his gaze.

"Torgan will catch us," he said. "Just hold on."

She nodded, feeling better as she stared at him. He parted his lips and breathed slow and steady, encouraging her to match his rhythm.

When she started to calm down, he nodded in approval. "Expect turbulence. This one is always a rocky landing."

She kept her gaze on Nyle as the pod began to shake.

"Do not worry, my wife. I will protect you. This is my plan." Yevgen's hand rested on her knee. His metal skeleton added weight to his touch in stark contrast to Nyle's gentler hold.

Payton ignored the guilt that tried to surface. Her body seemed to recognize Nyle's blood inside of the cyborg, more so now that her Roane heritage had shown itself. Maybe she had always sensed a connection to Nyle through Yevgen, but she wasn't attracted to the cyborg, not like she was to Nyle. Yevgen wanted to have feelings toward her, and sometimes she thought he might achieve it, but was Nyle right? Was the yearning Yevgen felt all a machine's programming? Was it some primal attraction inspired by Nyle's blood? And did it matter when Nyle's blood was now Yevgen's?

The pod jerked violently, bouncing them in their seats. Her hair reached up from her head as it turned upside down. Yevgen lifted off the floor, and she pushed her foot against his thigh to try to hold him steady.

Payton considered herself to be brave. She'd fight anyone she had to. Spiraling through space inside a small metal ball was not her idea of a grand adventure. Payton closed her eyes to picture the open Var forest and tried to attribute her quickening heartbeat to running through the trees.

"If the gods wanted cats to fly, they would have given us dragon wings," she whispered, willing the ride to end.

Torgan Black Market

Marketplace City of Madaga, Planet of Torgan

After seeing the giant dust ball of a planet from the high skies, Payton didn't expect much from being on the surface. Although there was some comfort to the sand shifting beneath her feet as she paced around the pod. The cylinder had landed none-too-gently in the desert docking lot on the outskirts of Madaga. A series of adobe structures spread out of the desert as if serving only to show-case the impressiveness of the main complex. It reminded her of Qurilixen's shame, of the ruins of Shelter City beneath the metal gaze of the Federation stronghold lording over them. She'd spent years in the city, hoping for the day to finally eject the

Federation's dictatorial rule off the planet once and for all.

That was what they were doing here. That was all that mattered. They needed to get Yevgen home.

"Payton?" Nyle's concern filled his words.

She felt an invisible thread pulling her toward him. She resisted.

Yevgen did not move as he sheltered close to the pod. He didn't appreciate the bright sunlight.

Sand pelted her exposed skin, stinging her hands and neck even as the breeze was light. The desolate environment held a subtle beauty when showcased by a hint of rings arching in the planet's sky, but she was too preoccupied to fully appreciate it.

As the breeze picked up, she covered her nose and mouth. She coughed the inhaled dust particles and turned her back to the wind.

The sand was made worse by the intense heat. She felt the sweat-adhered granules coating her cheeks as she held her hand against her face. The open pod would have offered a little shelter, but she'd rather be out in the elements than return to the small space.

"Should we walk toward the complex?" she asked.

Shifted, she could make the trip faster, but after hearing stories of how they wanted to sell her caged father, she felt it best not to reveal her natural abilities. The last thing they needed was to be hunted by opportunists looking for a pet.

"No, they'll send a retrieval team, and we'll sign over the pod in exchange for space credits," he said. "Yevgen, I need you to take ownership of the pod. If they insist that you sign, make sure their electronic clipboards glitch. We don't want a record of our being on-world."

Payton pulled one of the blasters from her waist to hand it to Nyle. He tucked it into his waistband under his shirt. She handed the second one to Yevgen. "Keep that hidden."

Yevgen lifted his shirt to reveal he still wore the compression wear beneath. He tucked the blaster like Nyle had. "I will tell them I am a crime boss and wish—"

"No," Nyle interrupted.

"Space pirate, then," the cyborg reasoned.

"No."

"Medical mafia boss," Yevgen insisted.

"No. Don't tell them you're anything," Nyle ordered.

"But I must be undercover to blend into this

environment." Yevgen stared at Nyle in irritation. "You cannot tell me how to act. This is my plan. I am in charge of this mission. I have it under control."

Nyle looked to Payton for help.

She frowned. "He's right, Yev. Say as little as possible. Don't tell them who we are, even if it's made up."

"Very well." Yevgen stayed beside the pod, but it didn't protect him fully from the sun.

"Where is this pickup team?" Payton shaded her eyes and narrowed her vision as she focused in on the distance. She detected a man standing in the doorway of one of the adobes looking toward them with binoculars. "I see a man watching us."

"I'm sure there are several," Nyle said. "Remember, this is Torgan. People here do not do anything without motivation, usually monetary. It's all about self-preservation. Don't trust anyone. The friendlier they try to act, the less they want to be your friend. Don't look at anyone too long. Don't make conversation. Don't go anywhere alone."

"I know how to handle myself," Payton interrupted. "Aliens don't frighten me. We have visitors to Qurilixen all the time."

"Not like this," Nyle insisted.

Payton tried to respond but instead ended up coughing as she inhaled more dust.

Nyle came close to her. Dust coated his face and neck. "Don't take drinks that don't come directly from within the bar. Don't leave my side."

"Don't worry," she managed, her voice croaking a little as she continued to cough.

"Payton, I'm going to worry. You are a prize that many here would like to own." Nyle took her arm and held it tight as if silently trying to impart the depths of his concern to her.

"Because I'm a shifter?"

"That, but more so because you're a beautiful alien princess. A man would have to be blind not to notice you in this crowd." He eyed her. "Even hidden beneath this layer of dirt, your beauty shines through."

She couldn't help the half smile that quirked the side of her mouth.

"Stop flirting with my wife," Yevgen said. "I will protect her. Coming here is my plan."

Nyle dropped her arm.

Her feet slipped with each step as she resumed pacing. She turned her attention to the main trading complex. At least the building was in sight. She would hate to find herself isolated in the middle of this terrain.

She saw movement before detecting the soft hum of a motor. Pointing, she said, "There. Land craft."

"That would be our ride," Nyle said.

"Stand behind me. I am in charge. This is my pod," Yevgen stated, moving as if to shield them.

Nyle arched a brow. Payton lifted her hand, silently telling him to drop any argument before they started bickering again.

They stood in silence, watching the approach.

The land craft hovered over the ground without a roof, completely open to the elements. A woman drove, her clothing fitted tight against her to block the sand. A hood fit against her scalp and covered her ears. A breathing mask encased her nose but left her mouth free. A narrow protective band covered her eyes.

The man with her wore looser clothing, a mask, and eye protectors. His hair blew around his head. If she had to guess, he spent most of his time inside the complex, whereas the driver worked outside. The land craft approached.

"Welcome to Torgan. I am Dock Master Wye," the man said, his monotone showing little interest in the travelers as if this was just another task to be marked off his work list. "Is the pod for fix or for sale?"

"Sale," Yevgen answered.

Wye grabbed an electronic clipboard, stepped off the land craft, and went to the pod. He pulled a scanner from his pocket as he went inside. Payton heard him moving around. Soft beeps came from within.

Wye poked his head out. "Luggage too?"

"Yes," Nyle answered. "It's all for sale."

"Very well." Wye went back inside. More beeps sounded.

"Get on." The driver motioned toward them.

Yevgen went to the land craft and climbed on. Payton and Nyle followed him. Yevgen reached down for her as Nyle took her hand to help her up.

Wye came toward the craft and joined them. He showed the clipboard to Yevgen. "Fair market value. It is our only offer.

Yevgen nodded. "Accepted. Do you need my signature?"

Nyle's eyes narrowed. The cyborg should not have volunteered to make a record.

"No need." Wye dismissed as he pulled a chip

from his pocket and set it against the clipboard. "Ship parts do not require documentation."

The electronic clipboard beeped, and he handed the chip to Yevgen.

"Complete payment. Don't lose that. No refunds. No replacements." Wye motioned at the driver to return to the complex.

As they flew toward the compound, a hauler came past them to pick up the pod.

Payton took a deep breath and shaded her eyes as they moved. The shield on the land craft kept the sand from pelting them but did nothing for the wind whipping her hair.

Her eyes met Nyle's. He nodded in reassurance.

The craft sped them directly to the main complex, where they were dropped by metal steps leading up from the sand to a glass barrier. Nyle took the lead, waving his hand in front of the scanner.

The glass slid open to let them in, quickly shutting behind them. Ventilation turned on, blowing up from the floor to suck the dirt from their bodies. The cold air contrasted with the heat outside. After it finished, a door opened to let them into the complex. Metal grates gave way to concrete beneath her feet.

They came upon a large walkway where ships were docked. A roof closed overhead as a small spaceship came in for a landing. The loud sound of its engines reverberated over her to drown out everything else.

Nyle led the way down a row of parked ships.

"I don't suppose we can just take one?" Payton mused.

"I don't think we'd make it very far," Nyle said.

They passed a group of Corge warriors near an open ship. Black horns protruded from their blue foreheads. She'd met their kind before at the Var palace. The aliens emitted a sickeningly sweet smell that automatically caused Payton to hold her breath as they passed. It was made worse by the sensitivity of her shifter senses.

Payton kept her gaze forward, not making eye contact with any of them.

By the number of ships, the complex would be full. A mix of aliens moved along the center walkway. She could identify several of them, but she had not seen all of them at the Var palace. Some looked mostly human with a variety of protrusions covering their bodies. Others were covered with hair or scales, some both. A Lykan with matted fur gravitated toward her, and she stepped out of his way. He laughed, the gruff sound indicating he'd tried to intimidate her on purpose.

"You all right?" Nyle asked.

Payton nodded, and couldn't help herself as she answered loudly, "Yeah. Some people need to learn how to use a decontaminator."

The Lykan made a low growl, indicating he'd heard her insult. Hey, the truth could hurt. He did reek. She listened to his steps but didn't turn to watch him go.

Payton continued glancing over the crowds. She found wings and webbed fingers. A short green woman with horns poking out of her head looked as if she were seducing a tall, thin, translucent creature without any recognizable facial features.

They moved through the doors to enter the main complex.

On the surface, it didn't look as if anything nefarious was happening at the trading center, but Payton knew appearances were deceiving. Every unscrupulous businessperson, corrupt politician, disgraced doctor, bounty hunter, mercenary, pirate, slave trader, or overall degenerate ended up here at some point. She had even once heard it referred to as a fallen angel's playground. If it was illegal or immoral, it could be found here. Someone would be willing to sell it.

The crowd thickened around a center bar and cheering erupted over the complex. Holograms showed overhead, revealing several gamblers playing Frendle's Chips.

"That game does not look complicated," Yevgen said. "Do you want me to win it for you, my wife?"

"I think entries are probably closed," Nyle dismissed the idea.

"No. Let's try not to draw attention," she said. "All right, so we're here. How do we get a ride?"

"Give me the chip." Nyle held out his hand to Yevgen.

"I am in charge." The cyborg refused.

"I need the space credits," Nyle said. "I'll get us drinks and mention to the bartender we're looking to pay for a ride. Someone will find us."

Payton didn't think that sounded too safe, but she wasn't sure what choice they had.

"You go. We will get our own ride," Yevgen dismissed. "I am in charge."

"No," Payton interrupted. "I am. We're not splitting up. Give him the chip, Yev."

Yevgen did not look pleased as he did what she ordered.

13

NYLE KEPT AN EYE ON PAYTON AND YEVGEN AS he made his way to the bar. People crossed by his vision, and he did his best not to crane his neck to see past them. If he made it too obvious that he was worried about Payton, it would only draw attention to her.

Being as she was the most beautiful creature in all the universes, she didn't need help bringing attention to herself.

The one good thing about Yevgen is that he would do anything to protect Payton. The bad thing about Yevgen is that living alone for decades had given him little in the way of social graces. He didn't exactly blend into their environment. If the cyborg had his way, he'd be standing on the table announcing he was the biggest crime boss in the universes, and all must bow to him. Not exactly subtle.

Nyle watched bets being placed as a new round of competition was announced. He found watching Frendle's Chips about as entertaining as watching a robotic arm in an assembly line. The game required skill, but he didn't think it rose to the level of sport some people did. The game boards were a large grid with metal discs floating at various levels. In round one, the contestants took turns finger-sweeping discs off the grid without getting shocked by random electrical zaps. For round two, they then threw their gathered discs to knock out the opponents' pieces. Electricity would eviscerate the disc in play if they went even the tiniest bit off course. And back and forth the game went.

Boring.

It still didn't stop the wild crowd from placing bets on the winners. Aside from that, they also placed bets on how many drinks a player might have between rounds. Or who would get into a fistfight. Or lose a ship. Or who would disgrace themselves in any number of ways. Or even end up dead.

Nyle pretended to ignore the small fights breaking out around them after each play. He tapped the bar top to bring up a holographic drink menu and ordered two hydration shots.

"Fifty for the woman."

Nyle frowned at the deep voice coming from behind him. He ignored it as he glanced in Payton's direction. She was speaking to a couple.

A hand clamped down on his shoulder. Nyle glanced to see dark red fingers gripping him.

"I said fifty for the woman. Twenty for the droid."

"She's not for sale." Nyle slowly turned without finishing his order.

The red demonic creature's black eyes stared down at him from an impressive height. Though he had human features, he did not look like any human Nyle had dealt with.

"Everything has a price," the alien insisted.

An announcer's voice boomed over them, broadcasting the next round of games.

"Not her." Nyle pushed away from the bar and tried to cross toward Payton. The crowd thickened, and the rowdy gathering blocked her from view as they made their way toward the gamers.

The demon stepped into his path. "Eighty."

"No." Nyle wasn't sure he could take the man in

a fight, but he would try if it came down to it. He attempted to sidestep him.

The man put the tips of his fingers to his chest and said, "One hundred twenty."

Nyle slapped the hand away and quickly ducked around him. He pushed into the crowd, moving as quickly as he could through the dense press of bodies. He forced his way between fur and leather before coming out the other side near where Payton should have been.

Her table was empty.

"Payton?" he called out, panicked. He spun in a circle, searching the sea of alien faces. "Payton!"

His voice barely carried over the crowd. Nyle stood on a chair. He found her being escorted away from the bar back toward the docks. Yevgen walked beside her. She looked back over her shoulder, but someone took her by the arm and kept her moving forward.

Nyle pulled out his blaster and leaped from the chair. When those near him saw the weapon, they backed away to give him room. He shoved past those who didn't.

Desperation gripped his chest. He had to get to her. Nothing else mattered. The crowd thinned, and he was able to run faster.

Payton and her escorts passed from the main complex into the docking lot. He lifted his weapon, ready to shoot anyone who threatened her.

"Hold up there." An older man fell into step next to him as he passed through the doors, gripping Nyle by the arm as he tried to disarm him. Gray streaked his dark brown hair. He gave a self-assured smile. "No need to go off halfcocked."

Nyle jerked his arm down and spun away from the man's grip. He lifted the weapon. "Back off."

A dark blond beast of a man appeared next to the first. He carried himself like a soldier. "Stop playing around. We should take to the skies."

Nyle didn't lower his arm. He backed away from them, trying to run sideways as he went after Payton. The demon appeared through the doors and joined the others. He should have known the demon was the distraction.

"Payton," Nyle yelled, not seeing her. "Don't get on a ship!"

She appeared from behind the nose of a ship. He rushed to her, ready to pull her toward safety. A man stepped up behind her. Nyle lifted his gun.

"Oh, wait!" Payton jumped in front of the weapon with her arms lifted. "Nyle, don't. It's all right."

"But..." Nyle swung around to look at the three men following him.

"What did you guys do?" Payton demanded.

The older man laughed. "We're just having fun, starshine."

Starshine?

"Payton?" Nyle asked, confused. "You know them?"

"Nyle, these are my uncles." Payton pointed at the man laughing, "Rick," then at the demon, "Dev," and finally the soldier, "Jackson."

"How...?" Nyle frowned as Yevgen joined them. His heart still beat a little fast from fear.

"Well, as good as uncles. They were part of my mother's old crew," Payton explained.

"I told you, this is my plan," Yevgen stated. "I am in charge of this mission. I have it under control. She is my wife, not yours."

"Wife?" the man next to Payton demanded.

Payton kept an even expression. "Nyle, this is my brother, Ryland."

Nyle could see the resemblance. They had the same dark eyes and brown hair.

"Do our parents know?" Ryland demanded.

"We can talk about it on the flight," Payton answered.

"You are now my brother as well," Yevgen said to Ryland. The man looked appalled by the thought. The cyborg held his arms out as if Ryland should embrace him. "You may welcome me into the family."

"Seriously, Payton, you married a droid?" Ryland demanded.

She gave a light shrug. "Cyborg."

"Come here, love," Rick interrupted, hugging Payton. "I want to hear what you have been up to, but first, let's get out of here where it's safe."

"Good to see you, Princess," Jackson said, lightly cupping her cheek.

Dev patted her shoulder, nodding. "You are as beautiful as your mother."

"Are we fueled?" Jackson asked.

Ryland nodded, still eyeing Yevgen.

Dev pressed a button on the bottom of the ship and opened a hatch. A dim light shone down as a ladder lowered for them. "Everyone up."

Jackson and Rick went up the ladder. Ryland motioned for his sister to go. After she reached the top, he jumped in front of Yevgen to stop his ascent.

"If this is a joke, I don't find it funny," Ryland said.

"No joke. It is as I said in my transmission to

you. We are in danger," Yevgen said. "The Federation wishes for what is inside me."

"Ry, leave him alone," Payton yelled down.

Ryland moved aside so Yevgen could go up. He turned to Nyle. "What about you?"

Nyle didn't answer.

"He's not important. You can leave him," Yevgen answered from above.

"Let's go," Rick ordered. "Everyone!"

Ryland went up the ladder. Dev motioned for him to follow. Nyle climbed up the hatch into the ship. Payton waited for him at the top. The others had gone ahead.

"I'm sorry if they scared you," Payton said. "They were just playing around. I sent them to get you so you could meet us here. And I'll talk to Yevgen. He should have told us sooner that he had reached the crew. I don't know why he didn't. I think he might be glitching from the blood loss."

Nyle reached for her hand, needing to touch her. "As long as you are safe. That is all that matters."

Dev came inside and secured the hatch. Nyle let go of her and waited as the man passed by them.

"Your cyborg is jealous," Dev stated. He glanced

at their hands even though they were no longer touching. "Any fool can see it."

"He's a machine," Nyle said. "He doesn't feel emotions."

"You might want to tell him that." Dev gave Payton a small smile. "We'll contact your parents as soon as we're in the sky. It will be good to see them again."

"Are the others here?" she asked.

"No, just the four of us on this transport," Dev said. "We were on a supply run to pick up ship parts when we intercepted the message. The rest of the crew is docked on Letame, waiting for us to return."

Payton followed Dev into the passageway. "Thank you for picking us up."

Nyle walked behind them. Payton looked completely at ease with the demonic man.

"Always," Dev answered. "Besides, your mother has been demanding Ryland's return. We were trying to finish the repairs so everyone could make the trip."

14

Payton arched a brow at Ryland from across the mess hall table. Shifter men tended to be overprotective of women. Though she was the oldest, her younger brothers had inherited that anti-quated trait from their father. It came from a time when shifter women were scarce—as they still were —and the off-world brides who came to the planet were often no match for fangs and claws.

She wasn't sure what bothered Ryland more—the fact she'd been kidnapped or the fact she'd half mated a cyborg who couldn't return her affections. Ryland took the idea of marriage very seriously, and for her to marry a machine would make a mockery of it in his eyes. She also knew his concern came from a place of love.

Materialized slices of Qurilixen blue bread and meats were laid out on a tray between them. Yevgen sat beside her even though he was not eating. Nyle was across from her, next to her brother. She wished Nyle was closer, if only so that she could brush her hand against his.

Jackson and Dev were monitoring space to make sure they weren't being followed from Torgan, and Rick was flying. She had known the men her entire life and seeing them felt like visiting family.

"How did this happen?" Ryland asked.

"Nyle led mercenaries to me," Yevgen answered, even though Ryland was not directing questions toward him. "I am an important payload."

Payton rubbed her temple. "They would have come either way."

"I meant the marriage," Ryland stated.

"Technically we are half mates," Yevgen said. "But there are no other half mates. Mathematically the concept is not logical, as there can't be hundreds of halves, but there can be hundreds of half mates. I am told language and math do not have to coincide."

"Ah, see, Ryland, only half mates." Rick appeared in the doorway. "You're all worked up over nothing. We love whom we love."

Rick paused to kiss Payton on the top of her head. He had never been one to judge.

Ryland ignored the pilot. "Our parents don't know, do they? Or is this why they have been frantically sending for me to come back?"

"You were the last one I thought would be so judgmental, rocket boy." For some reason, she couldn't meet Nyle's gaze.

"I can't believe you're being so flippant," Ryland countered.

"And they've been trying to get you to come back because we've been waiting for the Federation to make their move," Payton said. "Though I don't know what our mother thinks you can do to help."

"Children, don't fight," Rick scolded. "Or we'll have to settle this argument like we used to."

"This ship doesn't have VR," Ryland dismissed.

"You're just scared I'll beat you again," Payton teased.

"You never beat me. I let you win." Ryland grumbled in frustration. "Stop trying to change the topic. How can you follow our misogynistic grandfather's tradition and take multiple spouses? Can you even have multiple? Wives were never allowed to in the past."

"That's because there were no female shifters," Payton stated.

"So this is your attempt to stir up trouble and prove something about shifter women being as strong as shifter men?" Ryland insisted. "Can you even marry a cyborg? He's a machine."

Payton finally glanced at Nyle. He looked like he wanted to fade into the shadows.

"Ryland, I'm done talking about this," she said.

"You are my sister. He's not..." Ryland followed her gaze to Nyle as if the man would support his view.

"I am the Prince of Shelter City," Yevgen interrupted. "So you don't need to worry, my brother. I will treat her as my princess."

Payton couldn't help her smirk as she bit back a laugh.

"He's not alive," Ryland finished.

"What is life? I bleed. I can be shut down," Yevgen said. "My consciousness can cease. I have living tissue."

"So do ceffyls," Ryland returned, "but you don't see anyone marrying them."

Ceffyls were native to Qurilixen. Locals used the horned animals for transport. Though they had reptilian eyes and a long slithering tongue, they had the bodies of mammals and made for a comfortable ride.

Rick picked up a slice of blue bread from the tray. "You know I am always up for an adventure, little one. Why don't you tell us what we're up against here?"

Payton sighed, grateful for Rick changing the subject.

"Yevgen has proof of the Federation's misdeeds at Shelter City. We need to get him home intact." Payton met Nyle's gaze. She couldn't tell what he was thinking, and he hadn't said much since they boarded the ship. "Nyle came to warn us. We were taken by mercenaries who wished to sell that information. They didn't intend to kidnap me, but I was there. After they had me, they wanted to sell me on Torgan."

No one spoke as they all watched her.

Payton continued, telling them about Captain Rita and how they'd managed to escape, leaving out any detail hinting at her personal relationship with Nyle. Her brother was already glaring at Yevgen. She didn't need to give Ryland a reason to also turn his bad mood toward Nyle.

Rick tossed his bread back onto the tray and went to the food simulator. "Won't be the first time we've had to outsmart the Federation. They're like a pus-filled infection the universes can't cure."

"How did you get involved with this?" Ryland asked Nyle. He gestured toward his temple. "Were you in Shelter City and saw the mercenaries when they came for them?"

"He does not live at Shelter City," Yevgen said.

"But you're..." Ryland again motioned toward his temple to indicate Nyle's markings.

"He is Cysgodian Nyle, bastard son of an unknown off-worlder and Diana," Yevgen stated. "He should have been dead, but he is not."

"Yevgen," Payton tried to warn him to stop talking with her tone. Not surprisingly, the cyborg didn't pay heed.

"He is my creator from Yeven Genetic Cyborgtronics Laboratories. That is where the virus originated in a cyborg tissue-growing facility. I also have evidence of these crimes," Yevgen said.

Rick's normally jovial expression dropped. "*The virus?* I thought no one knew how that happened."

Nyle shifted uncomfortably in his seat and looked at his hands.

"Nyle had nothing to do with its development," Payton insisted.

"That's not exactly true," Yevgen disagreed. "It was his cloned organs used for the—"

"Yevgen, stop," Payton ordered. "What is with you? Your programming seems off. Run a diagnostic or something."

"My system is optimal. Nyle should not have taken sexual advantage of my wife." Yevgen looked at Ryland. "Logic says he is of low moral character. These actions prove it."

Payton stiffened.

Nyle stood. "Maybe I should..." He made a move toward the door.

Ryland shot up from his seat, blocking Nyle. "What happened with my sister?"

Payton pushed to her feet. "Stop it. All of you. No one took advantage of me."

"I know something happened. I monitored the ship," Yevgen said. "I do not blame you."

"I chose to have sex with him," Payton stated. "He's my lover. I don't need anyone's permission."

Jackson stopped in the doorway and instantly turned around, leaving the way he had come.

"Uh." Nyle looked to be at a loss for words.

"Do I have a say?" Yevgen asked. "I would like to forbid it."

Payton took a deep breath. Frustration filled

her. "No—"

"Yeah." Ryland arched a brow, challenging her. "Doesn't your *husband* get a say?"

There were several responses Payton could give to that. None of them made her look very favorable. If she pointed out that their grandfather, King Attor, never had to ask his wives before taking more wives or lovers, she would be comparing herself to one of the most deeply flawed rulers in their history. If she admitted she was wrong, she would be saying her time with Nyle was a mistake, and no part of it felt like a mistake. If she suddenly denied Yevgen was a half mate, she'd look insane.

The full impact of her careless decision not to deny Yevgen when he announced their connection struck her like a fist to the chest. At the time, it had almost been a joke. She wasn't laughing now.

When Yevgen had declared that she was his half mate, she honestly hadn't cared. Why not let him have it? He wanted so badly to love her. Maybe he did, in his own cyborg way. What was love anyway but a belief?

Her eyes met Nyle's. Her heartbeat quickened.

No. That was wrong. Love was much more than a belief in something. It was a feeling.

"I..." Payton took a deep breath.

She couldn't look away from Nyle. Her entire life, she'd never met anyone who made her think she might want marriage or a family, who could make her heart beat faster and her thoughts spin. She liked running in the forest, the freedom of not having to answer to anyone but herself.

"I am done talking about my personal life," Payton stated. "We need to get Yevgen back to the palace before the Federation shows and attempts to muscle their way back onto our planet over some technicality. We all know they were only on Quril-ixen because they claimed guardianship over the Cysgodian people in Shelter City. If we don't prove they abused their power, they're going to use our throwing them off the planet as a reason to create a permanent base."

"There was nothing else King Kirill and King Ualan could have done." Rick crossed his arms over his chest and stared down at the table. "I remember that day the Federation came to ask for help on behalf of Cysgod. They said they would provide housing but did not mention they planned on setting up a base on-world. In hindsight, everyone should have guessed it. If there is a way to screw someone, the Federation will find a way to do that and more."

"It was those pictures of the children." Dev

entered the mess hall. Being as he was half Belvon, a demonic-looking race with intensely red skin, the man could strike fear into most aliens—and with good reason. Belvons weren't exactly known for their kindness. However, the man's human half gave him a compassionate perspective. "And the fact the blue radiation was one of the few things that seemed to help. Even if they suspected the Federation would try to take over part of the planet, the kings would not have said no."

"It's true," Nyle said, taking a step back from Ryland. "The blue radiation saved them."

Ryland sat back down. "According to Qurilixian honor, to do so would have been the same as killing the alien survivors themselves."

"Since you weren't in Shelter City with the others, how did you survive the sickness?" Rick asked Nyle.

"The virus was harvested on his cloned organs," Yevgen answered for him. There was a gossipy quality to his tone.

Payton frowned. "Those are the same organs you carry."

Great, now *she* was bickering with Yevgen.

Rick seemed to sense her need to end the conversation. "We'll get you back to the planet.

We'll call the palace and let them know we're on the way as soon as we get a clear signal."

Payton nodded.

"We should make a copy of the files," Dev said. "If something happens to the cyborg, we'll be able to prove what was inside him."

"I do not think—" Yevgen tried to deny.

"Do it," Payton broke in. "The future of Qurilixen is on the line. We're not taking chances."

"Come with me." Dev motioned at Yevgen. "I'll hook you up in the communications room, and we'll start the transfer. Might take a while. It's an old ship."

Payton listened to Yevgen's heavy steps as he followed Dev.

"You look tired. Come on, I'll show you where you can rest up." Rick draped his arms over her shoulders and steered her toward the corridor. "You too, Nyle. Unless you want to stay here and get interrogated by Ryland?"

"I think—" Ryland began to say.

"Quiet, cadet." Rick grinned. "I'm captain of this ship. Listen to your elders and let your sister rest, or I'll make you swab the decks."

"What does that even mean, old man?" Ryland muttered. "You are so strange."

15

Nyle wanted to say so much but to Payton, not her family and particularly not Yevgen. Whatever was going on with the cyborg's programming felt like more than a glitch. He was being petty, argumentative, and vengeful. These were not traits programmed in by Yeven Genetic Cyborgtronics Laboratories. Sure, cyborgs could sound assertive when they talked about facts, but there shouldn't have been anything behind it.

If Nyle didn't know better, he'd have thought Yevgen actually had feelings.

Nyle knew better. It was all sophisticated—*glitchy*—programming. That was it.

Then why was it bothering him so much?

He glanced toward Payton. She walked in front of him beside Rick.

It didn't take a genius to figure out why it bothered him. There was no point in his denying it. He wanted Payton. He wanted to touch her, hold her, make love to her, fly away into deep space with her. He wanted to go back to that moment when the world faded away, and it was just the two of them alone in the storage closet.

Nyle had accepted long ago that he rarely got anything he wanted.

"I don't need to tell you that I'll drop you out of the hatch into the deep black if you hurt her, do I?" Rick asked, not looking back at him.

"I would never hurt her." Nyle frowned. What was it with everyone threatening to eject him into space like trash?

Pay day. Payload. Space trash.

Rick stopped and gestured toward a door. "You can rest in there. Yevgen will be hooked up for a while with Dev. It looked like the two of you had some things to discuss. No one will bother you until we are able to call the palace."

Payton nodded. "Thank you."

Rick gave him a small nod as he strode down the hall. He hummed softly to himself before singing, *"Our birth was a hard one, or so we've been told, our mothers were harlots our fathers out cold. The doctor was drunk, lads, the bartender did pour, as we shot out with the thunder and came with a roar."*

"Your uncle is..." Nyle tried to think of a diplomatic word.

"Odd?" Payton chuckled. She began softly humming the same tune as she put her hand against the door scanner.

"Yes." Nyle breathed a little easier now that they were alone.

"Rick's always flown his own path." Payton went inside the room.

Like the rest of the ship, the quarters appeared well kept but old in design. He half expected loud clanks to echo through the walls, but the ride remained smooth. Faded paint on the metal walls marked the outside door. He'd seen similar symbols throughout the corridors. A faint vibration came from the floor as he stepped inside, as if the engine room was close by. Someone had taken care of this spacecraft.

"Are you coming?" Payton asked, prompting him to follow her inside.

The door slid shut behind him. A viewing

screen hung from the ceiling and buttons lined the wall to control hidden furniture.

"The crew seems to really care about you," he noted.

"I've known Rick, Jackson, and Dev my entire life. That story I told you earlier about how my parents met. Rick and Dev were there with my mother when she kidnapped my father. Jackson was on my Uncle Jarek's crew at the time, and they came to rescue him. It's how they all met. You know, now that I think about it, they all have interesting stories about how they met their wives. Maybe they'll tell you about it someday."

Nyle liked the sound of there being a someday for them, but he didn't see how that would be possible. "I'm sorry if I have made things more difficult for you with your family."

"Who, Ryland?" Payton waved her hand in dismissal. She pushed a button and the wall opened. A small couch slid out and the viewing screen lowered by a couple of feet. "He'll get over it. He's overprotective. It's one of his least endearing traits. But he's also fair. I think he's most upset about Yevgen."

"I can understand that," Nyle said.

Her expression fell by small degrees. "I know it's complicated."

He nodded.

She sat on the couch, rested her elbows on her knees, and threaded her fingers together. Her gaze trained on the floor. "I know I made a mistake."

He could tell that was difficult for her to admit. He didn't move as he stood in the doorway.

"I shouldn't have let Yevgen announce we were half mates. I should have told him no. I didn't think I'd want..." Payton took a deep breath and looked up at him. She slowly shook her head. "I didn't think I'd ever want anything like..."

He held his breath, waiting for her to finish, scared that if he exhaled the moment would be over.

"Anything like you," she whispered. A tear slipped down her cheek. "I'm sorry, Nyle. I feel like I betrayed you before I even knew you."

Nyle went to her and pulled her into his arms. The smell of desert sand scented her hair from their time on Torgan's surface. A hint of dust still smudged her cheek.

"I had no right to act with jealousy over Yevgen," he said. "You couldn't betray anyone. There is too much honor in you."

"You don't hate me for being half mated?"

By all the blessed stars, how could he resist the pull of her beautiful eyes staring up at him? How could any man be mad at a woman like her? He could no more hate her than he could wish to cut off his own arm.

"Hate you?" Nyle shook his head. "No, princess. If I had to name what I feel when I'm with you, I would say I'm amazed by you. You're attractive and brave and strong. If I were worthy of you, I'd fall in love with you."

Nyle could have easily said, *I love you.* It would have been the truth. It didn't seem fair to put that on her, though. There was no future for them. She was a princess. He was a space bum with a jaded past. In no reality was he worthy of her.

Oh, but how he wished he were.

When this was over, she would remain on Quril-ixen. He doubted her royal family would welcome him into their home, let alone their family. No part of him wanted to make that moment harder for her. It would already be torture for him when it came time to leave.

And he would have to leave. Someone needed to return to Cysgod to ensure the virus formula was destroyed before anyone got hold of that old article and went to the laboratories looking for it. Before, no one knew what they were looking for, and the dangerous trip wouldn't have been worth it. That damned newspaper chip was like a pirate's treasure map.

He should not hint again at loving her. Sometimes love was keeping the words inside, to forgo what one wanted for what the other person needed.

Her eyes remained on his. "What are you thinking just now? I can normally read people, but for some reason, there are moments when you're a complete mystery."

"I desire you," he said.

"Well, that part is obvious." Payton laughed. Her smile brightened her face, and it radiated over him. Her nearness pulled him like gravity, and he forever wanted to be in her orbit.

Her gaze dipped to his mouth. When she looked up at him again, her eyes had lightened with the threat of a shift.

"I desire you as well." The glow subsided as she suppressed the animal within. Her lips parted, and she leaned closer. It was all the invitation he needed. He would always give her whatever she wanted.

His heart quickened as their lips touched. The soft movements of their mouths encouraged the sway of their bodies. Time slipped away, just as it had in the storage room.

His fingers skimmed her clothing as he looked to free her. She held his face, keeping his mouth to hers. When she pulled back to draw a heavy breath, her hands slid down his neck to rest on his shoulders.

"Take off those clothes." Payton pushed the button to retract the couch and then pressed a second one that slid a bed from the wall. "I don't want to lose a second."

He obeyed. How could he not? Nyle kicked off his boots. He pulled his shirt over his head and tossed it on the floor.

Payton unbuckled her top and wriggled out of it. She took a deep breath. "I'm glad to be out of that thing."

Nyle gave a half smile. "I can't say I disagree."

She kicked her shoes and pushed her pants down her legs. Nyle did not turn away from the show.

Payton grinned when she caught him staring. She hooked her fingers into his waistband and pulled him closer. When she kissed him, it was deeper than before. Need filled him like a darkness desperate to feel the light.

She was that light.

Payton walked him back to the bed, leading him to the edge of the low mattress. Tugging at his waistband, she swung him around so that he landed on his back with a small bounce. Almost instantly, she appeared at the end of the bed. Deft hands pulled the pants from his hips and off his legs.

She crawled forward. Her hair hid her face as she came over him. The strands tickled his legs. Each brush was a tease.

Payton kissed his inner thigh, sending a shiver over him. He reached for her, wanting her close. He slid her up his body before turning to pin her beneath him. Her legs naturally parted, and he settled between them.

Nyle took his time exploring her body, kissing her neck before moving down the valley of her breasts. He felt the heavy beat of her heart hammering beneath his mouth, and he knew she was as affected as he was by their joining. Her fingers curled into his hair as if to navigate his movements. She steered him to one nipple and then the other.

Payton pushed his head lower on her stomach. She inhaled sharply as his mouth moved along her sex. His kiss deepened as he tasted her.

I love you. I love you.

His mind begged him to confess, but his mouth was busy.

"Nyle," she whispered.

Payton pulled his hair hard, dragging his mouth back up to hers. She squirmed beneath him until his body fitted as they were meant to. Everything about this woman captivated him.

She urged him onto his back so that she could straddle him. She grabbed hold of his wrists and pushed his hands down. Nyle wasn't sure if she wished to restrain him or simply needed something to hold on to. Either way, he gave her control.

Her warm flesh moved along his, stroking and teasing. He moaned in appreciation. She kissed his neck and chest before sitting up. She took his hands with her before placing them on her hips.

Nyle caressed her curves as Payton guided him inside her. That intimate contact sent a wave of anticipation through him like a rocket. The slow thrust nearly caused his heart to stop as he held his breath.

Nyle tried to beg, but no sound would leave his throat. He was under her complete control.

When finally, she began to rock back and forth, he inhaled sharply. Her hands pressed against his chest, and she remained upright. Their eyes met and held. He gripped her hips, lifting and pulling her back down. Pleasure built between them, centering on his stomach.

Her eyes closed, and her head tilted back. The soft overhead light illuminated her beautiful form. It caressed her parted lips and long neck. He would carry the image of her beauty with him into eternity.

Passion overtook them as she quickened her movements. He tried to resist, but his climax rocked through them, begging her to join. Payton stiffened, crying out softly as she trembled in release.

As the quivering subsided, she gave a tiny laugh and collapsed forward against him. She stretched her body along his and rolled to the side to lay next to him on the mattress. Her hand rested on his chest.

"I wish we could lock that door and never leave this room," she said.

He kissed the top of her head as she snuggled into him.

"And watch the universes just melt away?" he asked.

She nodded. "Computer. Lights."

The lights flickered and turned off.

She nestled closer. "From the second I woke up on Rita's ship, all I wanted was to get back home.

Now we're flying there, and I find I don't want to go. I want to stay here."

Nyle grinned at the admission.

"Why are you smiling like that?" Payton asked, poking his side. "You're looking very proud of yourself."

"Who said I was smiling?"

"Shifter eyes have great night vision. I see everything."

Nyle's grin widened. He felt around in the dark to find her face. His fingers found the flesh of her neck and slid upward. He cupped her jaw and ran his thumb along her bottom lip as he guided her mouth to his.

A HARD JERK DREW PAYTON FROM THE WARM fog of sleep. Her body tilted, and she slid toward the foot of the bed. Her arms flailed, and she caught Nyle as he moved beside her. Before they launched off the end, the ship pitched in the other direction, and they glided toward the head. Payton managed to catch them as the flat of her hand struck the wall with a loud thud.

"Good morning, shipmates," Rick's voice announced on the ship's comms. "Sorry about the rough skies. I recommend you find," the com-link crackled, "hold on to. We're going to microgravity as we divert power—*blast it!*"

The ship lurched again.

"Lights on!" Payton held on to Nyle as they slid. The room lights flickered to illuminate the quarters.

Nyle grabbed the edge of the bed and kept them from sliding off. When the ship righted, he pulled himself up and hurried to get their clothing from the floor. He tossed her shirt next to her on the bed.

"Don't want you to worry," Rick's voice resumed. "The ship shooting at us is a short ranger."

"Someone's shooting at us?" Nyle repeated in surprise, tugging on his pants.

"Rick's the best pilot that I—" The ship jerked and trembled, cutting off her words. They remained upright.

"We'll outrun them," Rick stated.

Payton followed Nyle's lead, pulling on her clothes. She didn't buckle the shirt.

The ship continued to shake.

"This is not how I thought we'd spend the morning," he admitted.

Payton had enjoyed sleeping in his arms. She should have known it wouldn't last. She tugged on her boots.

Nyle opened the door and stepped into the corridor as the ship jarred again. He held on to the frame. "We should get to the cockpit."

"We need to find Yevgen and keep him safe," she countered.

The ship trembled violently, and a grinding noise came through the walls. The lights turned off in the sleeping quarters, and the corridor lights dimmed to a soft green that came from beneath the floor grates. Her eyes adjusted easily to the shadows.

Nyle reached for her hand and pulled her behind him as he rushed toward the cockpit. Her feet suddenly lifted off the ground as they tried to run, and her stomach lurched. She felt suspended for a brief second before gravity pulled her feet down once more. Nyle stumbled with her and tried to run forward. They made it a few steps before they again lifted off the ground, floating weightless in the corridor.

Payton felt like she was falling. She kicked her feet, but it didn't seem to make much of a difference as she barely moved. If she didn't see the floor beneath her, she would have assumed she was upside down.

Nyle pulled her through the air. He pushed his hand along the wall to launch them forward. They swam through the corridor as if suspended in water without moisture. Her legs lifted behind her, and she became parallel with the floor.

Dev appeared from around the corner. "Are you unharmed?"

"I haven't done this since I was a child," Payton said, trying to float to a stop before they crashed into him. Without something solid to push against, her flailing did little good.

"Who is chasing us?" Nyle asked.

"Looks like a Federation scouting ship. It isn't made for deep space travel, but it's fast. There will be a mother ship behind it." Dev moved back the way he'd come and led them around a corner. "We need to get you strapped in. Rick's going to outrun them, but it'll be a bumpy, dark ride. We're diverting all power to the engines."

Nyle grabbed the corner and pulled them around after Dev. Her feet overshot the turn, and she kicked off the wall. Ugly creaks reverberated through the metal. They floated in the air, physically unaffected by the shaking vessel. Dev reached a doorway and grabbed the frame before holding his hand out for Payton. She took it, and he pulled her through the door. Her hand slipped from Nyle's as she went into the small communications room.

"Buckle in," Dev ordered.

Yevgen already waited, strapped down in a seat with two disconnected wires suspended next to him.

"You should not worry, my love. I have calculated a sixty-seven percent chance of survival."

The lights flickered, and the ship lurched, whipping Yevgen's head forward.

"Fifty-six percent chance of survival," Yevgen corrected.

Payton pulled herself into a seat next to Yevgen. Her body hovered weightless over the cushion as she struggled to grab the straps floating in the air beside it. Yevgen pushed on her thigh to steady her into the chair. Her hair drifted around her head.

"You too," Dev ordered Nyle. "And don't move from the seats unless we tell you to."

Dev pushed out of the room.

Nyle pulled himself into a seat across from her. His eyes locked on hers. He strapped himself in as if he'd done it a million times. The ship continued to shake, each vibration rocking through her now that she was held down.

"Do you think Captain Rita somehow contacted the Federation, and that's how they found us?" Payton asked.

"That was an alien ship that—" Nyle began.

"Fifty-three percent chance of survival," Yevgen interrupted.

Nyle glared at the cyborg. "Anything is possible.

Even Yevgen had a difficult time with the technology on *World Traveler*."

"I rescued us," Yevgen corrected.

Nyle turned his attention to Payton, pointedly ignoring the cyborg. "Rita or one of the crew could have escaped before Yevgen's lockdown ended. Or the Federation had someone waiting for them at Torgan and when the *World Traveler* flew past, they went to investigate. I don't think it matters. This is where we're at."

"Forty—" Yevgen put forth.

"I will disconnect you," Nyle warned.

"It's not helpful," Payton told Yevgen in a softer tone. She felt the gravity beneath her fluctuating, becoming stronger to hold her against the chair.

"But—" the cyborg said.

Payton held up her hand. "We need to focus forward, not dwell on the odds of our death."

The ship pitched, giving the sensation of turning her on her side in the seat. The low gravity kept her weight from pulling her down even as the seat kept her strapped in. Her hair reached to the side. She held her breath and gripped as they bounced. A metal bolt fell slowly close to her head.

"There is a forty-nine percent chance of us going forward," Yevgen stated.

She felt Nyle's hand on her leg. The contact calmed her even as the ship rotated them upside down, moving the strands of her hair to indicate the ship's direction before they flipped back upright. The sensation of falling in place returned as the gravity lessened. Her head lightened, and her insides felt strange like they jumped around in her stomach.

She'd seen the dragon-shifters on her planet flying erratically in the sky, flipping, diving, and turning every which way. This flight reminded her of that. Every time she witnessed their reckless stunts, she was grateful to have her feet firmly on the ground. Cat-shifters were not meant to be higher than they could jump or climb.

Her thoughts churned, but she refused to let fear creep into her heart. She had to focus on the future. Her homeworld needed the information in Yevgen's head. It was that simple. How could she fear for herself with so much on the line?

Her eyes met Nyle's. But she *did* fear for him. She didn't want to lose him.

"Payton...?" Nyle looked as if he wanted to say much more. He glanced at Yevgen.

"This is where we are, and we know where we need to go," she answered, the vibrating ship causing her words to tremble. She thought of what her father would say, before adding, "When battles seem to be at their lowest and most dire, focusing forward is the only way through."

Nyle nodded, as if seeming to understand.

"Rick will outrun them," Payton continued, not sounding very reassuring as the jerking ship caused her voice to quiver. "My mother said he is the best pilot she has ever seen."

She released the arm of the chair and placed her hand over Nyle's on her leg. Seconds later Yevgen grabbed her hand from above and curled his fingers around hers.

"I understand now," Yevgen stated. "I found Rick's collection of intergalactic transmissions."

Gravity locked her back into the seat as the ship pitched again, twirling them upside down. Payton pulled her hand from between theirs and closed her eyes, willing the ride to be over. She gripped the arm of the chair.

"Most of his transmission featured women who kept accidentally losing their clothing," Yevgen stated. "It seems to be a unique problem from Old Earth. Or perhaps their alien greeting when service workers came into their homes."

"Yev—" The ship jerked, cutting off her words.

What in the universes was the cyborg going on about?

"They often seem surprised by it. Perhaps they needed better seamstresses," Yevgen continued, completely unaffected by the fact they were spinning in circles on the run from the Federation.

"I think he's broken," Nyle said, raising his voice over the rattling metal.

The ship flipped back around.

"You are not at ease, my love. I should help fly." Yevgen reached for the two wires that had been floating when they first came into the room. He jabbed the tips into his arm. The cyborg's eyes flashed.

"Yev, don't," Payton managed.

The ship's path smoothed, and the lights flickered on. Payton took a deep breath but barely released it before a loud explosion echoed all around them, followed by the sound of static.

"We took a hit. Get that blasted machine out of my controls before he fries us all," Rick ordered over the comms.

Yevgen lifted his arms from Payton so she couldn't take his control away.

Nyle unhooked his straps and surged forward, jerking the wires out of Yevgen. The lights dimmed, and gravity released. Nyle's feet lifted from the floor. Yevgen kicked the man's shin, sending him upward. Nyle flailed his arms. Payton grabbed his shirt.

"I got you," she said, trying to pull Nyle toward her.

Gravity returned, causing Payton's arm to drop faster than she intended. Nyle was forced downward. His knees struck the floor hard, causing the metal to clank at the contact. His head barely missed the arm of her chair.

Payton instantly wrapped her arms and legs around him the best she could to clasp him against her in the chair as the ship continued to pitch back and forth. He grabbed her straps to help her hold on.

"I got you," she repeated, gripping him tight. "Don't worry. I won't let go."

17

"I won't let go."

Those words repeated themselves in Nyle's mind, as the feel of Payton's fingers dug into his arms and back as she kept him from slipping away. His head was buried next to her thigh. The metal arm of her chair bumped his temple. The ship pitched back and forth. He kept hold of Payton to keep from being tossed around. Pain radiated from his knees. Gravity lessened and tightened its hold, unpredictable in its rhythm. Each time it pulled him down, the pressure made the pain worse.

Don't let go.

The jerking lessened, and the gravitational pull seemed to settle. He wasn't sure how much time had passed before the flight smoothed. Her fingers stroked his hair. He lifted his head to look up at her. Lights flickered, struggling to come on.

"I think it's over," she whispered as if afraid saying the words too loud would somehow cause more damage to the ship.

"Whoo-hoo, that's right, ladies and gentlemen," Rick exclaimed over the comms. "That's how you fly."

Payton gave a small laugh and visibly relaxed. The lights continued to flicker. "I told you he was the best pilot we know."

"Ryland, Jackson, check the engine room and try to fix whatever damage you can to the bio controls. I have lights flickering and have to take the viewing screen to manual," Rick continued, his voice a little staticky. "Since *someone* tried to take over flying, and we ended up taking it hot and hard up the ass."

Nyle frowned at Yevgen.

"Payton, you and your friends kick back and take things easy. We'll be right with you. And keep your cyborg out of my ship." Rick's words were punctuated by the sound of the comms clicking off.

Nyle slowly pushed up, his knees aching as he sat back in the chair. He rubbed his thigh and took a deep breath.

"Qurilixen has ties to Old Earth, does it not?" Yevgen asked.

"What are you going on about?" Nyle frowned. Actually, he wasn't sure he wanted the cyborg to answer that.

"I am trying to understand my wife's need for your company," Yevgen said. "She has not taken you as a half mate, and yet she is showing you favor. The Old Earth transmissions stored by Uncle Rick indicate some women wish to be with two men at—"

"Stop talking," Payton ordered.

"But—"

She held up her hand to cut off his words. "Yevgen, I'm serious. We're not having this conversation."

"You have never been this short-tempered with me," Yevgen stated. "The only logical answer is you are stressed by nearly dying in space."

Payton closed her eyes and shook her head as she took a deep breath.

Nyle stopped rubbing his legs and waited to see what she'd say. He wanted her to tell Yevgen they weren't married, that it had been a mistake to allow him to think that.

Instead, Payton took Yevgen's hand. "We have been through much, old friend. Let's get through this. Let's make sure the Federation never comes back to Qurilixen. Let's protect the Cysgodians. *That* is what matters and what we will focus on."

Yevgen nodded in agreement. "Yes. We must protect the Cysgodians of Shelter City."

...of Shelter City.

Nyle hid his reaction. The cyborg wanted Nyle to know that he did not consider the man worthy of his protection.

"And I must protect you, my love," Yevgen stated.

"I'm going to find a medical booth. I landed on my knees." Nyle said the first excuse he could think of. He had to step away from the cyborg before trying something stupid, like ripping Yevgen's wires out through his nose.

"Let me help." Payton reached for him.

He pushed to his feet. It hurt to stand and even more so to walk.

"Perhaps we should attempt to send a communication to the Var palace," Yevgen said.

"Dev will take care of that," Payton answered. "You heard Rick. He doesn't want you messing with his ship."

"Maybe you should stay here." Nyle stopped her from coming with him. Someone needed to babysit the cyborg and keep him from causing trouble. "I'll be fine. I know where the booth is located. I won't be long."

Nyle wasn't sure how he managed to make it out of the communications room without limping, but he suspected it had something to do with pride. Payton didn't follow him even though she'd looked like she wanted to.

"I believe this is cosmic justice for his trying to remove my legs." Yevgen's voice followed Nyle.

"Trying to save our lives does not rise to the level of needing cosmic justice," Payton dismissed. "Because that's what Nyle was doing in that lab. He wanted to make sure we could carry you off that ship."

Nyle slid his shoulder against the wall in an unsuccessful attempt to support his weight as he limped down the metal corridor. The sound of their voices faded. He made his way to the medical booth.

All he wanted in the universes was to be worthy of Payton. And it was the one thing he could never be.

He pushed a button and slid onto his back inside the unit. An ache formed inside his chest, worse than the pain in his legs. There was nothing the medical booth could do for his heart.

18

"WHAT DO YOU MEAN HE ISN'T WAKING UP?" Payton demanded even as she pushed past her brother to run down the ship's corridor. "Nyle!"

Her heart beat violently. This had to be a joke. It couldn't be real.

"It was just his knees," she reasoned. "I should have insisted I go with him. He said it was just his knees."

"Payton," Ryland called after her.

The tone of his voice made her stop and turn around.

"In here," he gestured into a room.

She didn't think as she turned to go where he indicated. "Nyle?"

Payton stepped into the sleeping quarters. She looked around, confused, not seeing him.

"I'm sorry." Ryland's apology was followed by the sound of a door sliding shut. "It's for the best."

Payton felt the animal surging to the surface as she leaped to stop the door. Her hand hit flat as it latched shut. She stood, half shifted, and clawed at the metal to force it open. She slammed her hand against the wall scanner, but it didn't light up.

"Ryland," she yelled angrily. "Sacred cats! Let me out of here!"

She continued to assault the door, scratching the metal's finish.

"Ryland!"

Breathing heavily, she searched the small quarters. Was this some sort of brotherly prank? Did that mean Nyle was unharmed?

She paced around the room, pausing a few times to put her hand against the scanner. The door didn't open.

"Payton," Ryland's voice came over the ship's comms. "I know you're upset—"

"Livid!" she yelled over his words.

"—but I'm doing this because I care about you. You're not thinking straight—"

"I'm thinking fine!"

"—and are making questionable decisions. I—"

"You're a questionable decision!"

"—know you would do the same for me if you thought I was in trouble."

"Oh, you *are* in trouble, Ryland. When I get out of here, I'm going to kick your furry ass!" Payton slammed her hands against the door. "I want to see Nyle! Open this door. I need to see Nyle!"

Her heart pounded, and she tried to catch her breath.

"Yevgen!" she yelled, knowing the cyborg had great hearing. "I need you. I'm locked in a room. Come get me out—"

"Hello, my love. This is Yevgen," the cyborg said over the comms as if she wouldn't know him.

Payton looked toward the ceiling as if she could somehow glare at his voice hard enough to let him feel her anger.

"My new brother Ryland and I have discussed the situation and have agreed that you have been acting out of your normal character. You are not one to take a lover. Especially not a man who has a connection to Yeven Genetic Cyborgtronics Laboratories. And you are not one to disregard the traditions of marriage, even if it is a half mating. He has explained what it means to be a Var husband. As a shifter, you are physically strong and worthy of battle. However, as your husband, it is my duty to protect you and intervene in mental health matters. I promise to help you."

Payton threw up her hands and growled low in her throat. What in all the universes was this nonsense? She paced around the room, trying to calm her breathing. It felt like she'd stepped into a parallel world where her brother and best friend had lost their damned minds.

"Good news. We're flying clear skies and have most of our life support systems intact," Rick announced. "Dev tells me we might lose lights again as we divert power. Don't panic. We're going to try to burst a transmission to the Var towers and let them know we're on our way. As to the current travel arrangements, I can't say that I agree, but Payton you rest easy. We'll get it all settled once we land. I'll let you know as soon as Nyle is out of the medical booth."

Payton closed her eyes and tried to feel relief. Nyle was in the booth. He was receiving care. Logic said her brother stirring up panic had just been a ruse to get her into this cage. Still, she couldn't completely tamp down the fear that remained, the thoughts that whispered, *what if?*

What if he didn't wake up?

What if Ryland removed Nyle from the ship before she could talk to him?

What if he told their elders what he believed to be the truth?

What if she didn't get a chance to explain? A chance to defend Nyle? A chance to tell him she...

"Nyle, I'm sorry," she whispered as she dropped to the floor. "I should have been better. I should have made better choices. Everything's a mess."

Payton was sorry she'd half mated with Yevgen. She loved her friend, but she wasn't in love with him. Shifters did not take mating lightly, but that's exactly what she had done. She never thought she'd find that kind of love. All her life she'd been focused on running wild and helping the Cysgodians any way she could. She was about adventure and freedom.

Now she was trapped in a marriage. It wasn't like she could simply change her mind and get out of the decision. There was a process—a long embarrassing process—and no one would prioritize it with the threat of the Federation looming and the future of so many people on the line.

She wasn't sure how long she stayed on the floor before movement sounded overhead. The lights flickered and turned dark. A soft glow illuminated the room. She looked up to where the viewing screen had lowered.

The picture of a young Nyle amongst the Cysgodian scientists appeared. She'd seen it before.

Payton slowly stood. She pushed the button to bring out a bed.

"I already know who he is," Payton yelled as she sat on the bed. Her brother and Yevgen were most likely listening. "I've seen this before."

She tried not to look up, but the light flashed, and she had a hard time ignoring the screen.

Images of Cysgod showed overhead. She knew what they were doing. Ryland wanted to make sure she'd seen them, and Yevgen appeared only too eager to help.

She didn't need to see the bodies lining the street or the funeral bonfires. She knew the toll the virus had taken on that planet. She had seen the agony and the long-term damage of the survivors.

Still, as she watched the raw grief, the suffering, the heartache, a tear slid over her cheek. How could she think of her own happiness with so much on the line?

Ryland and Yevgen had made a point. It might not be the one they wanted to make. She didn't hate

Nyle or blame him. But there were things in this world beyond the desire of two people to be together. This path she was on wasn't about her happiness. It was about the Cydgodian survivors. It was about protecting Qurilixen from the Federation occupation. That is what she needed to keep focused on. Anything else was just background static.

19

PAYTON DETERMINED A FEW THINGS WHILE locked in her cage of a room.

She hated space travel. The constant vibrations of ship engines and the sound of flickering lights felt like torture. She missed the dull thud of the earth beneath her feet and the wind whispering in the trees.

She hated the claustrophobic nature of spaceships. The air did not move inside a locked room. If she tried to imagine beyond the walls, her mind conjured images of the deep and endless black. If she never left the planet's surface ever again, she would not complain.

And she loved Nyle.

Payton wanted to rewind their time together to

handle herself differently. When Yevgen made his claim, she would have politely corrected him. When she'd met Nyle on the path toward Shelter City, she would have spoken to him and learned what he was doing on Qurilixen. Maybe then she could have alerted the shifter guards, and they could have fought off the mercenaries together.

Thinking of the past with longing wasn't helpful. Not when the future needed them.

Payton stood, staring at the door as she waited for it to open. The ship had landed. She felt every jerking shake of reentry. Rick said they were home, but she couldn't smell the fresh air or feel the heat of the suns.

"Are you calm?" Ryland's voice came through the door.

Payton felt her claws trying to extend from her fingertips. "Yes."

"You don't sound calm," Ryland insisted.

Her eyes narrowed. "Open the door."

She heard footsteps. The door slid open. Payton pushed her way out, ready to grab hold of her brother. She managed to land a kick right above his ankle as Ryland jumped back out of the way.

"Payton." The sound of her father's stern voice stopped her from further attack.

She instantly retracted her claws and turned toward him. She tried to pretend like she hadn't been caught assailing her brother. "Father."

Commander Falke stood at rigid attention, but she saw the relief on his face. "I was surprised to receive Rick's message. We didn't know you had left the planet. The guards said they had tracked you into the forest. What happened?"

"Mercenaries. They wanted Yevgen." Payton glanced back at her brother.

"The cyborg." Falke frowned.

"He has been putting together evidence for us to fight off the Federation," Payton explained. "The Federation found out he was going through the files and sent a team to stop him. I was collateral damage, as was a Cysgodian man named Nyle. He tried to stop them."

Ryland cleared his throat. Payton ignored him. As Commander, their father would demand access to everything Yevgen discovered. He was the highest-ranking Var military official. If they went to war, he would lead the charge.

"Did they succeed?" Falke asked. He made no move to leave the ship.

"No. They failed their mission. Nyle helped me escape." Payton watched her father carefully.

Nothing she said seemed to surprise him, and she had the feeling her brother had already given a version of events.

"And this Nyle, he was in the newspaper chip from Cysgod's evacuation that Nova gave the cyborg," Ryland added. "He was one of the men responsible for the virus."

"That's a misrepresentation," Payton disagreed.

"He was not pictured?" Her father asked.

"Yes, but—"

"We will show all the evidence to the family," Ryland interrupted. "You will judge for yourself."

"Where is he?" Payton kept her eyes on her father, but she felt her brother behind her. "Where's Nyle?"

"He will be treated well." Falke lifted his hands to cup the sides of her face. "I feared for you, little one."

"I'm safe," she said. "I remembered what you taught me. I kept my mind on the future, to what needed to be done."

Falke nodded at her words. "Your mother is waiting for you. Go to her." He turned his attention to his son. "Both of you. Go. She will not forgive me if I keep you much longer."

Her father held her face for a moment more

before dropping his hands and turning to lead the way off the ship.

"Where's Nyle?" Payton asked, dropping back to glare at Ryland as their father turned a corner.

"Inside the palace," Ryland answered. "With Yevgen."

"Did you hurt him?" She grabbed his arm. Her claws extended, and she couldn't control them. She shook with irritation.

Ryland's eyes flashed at the pain her grip caused but he didn't fight her off. "You don't have to ask me that. You already know I didn't. But that man is dangerous. I don't think you're seeing clearly."

"Stop arguing," Falke ordered, his voice carrying. "Your mother wishes to see you. Do not keep her waiting."

"You had no right to lock me in that room," Payton fumed, releasing his arm.

"You're not well, Payton," Ryland countered. "You think you're married to a cyborg and you're sleeping with—"

"And you're a coward. You had to get our father before letting me out because you knew I'd kick your furry ass up and down this corridor." She thrust her fist toward him before marching to follow their father off the ship.

"I love you, Payton," Ryland said, not bothering to yell after her. She heard his soft voice easily. "I don't care if you're mad at me. I won't apologize for helping you when you need me."

The first smell of forest air, as she exited the spaceship, caused her to pause and take a deep breath. It felt amazing to be home, but for some reason, she hesitated before stepping off the ship and crossing over the stone landing platform toward the steel doors that would lead inside.

The dock was an extension of the cat-shifter palace, reserved for honored guests and visiting dignitaries. The wide, flat area was high off the ground, with stone turrets providing a lookout from above. King Kirill's banner, a dark blue flag with the head of a panther hung down the side of each one.

Wind whipped her hair around her head. A softer blue-green light said that it was evening though it wouldn't get much darker at night.

She looked across at the short wall railing around the edges. She heard the faintest hint of voices on the wind. They came from the village outside the palace.

The castle palace jutted above the trees. Centuries of craftsmanship had gone into the design. The forest below stretched into the distance.

Normally, she'd be calculating the fastest route into the trees, which meant scaling down the side of the exterior palace wall. There were no stairs leading down from the platform, only steel doors.

"You won't run," Ryland said, drawing her attention back to the platform.

She hadn't realized she'd stopped walking to stare at the trees.

"When we were children, it felt as if this was everything," he continued. "Now, after having seen much of the universes, it all feels so much smaller."

"Our lives here are not small," Payton argued.

"I didn't say they were," he defended. "The planet itself feels smaller. It's about perspective."

She wasn't inclined to agree with her brother on anything at the moment.

Payton strode toward the doors. "Don't think you're worldly just because you left us to play around in the skies."

"Is that what I was doing?"

She heard the irritation in his voice. It made her feel a little better.

"As opposed to what you're doing?" he countered. "Running feral in the forest because you can't be bothered to say hello to a few visiting dignitaries?"

"I've been here, paws on the ground, helping to protect the people of Shelter City." She pulled one of the doors open just enough to slip inside. The weight pulled shut behind her, almost closing her brother outside before he caught the handle to follow her.

"Hey." He grabbed her arm to stop her from striding down the corridor. "You're my sister. I love you."

"I love you, too." She jerked her arm away and balled her hand into a fist as she turned to glare at her brother. "I also want to punch you in the face."

"My sweet babies!" The sound of rushing footsteps came up the hallway.

Payton instantly unfurled her hand.

"Hello, Mother," they said in unison as Payton turned to greet their mother.

Princess Samantha might be a humanoid who married into the shifter family, but she was a force to behold in her own right. Her father had been a Ticara royal, and because of that heritage she was a natural healer. Using the ability took much out of her, but that didn't stop her from reaching for her children's faces and using her healing magic to search for injuries.

Payton covered the tingling hand on her cheek and pulled it back. "We're unharmed."

"You aren't eating enough," her mother answered before looking at Ryland. "And there's something wrong with your ankle."

"That's what a medical booth is for," Ryland dismissed.

Samantha dropped her hands. Seeing they were, for the most part, uninjured, her expression instantly changed from concerned mother to aggravated royal.

"We've been sending for your help. What took you so long?" Samantha asked Ryland.

"We were repairing the ship." He pointed behind him toward the landing platform as if that would reinforce his excuse. "We rescued Payton. Saved her life. If not for me, she'd still be stuck for sale on Torgan."

Samantha instantly turned toward her daughter. "That wouldn't have been necessary if you had told us where you were going. We didn't even know you were off-world until Rick sent a message to tell us he had you. Torgan? Do you know how dangerous the black market is?"

"Isn't that where you took our father after you kidnapped him?" Payton asked, trying to smile.

Samantha was not amused.

"Ryland locked me in a room and didn't feed me," Payton tattled. "And I wasn't for sale. I was well on my way to escaping."

"Ryland," Samantha scolded.

"No, it was just—" Ryland protested.

"It's obvious your sister hasn't eaten enough." Samantha waved them to walk with her. "The family is in the banquet hall. You can explain to them why you imprisoned your sister."

"Payton married a cyborg," Ryland blurted.

Payton grimaced.

"Yevgen?" Samantha arched a brow. "That friendship advanced more than I thought it would."

Ryland held up his hands behind their mother's back and mouthed, "Truce?"

Payton narrowed her eyes at her brother and shook her head in denial.

"So, um, I have to ask..." Samantha kept her eyes straight ahead as they walked. "Which parts of him are of human origin?"

This was not a conversation she wanted to have with her mother. Or brother. Or anyone. Ever.

"Can he give you...?" Samantha continued.

"No, sorry. No cyborg grandchildren," Payton interrupted.

Ryland jerked a little and covered his mouth to suppress a laugh. "Maybe he can build one out of spare food simulator parts."

"Maybe Ryland can marry and give you many grandbabies," Payton countered, mocking his voice.

"As long as you have love, I am happy for you." Samantha lightly touched Payton's arm. "We will be sure to welcome him properly to the family the first moment we can."

"But..." Ryland quickened his step. "You can't be all right with this. He's a machine."

"And human," Samantha said. "If Payton loves that human part enough to marry him, that is all I need to know. All I want is for my children to be safe, healthy, and happy."

"Half mated," Payton corrected quietly. She hated to admit it, but it was better to tell her mother now before they made it to the banquet hall.

Her mother tripped but easily caught her footing. "And what about the other guest? The one locked in a guest chamber? Is he one of the men who took you?"

"Nyle? No. He's helping us. Which guest room is he in?" Payton asked.

"West corridor," Samantha answered.

Payton began to jog down the hall.

"You won't be able to see him now," Samantha called after her. "Your father's orders."

Payton stopped and hurried back. "You must talk to him. I don't know what Ryland told you, but he's wrong. Nyle is not a threat. He shouldn't be locked up."

"Your husband showed me the evidence," Ryland countered. "Was I supposed to ignore it? I'm worried about you, Payton."

She didn't care how sorry he appeared. That hadn't stopped him from snitching on her like a child reporting a list of perceived infractions.

Samantha held up her hands to stop their talking. "To the dining hall. The family is waiting."

"Everyone?" Payton asked.

Her mother nodded.

If her cousins, brothers, aunts, uncles, and parents were all in residence, they needed the dining hall to fit everyone. Payton fought the urge to run into the forest to avoid what felt like upcoming inquisition. This was not going to be pleasant.

Payton forced her expression to remain neutral as she stood in the arched doorway to the vast dining hall. Life in the Var palace starkly contrasted with that of Shelter City. The surfaces were clean, and nothing was allowed to remain in disrepair. There were times when being inside the palace walls made her feel guilty. Why should she have everything when so many had nothing?

The cat-shifter royal elders sat at the high table as if ready to pass judgment on those below. Their table was on a raised platform so that they could see when guests filled the hall. Now it was mostly family with a few trusted guards stationed at the entrances. The majority of the tables stood empty.

King Kirill and Queen Lyssa were flanked by

Payton's parents on one side, and Uncle Quinn and Aunt Tori on the other. There were two other siblings to that generation, but Reid and Jarek were off in space. The Federation wasn't the royal's only concern, just currently the direst.

Rick, Dev, and Jackson were next to her mother. The four of them were in animated conversation with Rick's laughter ringing out every so often.

In front of the high table, beneath the platform, her cousins waited. Roderic and his new wife, Justina, were in a low conversation with twins, Emma and Aliya. Like Payton the twins shifted into tiger form, but theirs was a distinct orange to her white.

A shadow moved across the floor, and she glanced up at the rounded glass ceilings. The domes diffused the light of the three suns, illuminating the gauzy strips of material that flowed from the ceiling and anchored to the walls. As she watched, she saw a dragon sweep past, casting another shadow. It was a brief glance at who it might be, but if she had to guess, she'd say the heir dragon prince, Grier, was surveying the area. Three more dragons appeared behind him, flying past the window.

"Payton," the king stated, his voice abnormally loud over the quiet murmurs.

She stiffened in surprise and turned her attention away from the dragons.

"Are you joining us?" Kirill asked, waving her toward him. She dragged her feet a little as she stepped further into the dining hall. All eyes turned toward her. It reminded her of the time one of the dragons had set a room on fire after she'd snuck them into the palace, and they'd found a case of Old Earth whiskey. She'd been called before a tribunal much like this one.

The queen placed her hand on her husband's shoulder and whispered to him. She was still technically an HIA liaison. Her stint working for the Human Intelligence Agency as an undercover agent made her particularly adept at diplomacy. They were depending on her contacts to help push back against the Federation.

"Greetings, family," Payton said, forcing her feet to lift higher so they didn't drag along the floor. Her cousin Roderic caught her attention and gave her an encouraging smile as if to say he was on her side. The look was meant to give her comfort, but the fact that he thought she needed it made her worry more.

"It's good you're home safe." Kirill smiled, but it did not hide his concern. The king's love of his family had never been in question, but neither had his love of his people. He took his responsibility very seriously.

"I hope you gave them hell," Queen Lyssa added.

Payton relaxed a little. They didn't seem upset with her.

"She locked those mercenaries up tight on their own ship and crash-landed an ejection pod on Torgan," Rick stated, giving her a wink.

Her father tapped his fingers on the table near his goblet and released a measured breath.

"She did her family name proud," Rick continued. "Reminds me of our own adventures in space, don't you think, Falke? Like father like daughter."

"Crash landing sounds more like you, Rick, than Prince Falke," Dev stated.

"And she did not marry her captor," Jackson added.

Payton knew she should keep her mouth shut, but she couldn't help herself. The corner of her lip twitched, and she said, "Well, Captain Rita wasn't really my type."

Rick laughed. Dev and Jackson suppressed smiles. No one else reacted to her joke.

"I would like permission to talk to Nyle." Payton

pointedly did not look toward Ryland. "He saved my life. He shouldn't be imprisoned."

"He's in a guest suite," her mother answered. "He's being treated well."

The king lifted his hand and motioned toward the guards. They instantly went out of the dining hall and shut the doors to leave the family alone. Kirill stood and led the way down from the platform table to join her cousins. The other elders followed.

"We're going to go get some rest. Will be nice to sleep in a real bed," Dev said, as a delicate way of excusing himself from the family discussion. He lifted his arms to gesture Rick and Jackson toward the doors.

"I'll be by later," Samantha told them.

"Bring the Torganian rum," Rick teased. "Let's see what kind of trouble we can get into."

"What is your interest in this Nyle?" Kirill asked when the men had left, motioning Payton to come closer.

Coming from a tight-knit family had its advantages. Having everyone know your affairs wasn't one of them.

"He's a good man. He saved my life." Payton went toward the king. He pulled out a chair for her at an empty table that put her in view of the others.

"We heard you were close." Kirill pressed his lips tightly together before adding, "Is he your second half mate?"

Payton's breath caught as she slowly sat down. She folded her hands in front of her on the tabletop. She wanted to say yes, but that would have been a lie. The denial trapped in her throat.

The elders sat across from her, except for her parents who came next to her. Emma and Aliya pushed up in their chairs, sitting on their knees to watch over Quinn's head.

"The cyborg said that you and he were..." The king shook his head, not finishing.

Queen Lyssa put her hand on her husband's shoulder. "We're a little confused about Yevgen. The choice is not, uh, conventional."

"She means we didn't think you were considering taking half mates." Tori tried to smile, but the look in her eyes held pity and sadness.

"If not for the Myrddinians, the practice would have died with your grandfather," Kirill stated. "We had been discussing outlawing the practice."

Payton knew not to take the king's words personally, but they stung. The royal family led by example, and they were proud of putting away the practices of the past, like taking hundreds of half mates. The Myrddinians were named after a sadist, Lord Myrddin. He'd been a close advisor to Payton's grandfather, King Attor. The old noble believed in shifter purity, which basically meant cats and dragons didn't mix, and the taking of many wives. No one in the family would want to be compared to him.

"You never indicated you had an interest in that lifestyle before." Quinn reached across the table to pat her folded hands.

"Have you given up on finding a true mate?" Tori continued, shaking her head in confusion. "I know that it must be difficult to be alone much of the time with so much pressure to act as a guardian to the Cysgodians. There haven't been many opportunities to meet potential life mates. Perhaps that is our fault?"

"We should have invited more dignitaries to the planet," Lyssa agreed. "Or maybe asked the dragons about their Galaxy Brides' contacts. If the corporation is willing to bring brides, surely, they would bring potential grooms."

Many years ago, the queen had snuck onto the planet pretending to be one of those dragon brides. Fate brought her to the cat-shifter side.

Seeing them staring at her, Payton lowered her

head and pulled her hands onto her lap. She was aware of her parents next to her and wondered why they didn't speak. Were they that disappointed?

"I understand that you're worried about the example it will set for the people, about what it means for a member of the royal family to have half mates. I didn't intend any dishonor." Payton tried to keep her voice steady, but it wavered. "I didn't think things through. I didn't believe it would matter as much as it does. Yevgen is... He cares... I, ah..."

"I think what everyone means to say is many blessings on your marriage." Roderic stood and came closer so she could easily meet his gaze. "All we want is your happiness."

"Of course," her mother stroked her back. "Many blessings. We are not here to judge you."

"Or question the will of the gods," her father added. The commander did not sound convinced.

She already felt bad about what she'd done. This was only making it worse.

"Yes, many blessings," a few of the elders added, their words mumbled.

"I'm not—" Ryland began.

"We're happy for you," Roderic interrupted. "Yevgen has proven himself a friend of the Var and of the Cysgodian people these many years. Without him, we might have lost Shelter City on several occasions. We owe him much. And I, for one, am eager to hear what information he was able to collate for us from the Federation databases. We are in his debt."

Ryland looked like he wanted to argue but instead shut his mouth.

Payton nodded at Roderic, grateful for his support. He had firsthand knowledge of what Yevgen had done, and it went beyond just saving a few lives and freeing the Cysgodians from Federation tyranny. The cyborg had assisted in eliminating the threat of mass destruction when he helped Payton and Prince Grier locate a bomb hidden in one of Shelter City's alleyways. The explosion would have killed everyone in the city. He had also helped locate one of the future dragon princesses being illegally held prisoner inside the Federation facility. The list of his deeds was endless.

"I will not dictate your choice in husbands," Kirill said.

"Thank you." Payton really wanted to stop discussing the subject. All she could think about was Nyle. "I have no intention of being like King Attor. I will not shame the family."

"No one would accuse you of shaming us." Her

father's tone was firm. "If our people have a problem with it, they can speak to me on the matter."

No one would be foolish enough to take him up on that offer.

"I love you, too," Payton whispered to him.

"You haven't asked where Yevgen is," her mother observed, stroking a piece of Payton's hair away from her face.

"Where is he?" Payton forced her gaze to move around the group of elders. Of course, she should have asked that. He was her husband. No wonder her family was confused by her choices.

"We gave him some parameters, and he's organizing the information he discovered into a coherent presentation. He's in my office for privacy," Quinn answered.

Payton pressed her lips together and shared a look with Roderic. "You left him alone by a computer port?"

"He doesn't have high-security clearance," Quinn said. "Will he damage our system?"

"Father, Yevgen likes collecting data," Roderic told Quinn. "He'll be inside any archive he can hack into, copying them."

Payton gave a small nod of agreement. "It's true."

"Do we need to isolate him?" Kirill asked.

"He won't betray us," Payton said.

"Payton and I will go make sure he's behaving," Roderic offered, moving toward Payton.

She stood, thankful for an excuse to leave.

"You haven't eaten yet," her mother protested.

"I promise, I'll make sure she does." Roderic hooked his arm through Payton's and pulled her with him toward the dining hall door.

"We have much to discuss," Kirill said.

"We'll be back." Roderic walked faster.

When they pushed open the doors, they were met by two guards. Both were half shifted into upright cats. One nodded. The other tried to suppress an annoyed growl.

"Not now Natan." Payton held her hand up to block his face from her view.

Roderic chuckled and continued to pull her with him. "What did you do to that poor man?"

"I don't remember," she lied.

"Tell me, or I'll stop this rescue and walk you right back into the inquisition." Her cousin slowed his steps and began to turn around.

"No, wait!" Payton pulled his arm hard to turn him around and mumbled, "I...*shamahim*.

"You what?"

"I shaved him," she answered in mock exasperation.

Her cousin began to shake as he suppressed his laughter. "I need more."

"My father left him to watch my brothers and me. He was new and scared of angering the commander. He really wanted to do a good job, so we convinced him to shift to play hunter. We were supposed to hide in the palace gardens, but I set up a rope trap, and when he was hanging upside down, I shaved him."

Roderic laughed.

"Then we ran off," Payton continued.

"Oh, no." Roderic's laughter died. "You didn't...?"

"My mother cut him down," she said.

"Oh, Payton."

"The fur eventually grew back," Payton defended. "He's the one still holding a grudge. It was sixty years ago."

"So you were...?"

"Like ten or twelve when it happened," Payton said. "He was a soldier. He shouldn't have let me take advantage."

"A new soldier. And you expected him to go up against the commander's children?" Roderic kept an even pace as he led her toward his father's office. "Have you apologized?"

"I tried a few times, but he keeps growling at me." Payton avoided her cousin's gaze.

"What else?"

"I might have escaped a few times on his watch over the years. I told you the man holds a grudge." As they neared Quinn's office, she stopped. "Thank you for getting me out of there."

"You looked like you were drowning a little," Roderic said. "Seriously, Payton, did you say yes to Yevgen? I know he's your friend, and he has some kind of bizarre cyborg crush on you, but I never thought you'd—"

"It was a mistake." She lowered her head and closed her eyes. "I've made a mess out of everything. Yevgen made the declaration. I wasn't thinking clearly. I let it happen. Then the mercenaries were coming, and I got irritated with Nyle and confirmed it, and now..."

"Nyle." Roderic lifted her chin to make her look at him. "Ryland said he was a bad man. Who is he to you?"

Her expression must have answered for her because Roderic nodded.

"I see." Roderic sighed heavily.

"My brother doesn't listen. Yevgen must have given him only part of the story." Payton glanced back and forth down the hallway before stepping closer and lowering her voice. "Nyle isn't bad. He was a scientist on Cysgod. They used his cloned organs in the cyborg facility. Then they started doing experiments. The virus wasn't his fault."

"It came from his facility?" Roderic frowned. "You're sure? You have proof of origin?"

"Not *his* facility," she corrected. "The facility where he worked. He was in a different laboratory."

"Even if it wasn't his department, people are looking for someone to blame." Roderic shook his head. "This isn't good. They want someone held accountable. The Federation will not let that go."

"Let's hope they don't find out. Nyle is not a bad man, Roderic," she whispered. "Please. Trust me."

"I'm not the one you have to convince, but I am on your side." Roderic put his hands on her shoulders and looked as if he wanted to hug her. "You love him, don't you?"

A tear slipped down her cheek, and she nodded.

"Then keep faith that the gods know what they are doing," he instructed. "I didn't think Justina and I would ever find a way, but we did. We were written into two different stories, and somehow, we found our way to each other. The odds were impossible."

She wished she had his kind of faith. "I've made a mess of everything. I don't know how Nyle feels about me, and I have no right to ask him. I'm half mated. He deserves more than that, and the family is already humiliated by the idea of me taking multiple husbands. One half mate might be overlooked in time as a quirk, but not multiple. Multiple is a statement."

"Don't lose hope." This time he did hug her. "We never know what tomorrow will bring. Once we deal with the Federation then, who knows? If you are meant to be with him, then the gods will find a way to make it so."

Nyle was convinced he could feel the world moving beneath him, as the songs of the universes buzzed in his ears. When he opened his eyes, it was to flashes of light, colors that drifted like they were carried by the wind. When his eyes closed, it was to a swirl of dreams that made no logical sense and yet conveyed everything within them that mattered.

He saw the shine coming off the tall buildings of his youth. It flashed like a smile from a pretty woman. Faltering and brief.

He lingered in a memory of being in the laboratory, holding delicate instruments in his hands as he created the most beautiful machines. Yevgen had been born there. He'd seen his eyes open and light up for the first time and heard the monotone voice repeating test sequences before they gave him a personality.

And then there was Payton. The princess reigned over every moment, present even when she was not. She was a feeling more than an image, a part of himself he could not survive without. She had been his salvation all those nights in space, alone as he watched the scraps of transmissions from Yevgen for a glimpse of her. He remembered watching her stalk down an endless metal corridor, paws moving soundlessly over the grates, turning to feet and then back again.

The soft bed he now inhabited was much better than the hard cot he had been on. At least, from what little he could remember between doses of sleep. Payton's brother really didn't care for him. Ryland had kept him under chemical restraint for the entire flight, and Nyle was just now starting to come out of it.

He lingered in the twilight, not ready to leave the dream world where Payton existed just for him. But reality beckoned, as it always did, to ruin the perfection of fantasy.

The buzz in his ears softened. The world settled and stopped swaying.

Nyle stared between the two open curtains. The thick material hung around him as he lay on the large bed. Closed, they would cloak him in darkness.

A gentle light came from a domed window above. Small mirrors caught the reflection, sending it around the room in oval patterns that shimmered on the walls. The furniture looked like it had never been used, and the thick white cushions were too pretty to sit on. Two dark blue banners hung over a fireplace. The silhouette of a cat's roaring head had been imprinted on one, and the figure of an upright cat with claws extended on the other.

He slowly rolled onto his stomach and crawled to the end of the bed. His fingers dug into the silky blankets. "Hello?"

No one answered.

He searched the suite and found it empty. Across the room, more curtains hung around a bathing tub. Small sculptures decorated several surfaces.

This was not a home. It was a waystation. It was a place wealthy people came for short periods but not to live.

Nyle frowned as he made his way to his unsteady feet. He crossed to a pair of tall double doors and pressed his hands against the carved cats in the wood. They refused to open. He then ran his hands over the walls, looking for hidden scanners.

"Open," he ordered.

The doors did not obey. He was locked inside.

Looking up at the sky, he reasoned he was on Qurilixen. The green-tinted daylight gave it away, as did the fact that was where the ship had been heading.

Where was Payton?

He had a hard time believing she would let him be drugged and detained on the ship.

Nyle examined his body. He remembered being in the medical booth for his knees. Had it found something worse?

No, that didn't make sense either. He'd just been checked by the unit not long before they lost gravity.

This room hardly seemed like a prison, but then why couldn't he leave?

"Hello?" He called louder. "Computer? Is there a computer?"

Nothing answered. He wasn't surprised. The room didn't appear to be fitted with interactive technology.

It felt futile, but he started looking for an escape. His wristband was missing, and he couldn't cut his way out. He ran his hand over the walls and lifted the sculptures to see if they'd trigger some hidden passage. He wasn't sure where he'd go if he escaped, but he wanted to find Payton.

He lifted one of the banners and found a button. He pressed and held it. "Hello?"

The wall began to move. A food simulator appeared in a hidden alcove. The button wasn't for communication.

"I am Prince Falke, Var Commander, and Princess Payton's father."

Nyle spun around in surprise at the booming voice coming from the doorway. He hadn't heard anyone enter.

The man's wide stance and narrowed, glowing gaze made the commander's imposing figure even more fearsome. His eyes were the only thing that shifted, but it was enough to pose a threat. Two guards stood behind him, partially shifted into their human cat forms. They wore matching clothes, black uniforms with cross lacing up the sides of the legs and from armpit to waist. The commander wore an emblem on his chest that set him apart from the others.

Falke gestured a finger without fully lifting his hand, and the guards instantly pulled the doors closed.

"Is Payton well?" Nyle asked, eager for word of her.

Falke nodded. The man continued to stare for a long moment.

"I am called Nyle," Nyle finally said, wondering if the man was waiting for him to speak.

Falke continued to watch him.

Nyle tried to look away but couldn't. Fear crept in. He'd seen Payton shift. If that was any indication of what this man might become, he could be in trouble. He straightened his shoulders and said, "I'm Cysgodian Nyle."

Falke tilted his head and crossed his arms over his chest.

"Cysgodian Nyle, bastard son of an unknown off-worlder and Diana." Nyle hated his full name. He had gotten past not knowing who his father was long ago, but it didn't mean he liked announcing it. "But I prefer Nyle."

"My daughter said you assisted in bringing her home." The man didn't move, and still it felt as if he loomed forward.

Nyle gave a small nod. "I did what I could. Payton is resourceful. She didn't need saving."

"Yes. Payton is that." Falke dropped his arms and stepped closer. The movement relaxed his stance some as he came toward the couch. His gaze moved to the food simulator and then back to Nyle. "You're a scientist."

Nyle nodded. "I was in another life."

"There is only one life," Falke answered, "with all its honors and all its failures. There is no separating the beginning from the end as time cannot be severed."

Nyle tried to give a small nod of agreement. What in the universes was he supposed to say to that? The man was the highest-ranking Var military royal. It's not like he was going to argue philosophy with the man. One slap and Nyle wouldn't be waking up. Plus, he was Payton's father. One word and he could keep Nyle from ever seeing the princess.

Maybe it would be best if he didn't speak. Commanders were used to being heard.

"You don't agree?" Falke inquired when Nyle remained silent.

"Uh, yes. I know of no scientific way of severing time," Nyle answered. He didn't add that in a way there were methods of stopping time, at least for an individual—stasis pods, and an old freezing technique that turned prisoners into stone. Though, that last one came with some nasty side effects.

Falke let loose a loud breath and appeared disappointed. A claw extended from his fingertip, and he scratched the back of his neck. "I was speaking of honor."

"I don't know what you want me to say." Nyle focused on keeping his breathing even.

Falke dropped his arm to his side and tapped the tip of the claw against his thigh.

Of course, they had Yevgen. The cyborg had probably told them everything.

"You want to know if I think I should be forgiven for my past failures or if I have forgiven myself and believe my honor restored." Nyle considered lying. He thought about twisting his words, so they softened reality. He thought about defending himself, saying he'd watched the survivors from space and sent Yevgen to protect them. Instead, he answered, "No. Someone needs to take responsibility for what happened, and I am the only one left."

The faint impression of the dreams he'd had while drugged faded into the harsh reality of his memories. All those bodies haunted him. Those cries followed him, brought forth with every high-pitched whistle of wind or audible breath. Slamming doors triggered the memory of the locked

Central Hospital ward where people went to die. Smoke drew forth images of mass funeral pyres.

"Did you know?" Falke asked.

This was not a conversation. It was an interrogation. The thought should have occurred to him sooner, but he'd been focused on Payton when the man walked in.

"About the virus? Not directly." Nyle found no reason to lie.

"But you carry the blame?"

"I was in a different department, but I knew they were cloning my organs to use inside the cyborgs. They wanted them to be resistant to the dangers of space. They tested everyone for the project. My unknown off-worlder parentage made me the ideal candidate. My best guess is that was why I didn't get sick like the others."

"You donated your organs, and you believe you're responsible for what was done to them." Falke gave no indication of what he was thinking.

"All the cogs that made the machine possible hold responsibility—from the politicians and corporations who greedily pushed for more technology, to those cooking up diseases in the lab, to people like me who didn't know directly but went to work every day and made Yeven Genetic Cyborgtronics Laboratories money to continue experimenting. I should have asked questions. I should have snuck in and looked at the files. I should have done something."

No. He should not be forgiven. None of them should be.

Nyle wanted the screaming echoes to stop. They wouldn't.

"And by that logic, the citizens who voted in the politicians were also to blame?" Falke asked.

Nyle frowned and took a small step forward in challenge. "Don't be ridiculous."

Falke arched a brow.

Nyle caught himself and evened his tone. "What I mean to say is, they have paid enough of a price. No one could have expected them to be reasonably aware of what was happening. Security on the project was kept tight."

"And..." Falke's eyes closed briefly, and he took a deep breath. "This *Yevgen* is one of yours?"

"I sent him to watch over the Cysgodians and report back to me so I could keep an eye on them. I tried to find a way to help, but no one outside of this planet wanted to get involved, not with the Federation running things, not with it being..." Nyle caught himself.

"Primitive territory in the X quadrant that has

little value beyond its ore and is definitely not worth angering the Federation over?" Falke finished for him.

"I wouldn't put it like that," Nyle answered.

"Others might." Falke seemed proud of the description, as if he liked that the universes underestimated them.

"I know the Federation is interested in mining your ore. Qurilixen isn't part of the Federation Alliance. I've checked. I assumed after they built Shelter City you would be."

"They've offered. We've refused."

Nyle figured there was much more to the story but didn't ask. Not many people said no to the Federation.

Falke continued to study him with his untelling expression. "This Yevgen. Can he feel?"

"I don't know how to answer that." Nyle tried to tell himself to stop talking. He didn't know what the commander wanted from him, and angering this man wasn't good for anyone.

Falke glanced around the suite before taking a seat on the edge of the pristine white couch. He held himself rigid. "You're a scientist. You helped make him."

"I programmed him to protect the Cysgodians.

That is his central focus. Everything he does is constructed around that." Nyle didn't take a seat to join the commander. The man looked as if he could still pounce at any moment.

"You gave him your heart, your blood, your tissue. Can he feel? It's a simple question."

Simple? Nyle frowned. There was nothing simple about Yevgen.

There was nothing simple about this conversation.

"He has nerve endings. Pain is a useful sensation. It tells us when we are injured," Nyle said.

Falke's eyes darkened.

"Some cyborgs are people who have body parts replaced with technology. But they were people first, and they have the flaws of people. There's a giant debate amongst cyborgeneticists over at which point in the artificial intelligence process the person ceases to exist and when you can call them a true cyborg. People can upload information into their brains, learning things they never studied but it's still their brain. Some purists argue that makes them artificially intelligent." Nyle looked at his hand, flexing it to see the movement beneath the skin. "But Yevgen was never a man in that sense. He is a sophisticated machine. Half built, half grown. His programming was a work of art, and it was left unattended for decades. It grew, and learned, and morphed. He reprogrammed himself and rebuilt himself. He improved. There is no other cyborg like him."

Nyle knew this wasn't the answer the Var commander sought. He dropped his hands and met the man's gaze.

"Why won't you answer my question?" Falke's claws extended and then withdrew back into his fingers.

A threat? An involuntary gesture? Nyle wasn't sure.

"If you're asking me if Yevgen is alive, then I would have to ask you what your definition of life is," Nyle said.

"Does he feel?" Falke pushed to his feet, resuming his previous stance. "Can he love my daughter?"

Nyle felt the words like a slap, and he held his breath. He thought about what Payton had once said, *"All he wants is to understand love. Sometimes the yearning for something is enough."*

A father would not be comforted by those words. Payton deserved the love of a man who would give everything for her.

"I wish I had a definitive answer. If Payton believes it is possible, then perhaps that is all we need to know. Yevgen is my creation, but he's her..." Nyle wanted to say the right thing, the comforting thing. He wanted to put the man's mind at ease. "I'm sorry. She deserves better. She deserves everything. I can't imagine any man being worthy of her, but Yevgen will be loyal. He'll give himself to protect her. He'll be attentive. He will try to love her as he understands it."

Before he arrived on Qurilixen, Nyle would have said without a doubt that the cyborg couldn't feel emotions. Yevgen could mimic them, quite convincingly, but it all came down to computer programming.

But clearly Payton felt some kind of attachment. Who was he to negate what she felt? And Yevgen acted like a man in love, mostly. He showed jealousy and a desire to please.

He felt the commander's eyes on him, as if analyzing his every movement.

"I'm not the right man to ask about this," Nyle said, unconsciously stepping back. "You should speak to your daughter about her relationship."

"What is your relationship with my daughter?"

"You should ask her about that too," Nyle said.

"I've already said too much. I have no right to speak about her choices or on her behalf."

"By not answering, you imply there is a relationship."

"I would never presume. She's married. I would never dishonor her by implying such a thing." Nyle wondered what the odds were of him getting Falke to leave. He'd rather face the man's fists than his words. At least with a punch, the torture would be over quickly.

Falke stared at him for a long moment. Nyle tried not to shift his weight as he waited.

"The Federation is coming," the commander stated. "They want control over the Cysgodians, and they want their alliance with Qurilixen. They'll try to lay claim to the planet if they can't have an alliance. They are prepared to take it by force as long as they can claim righteousness in doing so to the rest of the universes."

"You can't let that happen," Nyle said. "The Cysgodians will not survive Federation rule. The Federation wants Cysgod. They'll make sure no one is left to lay claim."

Falke studied him.

"I'll do anything to make sure that never happens," Nyle insisted. He wanted the nightmares to end. "Anything. Trade me to the Federation. Let them make a public example of me. Let them blame me for the virus. Let them look like heroes. I won't fight it. Just make sure they agree to give up all claims to my people."

Falke continued to stare as if contemplating everything Nyle had said. Finally, the commander nodded and turned toward the doors. He gave a soft growl low in his throat, and the doors automatically opened to the sound. The guards waited for the commander to pass and then closed the doors behind him.

Nyle took a deep breath and relaxed his stance. That conversation could have gone better, but he said what he needed to.

"Father?" Payton stopped short on her way through the corridors. "What are you doing here?"

She'd checked on Yevgen long enough to tell him not to break into the palace system but quickly excused herself to find Nyle. She looked behind him to where two guards stood outside the guest suite doors.

"I could ask you the same," Falke said.

"Were you talking to Nyle? What happened? What did he say?" She couldn't take her eyes away from the door as if waiting for him to appear while knowing he wouldn't.

"I went to hear the truth from him." Her father crossed his arms over his chest. The stance would have been intimidating to most, but she had made a childhood out of pushing his limits. His demeanor didn't frighten her. His talk with Nyle did.

"What did you learn?" She drew her gaze back to him.

"You know what I learned."

Payton shook her head. "He should not be blamed for what happened on Cysgod. He's been trying to make it right."

She felt like she kept saying the words, but no one was listening to them.

"I believe that." Falke put a hand on her shoulder. "I also see a man hollowed by guilt who wants to be punished."

"It's not Nyle's fault."

"You should be with your husband." Falke dropped his hand. "I will not pretend to understand your choice, but I will support it. Marriage is the most sacred thing you will do in your life. My bond with your mother makes my life complete. She is my soul, my very breath, and she blessed me with you and your brothers. All I want in life is to see the three of you settled the same."

Payton tried to tell him she'd made a mistake with Yevgen but couldn't force the words out. How could she after that testament to marriage?

"Rick said the Federation ship wasn't far behind. We're locking down the palace and village. The Cysgodians are being kept indoors," the commander said.

"I understand. You must go." Payton nodded. She was used to the demands of her father's time.

"Right now, I need to talk to my daughter." He stopped her from stepping around him. "Can I rely upon you to stay here at the palace where you and your husband are needed?"

"Of course."

Falke gave her a small smile. "Do not say of course as if it was a given, my little runner. I can count on one hand the times you did *not* escape to the forest when dignitaries were on their way."

He was teasing, but it still stung a little. The Var were all about duty and honor, and the words made her feel as if she had skipped out on hers. "These aren't dignitaries, and this isn't some meet the Lithorian chocolate suppliers' tasting banquet. If the Federation is coming, I will be here."

He arched a brow. "Have we had a meet the Lithorian chocolate suppliers' tasting banquet?"

Payton chuckled. "No. That one I might have gone to."

Falke lowered his voice and leaned closer.

"Women swarming over chocolate samples? That one I might have staged a war to get out of."

Payton laughed a little harder.

"It is good to hear you laugh, little one. I have not liked the expression in your eyes since you returned home. It does not belong there."

"I'm just tired. Ryland locking me in a room without windows and fresh air will do that," Payton dismissed.

"Resignation," Falke corrected.

"What?"

"I see resignation, not tiredness. I know the fighter I have raised, and that look does not belong on you. You are fearless, my daughter, with a fierce heart. You always have been. You're braver than most of the soldiers I have trained. Even when you were just a cub, you would stand up for anyone you thought was being treated unfairly. You'd take on an entire planet in defense of something you cared about. I have seen your many moods, but resignation has never been one of them."

"I'm not resigned." Her eyes again strayed to the door. "I'm preoccupied. As you said, the Federation is finally coming. We need to stop them. That is all that matters right now."

That was all that *could* matter right now. Too much was on the line—shifters' futures, Cysgodians' futures. They needed to prove to the universes that they had every right to eject the Federation from the planet and take over Shelter City.

She had to stay focused.

"You can see your friend if you wish, but we must prepare for our visitors." Falke stepped aside. He lifted his hand to gesture at the guards. "Don't take long. It sounded as if you need to keep Yevgen focused on his task and out of the palace mainframe."

"Thank you." Payton nodded as she moved past her father toward the guards. They reached to open the door for her.

Nyle stood at attention near the fireplace. His eyes met hers, but he didn't relax.

Payton felt a rush of emotion flood her. She lifted her hand, gesturing at the guards to shut the door behind her.

When they were alone, she hurried toward him. "Are you harmed?"

"The drugs are wearing off, and my head is clearing." He seemed upset. She could hardly blame him.

"Drugs?" Payton stopped near the couch. "I'm sorry about my brother. He thought he was protecting me. He locked me in a room on the spaceship. I didn't know what was happening to you."

"He doesn't think I'm worthy of you." Nyle ran his hands through his hair. "He's right. We weren't thinking clearly. Maybe the danger of being kidnapped in space brought us together."

"What?" Payton shook her head. "No."

"You're a princess. I'm..." He gave a weak shrug. "I'm—"

"Don't finish that sentence. Whatever it is you were about to say, don't." Payton lifted her hands.

"I met your father." Nyle crossed his arms over his chest, as if trying to keep himself rigid and unwelcoming. "He seems like an honorable man. Terrifying but honorable."

"He stared at you without speaking, didn't he?" Payton tried to close the distance between them, but he stepped away every time she stepped forward. "I hate when he does that. He knows people have this need to fill the silence. So he just intimidates and sees what falls out. What did you tell him?"

"The truth."

Payton bit her lip. "Everything?"

"Nothing that would dishonor you."

Payton stared at him, willing him to smile. She hated the sadness in his gaze. She hated this situation.

She wished he would ask her to run away with him into the forest, into the sky, into the bed, anywhere that they could be together.

It couldn't be.

She'd promised her father she wouldn't hide in the forest, not with the Federation looming.

The high skies were an awful place without air, and her soul would wither trapped in the deep black.

And the guards would hear them in the bed.

Payton wasn't ashamed to have him as a lover, but she would be ashamed to dishonor her family by letting it be known she had a half mate *and* a lover. No, not just her family. She would dishonor herself. She would become something she resented. She would become like her grandfather and the Myrddinians, making a mockery of what was most sacred —love.

Everything they had in life, all the power, the wars, the very castle around them, the forest. In the end, it meant nothing if you didn't respect the one thing that mattered most.

Love.

A tear slipped down her cheek. "I'm sorry, Nyle."

He finally came closer, lifting his hand. "Don't. You have no reason to be sorry. You have done nothing wrong."

Payton forced herself to keep their distance. If he touched her, she wouldn't be able to let go.

"I don't expect you to understand this, but I betrayed you before I knew you." Payton lifted her hand to keep him from advancing.

"You're right. I don't understand why you would say that. It's not true."

"I didn't believe in you. I didn't believe that I would find you. I didn't want to find you. Part of me thought that I was beyond needing to be defined by love. So I threw our chance away." She lowered her voice. The guards were trained not to listen, but who could really know for sure? "I married Yevgen, and I think the gods are going to punish me for it."

"Oh, Payton. No." He closed his eyes and wiped at a tear with the back of his hand before it could fall. He shook his head. "You didn't ruin anything. You didn't throw anything away."

She inhaled sharply and pressed her hand to his chest. The pain rolling over her should have killed her. "You don't want me."

"That's not what I said." He opened his eyes and stared into hers. "You didn't ruin anything because we never had a chance. Maybe you innately knew the truth. Maybe Yevgen is the only way any part of me could be with you. He'll do everything in his power to protect you."

Payton pressed her lips tightly together.

"Someone needs to be held accountable," he stated. "No matter how much I want things to be different, this isn't some story we get to make up. It's reality. Everything is bigger than the two of us."

Payton hated that he was right. She started to nod but failed. "Bigger than what we want."

"I've always known I was on borrowed time. If I could change the past, I would. All I want is to offer you everything." Nyle's hand finally made contact with her. He cupped her cheek. "Even if the Federation doesn't hold me accountable, the Cysgodian people will, as they should. They need closure. I need the nightmares to end."

She hated the picture he painted of reality. She didn't want to think about it. She wanted to run. Her leg twitched, and she felt the forest calling her. They could disappear and hide there.

"Maybe there's hope," Payton whispered. "A way we can't see."

"Sure." His sad smile said he didn't believe it. "Maybe."

They were lying to each other.

His hand remained on her cheek. She couldn't bring herself to sever the contact.

Payton forgot about the guards, about thoughts of duty and honor. Instead, she remembered what it felt like to be trapped alone on the ship without him, isolated and desperate.

"You once told me if you were worthy of me, you would fall in love with me," she said.

"I was wrong." Nyle brought a second hand to her cheek. "I am not worthy of you, Princess, and I have fallen in love with you anyway."

"That's good because I've fallen in love with you too, Nyle." Payton took hold of his shirt and pulled him toward her. "I need you to kiss me. I don't want to think of or feel anything else. Right now, I just want you to kiss me."

His thumb ran across her bottom lip, causing her to shiver. "As you command."

Their lips joined, but it wasn't enough. It would never be enough. Her hands needed to feel him.

Payton tugged his shirt over his head, resisting the urge to claw it off like a wild animal. Nyle tossed it aside before scooping her up into his arms. He carried her toward the bed, between the curtains, to deposit her onto the soft mattress.

She crawled back into the shadowed cocoon of the enclosed bed. He quickly undressed. She watched the seductive show through the part in the curtains.

Payton ran a claw down her chest and stomach, cutting open the shirt without nicking her skin. She pulled it off like a jacket before pushing the pants from her hips. The silken covers caressed her naked flesh.

"Come here," she ordered, beckoning him onto the bed.

Nyle obeyed, crawling toward her. The mattress sunk with the weight of his hands, causing her to rock gently back and forth. She felt his heat before she felt his skin brushing up against her.

"I wish I had the power to lock us in this very moment." He gave her a soft kiss.

Payton chuckled. "You might want to wait a few seconds. The next moment's going to be even better."

She ran her foot along his calf before hooking his thigh to pull him down against her. The intimate contact with his body caused her to gasp. She wanted to touch everywhere at once. Her legs moved up and down his. Her hands explored his chest and shoulders before her fingers threaded through his hair.

Their lips met, tongues frantically moving as if they could consume each other. Desperate pleasure erupted under each caress. It would be easy to forget the outside world when everything inside their little fortress was perfection, but the threat of it loomed, shining in on them like light from the parted curtains.

Payton wished she could freeze time and keep them in this moment. She didn't want to lose him. She didn't want to have to choose between love and everything else.

Nyle entered her slowly as if to prolong the experience. His eyes gazed down into hers. The light outlined his head, but her shifter vision easily cut through the shadows to fully take in his expression.

The slow pace could not last. They rocked together, harder with each thrust, seeking to fulfill that raw, primal need. As much as she wanted to stop time, her body wanted the exact opposite. All the stress and worry, and fear begged them for release. Climax washed through them, muscles tightened, and bodies shook in perfect unison.

The sound of their heavy breathing mingled in the quiet. Nyle pressed his forehead to hers briefly before rolling over on his side. He gathered her into his arms.

She listened to the sound of his heavy breath. A distant thump made her concentrate on his heart. She laid her hand on his chest, but the sound didn't match his heartbeat. The thumping became louder. One became two. Feet. Running.

Frowning, Payton pushed up on the bed. "Something's not right."

She slid off the end of the bed and crossed to the wall. Passing her hand over a seam, she tripped the sensors to open a drawer with clothes. She dug through the stack and found a shirt in her size.

"What is it?" Nyle stood at the end of the bed and pulled on his pants.

The sound of footsteps stopped outside the door.

"I'm not sure." She looked around before pointing behind him. "My pants?"

Nyle leaned over the bed and grabbed them before tossing them over. They quickly dressed in silence. There was so much Payton wanted to tell him, but what was the point? She'd said the one thing she needed to, that she loved him. The rest were just words that wouldn't change anything.

She heard a murmuring of voices but couldn't make out what the guards were saying.

A light knock sounded as she pushed her hair away from her face. The door cracked open, and a voice softly called, "Princess?"

"What is it?" she answered as she met Nyle's gaze.

"Your presence is required," the guard said. "A land craft is waiting at the front gate and will take you to Shelter City after you have a moment to change your clothing. Princess Samantha ordered a gown and a tray of food to your room. She asks that you eat something before leaving as she is sure you have forgotten."

Payton didn't answer the guard while keeping her attention on Nyle.

"They're here. They've come. It's starting," she said, the statement an acknowledgment of all they had been anticipating. The Federation had finally arrived.

She couldn't look away from Nyle. She wasn't ready to leave him.

"Go." He tried to smile as if understanding her inner turmoil. The expression didn't reach his eyes. Instead, she saw sadness staring back at her. "You have no choice."

"Nyle..."

What did she say to him? What words would unravel everything swirling in her brain?

"This is too important. Go." He glanced at the door. "I'd come, but I don't think those two are letting me out of here."

Her eyes moved to the food simulator. "There's food, clothes. If you need anything, tell them. It might not feel like it, but you're a guest, not a prisoner."

"Princess?" the guard repeated, slightly louder.

Nyle put his hands on her shoulders. "Payton, go."

She closed her eyes for a second and then nodded. Lifting on her toes, she allowed herself a brief kiss before pulling away. "We're not over. This is just—"

"I know." He nodded toward the door.

The door opened before she reached it as if the guards had been listening for her to leave. This is what it meant to be in the royal family. For all her escaping to the forest, when it came down to it, her life was not her own. She had to help protect her people, all the people of Qurilixen—shifters and Cysgodian.

At least Nyle would be safe in the palace until she returned.

23

ANYONE IN HER FAMILY WOULD EASILY SAY diplomacy was not one of Payton's strengths. The Federation proved that point and stretched her patience beyond all limits. The royal gown did not help. The layers of flowing fabric were beautiful, and she suspected her mother picked it to discourage shifting. At least the bodice was loose, and Payton could breathe.

The Federation mothership had stayed in space to drift over the planet like a threat. General Griggs and her crew had landed one ship at the palace and planned to take land crafts across the surface toward the fortress above Shelter City. Thankfully, the Federation had their own land crafts, or Payton might have shoved a few of them overboard along the way.

General Griggs had led her entourage to survey the Var palace as if they were gracing a hovel with their majestic presence. They muttered comments like, "Though it is a primitive stone, I did not expect there to be such a level of civilization here, being as it's impossible to fly to," and, "Think of where this planet could be in a hundred years with the right connections," as if the people standing in front of them couldn't understand the Old Star language.

The general then began speaking as if laying down decrees to the simple locals. Her words flowed like someone who enjoyed filling the air with the sound of their own voice. The Federation was there to gather evidence and had every intention of honoring their duty to the Cysgodians—whom they had saved from extinction, after all. This was to be a dignified meeting. The Qurilixen royals were to be reasonable and accommodating.

Then came the dreaded niceties and cosmic pats on the head. Things were said, but not really. Everything had a hidden agenda and double meaning. It had been kind of the shifters to watch out for Shelter City while the Federation made new arrangements. Things did not need to go badly as the Federation retook power and established a more permanent residence on-world.

The fake diplomacy and veiled threats were enough to make any self-respecting shifter wield their claws. Payton wanted to stand and shout, "You overstepped. You know it. We know it. If you don't want the entire universe to know it, get the fuck off our planet and leave us alone. This is not a negotiation. Don't let the claws stab you in the ass on the way out."

It was only the echo of Nyle's voice in her head saying, "*This is too important*," over and over that kept her from screeching and brandishing her claws.

Oh, but she wanted to scratch General Griggs's smug face off.

And maybe rip the heart out of the forked-tongue ass-kisser next to her. The slargnot repeated a version of everything the general said but added more slime to it. If those two weren't in some kind of fucked up lovers' situation, Payton was absolutely no judge of character.

I am the best lover, the general would say.

Yes, you are the goddess of all that is dominant, with gilded spanking hands of—

"Payton." Her father's whisper snapped her out

of her mocking thoughts. "Try not to glare at our guests."

The commander's eyes darted down to her hand. Payton instantly retracted her claws.

Roderic and Justina watched her from the small land craft's deck. The transport hovered over the ground and would make for a smooth glide over the terrain. Payton hopped up and stood next to the rail to stare at the Federation members climbing onboard their own craft. Others boarded behind her, but she ignored them.

"The general doesn't appear scary up close." Roderic joined her against the railing as they pulled away from the palace. His Cysgodian wife sat on the floor behind them, her arms crossed and her head down. The open craft let the air rush around them. Shifters didn't notice the chill, but Cysgodians weren't immune.

"And yet she is capable of causing great harm," Payton said. "Griggs is full of herself."

"Yevgen is going to send the data to the fortress once it's presentable." Roderic touched the bag hanging by his hip. "I have a communicator if there are any issues so he can contact us directly."

She nodded in acknowledgment. "You reminded him not to mention how the virus came to be? It's not pertinent to removing the Federation from the planet, and we don't wish to give them a reason to blame the Cysgodians."

Roderic nodded. "I reminded him."

Payton couldn't help but glance back at the palace as it faded from view. She'd run this path so many times, never looking back as she fled toward something else. Now, she wished more than anything to be back inside the walls, safely tucked away in Nyle's arms. She felt like there was more to say to him, and yet everything that needed to be said had been.

"I am not worthy of you, Princess, and I have fallen in love with you anyway."

"I've fallen in love with you too, Nyle."

His voice echoed in her mind. Each moment fought its way to the top of her memory. They had lived a lifetime of adventure together in a short span of time—mercenaries, crash pod landings, black markets, and a well-intentioned brother. Fear crept inside her. What if that is all the gods would give her? What if there was a before and an after, but very little actual love story?

Her hands shook, and she thought about jumping over the side and running back to him.

"This is too important."

Nyle had been right. If she ran from her duty now, how could she face him?

"Payton?" Roderic touched her arm. "Are you that worried?"

She realized she'd not schooled her expression. "I want today to be over."

He nodded in understanding. "It's been a long time due."

When the land crafts finally docked near the Federation stronghold towering over Shelter City, Payton couldn't help but whisper to her cousin, "They mock our palace, but their buildings are hardly a testament to beauty. It looks like a hard fungus that needs to be scraped from the surface."

Roderic's lip twitched at the corner, but he did not react otherwise.

The stark military buildings looked the same no matter which planet they were dropped on. They did not consider nature's shape or the landscape's flow. This monstrosity was what Griggs used as a gauge for true civilization.

Plus, how Griggs could look down her nose at them when her organization was responsible for the falling structures of rust and rot that they called Shelter City just below the stronghold was beyond Payton.

The general and her entourage led the way into the stronghold facility like the shifters were their guests. The white interior lacked style and craftsmanship. Unless one could call oppressive utilitarian military a style and white on boring white a color palette. Payton resisted pointing out that if Griggs wanted to control the building so badly, she was welcome to take the eyesore with her.

Because the white walls, ceilings, and floors needed constant cleaning, the stronghold carried the faint char of disinfectant lasers. The smell always made Payton's stomach curl, and she tried not to breathe too deeply.

The general led them to a conference room where a large table's glossy finish reflected everyone's faces when they gathered around it.

"You can wait there," a Federation soldier stated, blocking Justina from entering.

"She has every—" Roderic tried to protest.

Justina took hold of his arm and motioned for him to go inside. "I trust you. I'll be right here. Whatever it takes to get this over with."

For the dragons, King Ualan and his son Grier sat next to Commander Zoran. They'd been waiting in the conference room. She wished Grier's wife, Princess Salena, could be there since she was a truth receiver that no one could lie to. It would take two seconds for her to draw all the deceptions out of the Federation's representatives. Unfortunately, the former general had wrongfully imprisoned Salena and her sister, and Grier would not risk his wife to their exposure. Payton understood. She wanted to hide Nyle from exposure as well.

For the cats, King Kirill and the heir prince Korbin were next to Payton and her father. No one directly represented the Cysgodians.

"Be seated. There is no reason not to get through this quickly and with civility," the general said. Her entourage instantly obeyed the command, except for two soldiers who stood at the wall behind her.

"We should include the Cysgodian leader," Payton put forth, not taking a seat. "Justina has a right to be represented here."

Roderic nodded in agreement. "She—"

"There is no recognized Cysgodian leader. They are our wards. We will speak for them," General Griggs stated. The muscles along her eyes tensed as if trying to project control but failing.

"We recognize Lady Justina," Roderic said.

"As a leader or as a princess by marriage?" Griggs asked.

"Both," Roderic said.

"The Cysgodians are *our* wards," King Kirill corrected. "General Sten lost that privilege."

"I am not General Sten," Griggs said before sighing. "We both want a favorable outcome to these proceedings."

"Yes, favorable," the general's sidekick repeated as if those were the wisest words ever stated.

"I think we have different definitions of that word," Payton grumbled.

Falke placed his hand on her shoulder. He gave her a stern look before taking a seat, prompting her to do the same.

Payton reluctantly sat. Like the other shifters, she found it horrible that the very people who were held hostage on the planet by the Federation were given no say as to their future by that same organization.

"This is too important."

Payton realized her claws had extended, and she drew them back in. She pushed the tips of her fingers to her thighs under the table to try to keep the need to slash something under control.

"Shall we start? We have a long session ahead, and I'd like to get through it." The general held out her hand. A soldier placed an electronic clipboard in it. "I think we can all agree that this comes down to a contractual dispute. I'd like to begin with our agreement, and we need to be thorough."

"I don't think we all would agree," Payton grumbled. She couldn't help herself.

The general handed the clipboard back to the soldier, who promptly began to read aloud, "Cysgodian-Qurilixen Settlement Agreement between the Federation Military, the Royal House of Draig, and the Royal House of Var. Final agreed upon version star dated—"

"We've all read the document," King Ualan interrupted.

"We have marked pauses so that we may discuss any portion," the general said before motioning for the man to continue reading.

"Final agreed upon version..."

Time sometimes felt endless, the seconds, minutes, and hours stretching beyond their limits, more so under the droning monotone of arrogance. The man kept speaking, and Payton found it hard to concentrate on what the words meant. Not that it mattered. Once Yevgen sent his presentation, none of this would make a difference. Payton told herself they were merely humoring the Federation, all in the name of diplomacy.

"...off-world prisoner brought to, or captured on

this planet by visiting authority must be divulged to the royal shifter families immediate—"

"*Ughhhh*," Payton groaned, dropping her head forward onto the table to bounce against her folded hands. She lifted her head, realizing she'd groaned out loud.

General Griggs stared at her in irritation.

Payton took a deep breath. Since she'd already made a scene and stopped the reading, she might as well speak the truth. "Enough of this torture. We all know you were sneaking prisoners on-world. We have the logs. Save face with the universes and get off our planet already."

"Payton," her father stated sternly, the single word a warning.

General Griggs and her pet ass kisser glared at her. Payton fought the urge to leap over the table.

"Princess Payton, would you please check on the transmission," King Kirill added, his words gentler than Falke's.

Payton forced herself to stand, torn between the need to jump over the table to slap the general and the needs of her people. "My apologies for speaking between the designated discussion pauses."

The low words rolled from her throat like a sharp-edged stone cutting its way from inside.

Payton stiffly walked out of the conference room.

"She's passionate in her opinions, but she's not wrong," King Ualan said. "We have proof that off-world prisoners were being brought here against the terms of that agreement."

When the door opened, Justina pushed up from where she sat on the floor against the wall to greet her. The door closed. "What's happening?"

"I lost my patience," Payton said. "They kicked me out."

"You lasted longer than I thought you would." Justina gave a tight smile as if she wanted to laugh, but the situation wouldn't allow for it.

"I make a horrible ambassador," Payton agreed. "But that soldier kept droning on reading that stupid Cysgodian-Qurilixen Settlement Agreement word for word. Then everyone pauses and debates what is read even though everyone knows the Federation is in the wrong. It's like they keep hoping they'll discover a loophole that lets them take over the planet. There are intergalactic laws against this kind of drawn-out torture."

Payton stared at the door, trying to hear what was happening on the other side. Her shifter hearing should have been able to pick it up, but a light buzzing filled her ears instead.

Justina pointed to a device on the wall. "Noise dampener. They placed it as soon as the meeting started."

"I should have kept my mouth shut." Payton frowned, angry with herself. She reached to pull the noise dampener off the wall, but it zapped her fingers with electricity. Her claws automatically extended from her fingertips and fur sprouted up her arm as she jerked her hand back.

Justina lifted her hand to show red fingertips. "I tried that already."

"All I had to do was keep my mouth shut," Payton whispered, angry with herself. "Why couldn't I keep my mouth shut?"

"Some people are of physical action. Some are of talking. You never struck me as someone inclined to the art of conversation."

"That's a nice way of saying I'm a freaking space cadet." Payton considered charging back inside.

"This is too important."

Nyle's words echoed through her, and she felt like she'd failed him.

"I failed him," she whispered.

"Who? Yevgen?" Justina asked.

Payton shook her head. "Nyle."

"Oh." Justina placed a gentle hand on her shoulder. Payton hadn't heard the woman move behind her. "You married the wrong man, huh?"

Payton nodded.

"Then fix it." Justina gave her a firm pat.

Payton took a deep breath. "I told Nyle that I love him, and then I came here. I can't shake this feeling that I'm going to be made to choose between him and everything else."

"I know shifters generally live for hundreds of years, and that gives you a sense of all the time in the universe, but take a page out of the Cysgodian book. Time is never what you think it is. If you are with the wrong person, fix it. If you're in love with this Nyle, make it work. If you're—"

"A princess with more than my own selfish desires at stake?" Payton interrupted.

"King Attor had a billion wives," Justina countered. "Your father and uncles took one each. None of that affected the Var monarchy. You're still here doing the job. Times change. People change. I would think the Var people would respect someone who admitted they made a mistake and then fixed it. Honor and duty are important, but so is love. Take another half mate.

Divorce Yevgen and marry Nyle. Do something. Pretend the world is ending tomorrow because one thing I know as a Cysgodian, it very well might be."

"You should be in there with them, not out here with me," Payton said, countering Justina's advice with her own.

"I know. You're right. I'm trying to think like a diplomat, not the crazy lady yelling on the street at people. I know the Federation doesn't respect us. They respect the shifter royals. They'll listen to them. My presence—"

"Is needed. Be a loud diplomat," Payton said. "From what I remember of your streetside speeches, you do have a way with words. Maybe you're inclined to have the conversation."

Justina took a deep breath, appearing determined as she went toward the doors to push her way inside. "Good luck with your heart."

"Good luck kicking all their asses," Payton answered.

Payton glanced down the corridor. She listened to the distance. The conference room was blocked, but a slight shuffle sounded from where some of the Cysgodians now lived. They'd moved into the facility after the Federation was chased off. There normally were more sounds, but the current events caused people to slink into hiding.

Payton couldn't blame them. No one wanted to move back into the squalor of Shelter City. Well, no one but Yevgen.

Payton stared at the door. Justina was right. She was a woman of action. She needed to trust the diplomats to the diplomatic conversations. Yevgen would send his data over, and that would be that.

Then, after, she would figure out her life.

The loud sound of multiple footsteps drew her attention. The steady, firm rhythm was filled with purpose.

She automatically stepped toward it, eager to meet whoever was coming.

"Princess Payton," a Var guard greeted, pausing as she rounded the corner to appear in front of them. The dragon-shifter he was with took a few extra steps before he also stopped.

"Do you have the evidence?" Payton asked.

"We do, princess," the cat-shifter answered.

"We're bringing it now," the dragon added.

Payton felt the end of the nightmare was close. She motioned them to follow her. Their footsteps resumed the perfunctory stride.

She didn't stop as she reached the conference room doors.

When she went inside, Justina was saying, "The Cysgodians wish to retract their—"

"We have invested a lot of resources into—" the general talked over the woman.

"—request for assistance being the medical crisis has passed," said Justina.

"—honoring the terms of the Cysgodian rescue as agreed upon by the reigning parties at the time of the crisis," the general insisted.

"It could be debated that the Federation did not honor their part of the Cysgodian rescue agreement," Payton interrupted.

"Payton?" King Kirill asked.

Payton nodded. "We have the proof."

She stepped aside to let the two shifter guards into the room. One placed a holodisk on the table.

"We're not done reading the agreement," General Griggs stated.

"We're done listening to it," Prince Grier said, reaching forward to press the top of the holodisk.

"Greetings." Yevgen's face appeared as soft music played behind him. "I am Prince Yevgen, first husband of the beautiful Princess Payton." The holographic scene changed to show old photos of

Payton from around Shelter City. Small heart shapes exploded around her images.

Her father arched a brow as he glanced at her. Payton gave a small, embarrassed shrug.

Yevgen's presentation continued, "What you are about to see is indisputable evidence of truth."

"Is this a joke?" General Griggs demanded as Yevgen reappeared in a regal pose with a crown on his head.

"Evidence collection part one," Yevgen said. "General Sten, disgraced Federation leader, admits his primary goal is to wait for the death of the Cysgodian people so that the Federation may lay claim to their planet."

General Sten's face appeared over the table as a series of recordings played. "Estimates show that they will all be dead in twelve years, and we'll no longer have a Cysgodian concern. Once the virus clears and the planet is ruled safe to inhabit, which our researchers indicate should be in about a hundred years, no descendants will be left to lay claim to Cysgod. I believe the Federation is morally obligated to take over planetary rights."

Payton remained standing by the table as the two guards who delivered the device left them. She had seen this footage before. It continued to show the general and some of his men making plans to poison the population's food with a drug that caused an intense rage. Scientific charts and graphs replaced the general's face. They flashed too quickly to study properly, but Yevgen's voice narrated their importance. Then Justina appeared within a Federation prison cell in the images.

"You should know the medical scan found several abnormal growths," a guard threatened her. "The growths won't kill you right away, but..."

Justina reached to pause the recording. The Federation soldier's projected smile froze, and it felt as if he glared at them. "That's Sever. We have confessions of him admitting everything. This was when he tried to blackmail me into distributing the poison. Access to medical care was denied to many, even though working medical booths were just a short walk away from the city. Those, like me, who were allowed a scan were then blackmailed before care was given."

When Justina turned the holograph back on, a series of conversations and images confirmed her assertions.

The scenes came in a montage of information.

"Evidence collection part two." Yevgen reappeared in his crown. "General Sten, disgraced

Federation leader, poisons the population and administers birth control."

"Cut the food rations, up the dosage of birth deterrents, and post more guards around the city's borders to keep the population from sneaking into the forests to hunt," General Sten's voice stated over images of ruin and decay, of poverty and pain. "Patience. This is a long game. Every death must be explainable and the Federation blameless. When Cysgod is once more inhabitable, if there are no living descendants at that time, as the last remaining governance of the Cysgodian people, the Federation Military will be able to keep the planet on their roster permanently."

Sever's voice took over, showing him being inter-rogated by the shifters. "We cut food rations, gave out the aggressive agent, and lied to them about the medical booths. No one will question our records if we document a slow downfall over time."

Payton took a deep breath and released it slowly. Finally. It was happening. They were going to get rid of the Federation's presence on Qurilixen. She fought the urge to shout in happiness.

Yevgen's face reappeared, narrating a long list of shipping documents, memos, and other Federation documents as more proof of decades of wrongdoing.

If anything, the cyborg was very thorough in his documentation. He included everything—calculated food logs, food simulator cycle counts, and medical booth scan records. He even added the Medical Alliance for Planetary Health's recommended scan rates for optimum care for humanoid species recovering from a large-scale illness, which didn't happen to be the never-amount-of-times some of the Cysgodians had seen a booth.

When proof of General Sten's false data stating medical booth radiation would kill the Cysgodians, and that the population was not cured of their plague, General Griggs nodded at her ass-kisser who promptly reached forward to pause Yevgen's presentation.

"I don't think it's necessary to go through every shipping document," General Griggs stated.

"I think you would agree," Falke answered, never once revealing what he was thinking in his stoic expression. "We need to be thorough."

Payton's lip twitched a little, as she thought, *Shove that in your black holes, slargnots!*

"Unless you are willing to admit you are in violation of the temporary settlement agreement and immediately plan to vacate this planet," King Ualan offered. "We would welcome any Cysgodians who choose to remain with the understanding that they are no longer under Federation rule. They will be free to choose between leaving or becoming true Qurilixen citizens."

General Griggs's expression tightened, and she did not answer.

Falke leaned forward to resume the presentation. "We'll be sure to pause for discussion."

The general leaned to whisper to her soldier with the clipboard, "Go now," who then nodded in return and instantly left the room.

"Evidence collection part three." Yevgen did not wear the crown this time as he introduced the next segment, "Federation soldier crimes against women."

Nyle stared at the door where Payton had disappeared for so long that, when it opened, for a tiny moment, he thought he'd willed it with his mind. Seeing a half shifted cougar-man quickly corrected the thought.

Everything inside Nyle begged to see Payton again. He felt the absence of her skin. The memory of her smell lingered softly. He hated hiding in the palace suite while she went to deal with the Federation. Not that he had a choice, but it felt like hiding.

"Come," the guard ordered, the word between a voice and a growl.

"Where?" he asked.

"Come," the guard repeated with a gesture of his

clawed hand. It didn't appear as if the man was going to be forthcoming with the details.

Nyle nodded and moved to obey the command. He became very aware of the cougar's sharp claws as he stepped out of the suite. Though he doubted if the Var royals wanted him dead that they would ambush him in the hallway.

He followed the guard's gestures through the vast halls. They took a series of turns, which Nyle assumed was meant to disorientate him.

"I think I should get a jeweled crown. Red and blue stones to match my eyes."

Nyle barely suppressed a groan as he heard Yevgen talking.

"Will I be introduced as Prince Yevgen?" the cyborg continued. "I did not see anything in the palace database for protocol when introducing the half mated husbands of royal princesses."

"You weren't supposed to be in the database," a man answered.

"Then I wasn't." Yevgen stepped out into the hallway. Seeing Nyle, he said, "Greetings Cysgodian Nyle, bastard son of an unknown off-worlder and Diana."

"Uh..." Nyle frowned.

"See," Yevgen said into the doorway. "A title."

"Why aren't you with Payton?" Nyle demanded.

"I was not invited," Yevgen answered. "Did you know that this palace has—"

A muscled guard appeared in the doorway behind the cyborg. The lion cat-shifter looked as if he could punch a hole through the stone wall.

Yevgen glanced sideways and finished weakly, "—a roof?"

"I had noticed," Nyle answered.

To the guard, the cyborg said, "You can't prove I was in that database."

"Computer, update access logs," the guard stated.

"Ha! I deleted those," Yevgen said.

"Access logs restored and updated," a disembodied voice answered.

"And they say the future of the Cysgodian people depends on you," the lion guard answered with a slight curl of his lip. "They're worse off than before."

"Don't say that," Nyle put forth. "Yevgen's entire function has been to protect—"

"I'll take them," the cougar interrupted before motioning to Nyle and Yevgen. "We have a transport waiting."

Nyle had a strange feeling overcome him as he followed the guard's gesture. Maybe it was the way the man looked at him as if he expected Nyle to run at any moment.

Why would he have reason to run unless they were taking him toward something worth running from?

He had told Prince Falke he would do anything to protect the Cysgodians. If they were taking him to Shelter City, then there must be something they thought he could do.

"Come." The guard motioned for Nyle to move.

"Prisoner transfer?" Nyle asked the guard.

The man's only answer was to gesture for Nyle to walk down the corridor.

"There is no prisoner transfer in the computer," Yevgen said. "I sent a communication to the coordinates Prince Roderic provided, but they must need me to verify the information for them."

Nyle stared at the cyborg. For a smart machine, he sometimes lacked a deeper understanding.

"Me," Nyle stated. "I'm the prisoner being transferred."

"Because you had sexual relations with a married princess?" Yevgen asked. "My wife."

Nyle flinched. To the credit of the guards, they

didn't register that they heard the admission. He didn't want them gossiping about Payton, not because of him.

Nyle turned and made his way down the corridor. The guard fell into step next to him. He heard Yevgen behind them, the heavier thud of his mechanical legs unmistakable.

"I'm not going to run," Nyle said softly to the guard. "I have nowhere to go."

The feeling of numbness crept over Nyle's hands, and he clenched and unclenched his fists. He forced his legs to move, praying Payton was at the end of this journey. He wanted to see her face, hear her voice.

The guard strode ahead of them, and Yevgen stepped into pace next to Nyle. The fact that he turned his back said the Var shifter did not perceive them as threats.

"I'll tell them I do not wish anything bad to happen because of your time with Payton," Yevgen said, placing a hand on Nyle's shoulder. The heavy weight of it pressed uncomfortably. "We'll find a suitable punishment. An apology to me, for starters. You are not her second husband, and I did not approve of you beforehand as a lover."

The cougar guard opened a door, and a cool,

fresh breeze swept into the palace as the pale green daylight filtered over them.

Nyle put his hand over the cyborg's. "I love her, Yevgen. Make sure she knows I didn't want to leave..." His breath caught. "Whatever is at the end of my journey, take care of her like you did the Cysgodians. Take care of Payton. Consider her safety and happiness your new primary program directive."

Yevgen's eyes flashed from blue to red and then back again.

25

General Griggs stood abruptly from her chair as Yevgen's presentation continued to play. "I've seen enough."

Her ass-kisser minion instantly turned off the holographic disk.

"We're not finished. We also have documentation from scientists with the ESC about the chemical breakdown and effects of the drug compounds you administered to the Cysgodians," Prince Roderic said.

Griggs rudely held up her hand to stop him from talking. "You had no right to share private Federation documents and medicines with the ESC. In fact, most of your presented evidence appears to be documents obtained without permission. Regardless of what any of this indicates, the fact that you accessed them without proper authorization makes them irrelevant. I demand you return our stolen property at once."

Kirill leaned forward and pushed the disk toward her. "You can keep this copy. We have others."

"I vote we send copies to all our friends across the galaxies," Payton said. "Let's ask them if they think this evidence is relevant."

The general's eyes narrowed in anger.

"I will not be threatened by some animal who married a broken-down computer module," Griggs countered.

"Whoa," Grier pushed to his feet in warning.

"Watch the disrespect," Korbin added, not moving as he showed his claws. He hadn't said much as he watched the proceedings. "You will show respect as visitors to our planet."

"Confirm it," the general said to one of the soldiers standing quietly against the wall behind her. The man nodded and instantly left the room.

Payton gestured at Yevgen's recording. "Doesn't he need this?"

The general ignored her and didn't take it.

"General Sten and his actions do not represent

the high standard of practice the Federation is known for," Griggs stated.

Payton wanted to disagree with that statement but kept quiet. She thought of Nyle. The sooner this was over, the sooner she could go to him.

The general gestured at her ass-kisser sidekick, who in turn pulled a handheld device from within her jacket.

"The truth is we want your galaxa-promethium mines, but the cost of these negotiations has become more than they are worth. We will be sending a new purchase order for the ore at standard rates. I presume you will accept it, and we can expect the first fulfillment shipment in six months." The general glanced at her minion to make sure she was recording what she said. "We are willing to hand over the continued rescue efforts of the Cysgodian people to the Qurilixian royal families. In exchange, we rely on discretion, and the Federation must be able to act to preserve our good name as the primary rescuers and defenders of the Cysgodian people within the galaxies. We will make the announce-ment and control the narrative. General Sten's crimes will be punished. Quietly."

"How?" Grier asked.

"Rank stripped, imprisonment," Griggs

answered. "And if that is ever to change, a Quril-ixian diplomat will be invited to speak on behalf of this planet before a decision is made. In return for this consideration, nothing will be said about the details of these events."

Grier nodded, reluctantly.

"What about Cysgod?" Justina asked.

"It's uninhabitable," Griggs said. "You want out from under the Federation's protection, then we withdraw all support. The planet is yours. It is up to you to safeguard it until your return. We will not intervene. If, at the end of its quarantine, the planet becomes abandoned, then it's anyone's to inhabit."

The general meant it as a threat, and in many ways, it was. With a dwindled population and no one living on the surface, it would be hard for the poverty-stricken Cysgodians to maintain authority over it for a hundred more years. The general didn't realize that the shifters would do everything they could to help if the Cysgodians still wanted to return to Cysgod.

"Counterpoint. You don't have to enforce protection, but you will leave it listed under protected status to deter trespassers," King Ualan stated. "And if anything comes to your attention, you will immediately alert the Cysgodian authorities."

"Fine," the general agreed. "It's marked as contaminated and dangerous anyway. I doubt anyone will care to land inside a hot zone. Nothing left there is worth the risk."

"So you've been back?" Payton thought of the virus.

The general nodded. "We sent a medical team after the relocation to sweep the planet's laboratories and hospitals for any remaining contaminates. They discovered nothing worth noting about the source of the infection."

"We want any records you have about what you've found," Justina said.

The general swept her hand as if it didn't matter. "Anything else?"

"And this," Roderic glanced around, "building?"

"Keep it," the general dismissed. "It's outdated."

Payton wanted to point out that they didn't want the ugly structure but kept her mouth shut. The Cysgodians needed a safe place to live and had already occupied the fortress and barracks.

"Are we in agreement?" General Griggs held her hand toward the ass-kisser, who gave her the device.

The general took it and placed it on the table. "I'll need both kings' signatures."

"All the residents of Shelter City are free," Kirill said, his tone firm as he clarified the most important points, "and the Federation is relinquishing all rights to remain on Qurilixen. I want that in unmistakably plain writing."

"Yes." The general picked up the device and handed it back to her minion to add the words before she drew her finger over the handheld to sign it. Pushing it toward King Kirill, she said, "Sign it so I can withdraw from this planet. I have no wish to spend the night. We have a long flight ahead to the Zenni District."

Kirill held up the device, reading it. He looked at the dragon king. "It's all there. Everything she said. Do we agree?"

Ualan nodded.

"Yes," Korbin said. "Whatever gets them off this planet."

"Are you sure it's long enough?" Grier asked. "Usually, these Federation agreements require several hours and stone hard fortitude to plow through."

"The Cysgodians will be happy to have their lives back," Justina said.

"If they do not live up to the terms, we will release the truth," Falke warned.

General Griggs waved her hand in exasperation. "Threats noted."

"I don't trust them, but yes," Payton voted. "Whatever gets them off the planet."

Kirill and Ualan both signed.

"Confirm they're ready so we can finish this and go," the general said, moving toward the door.

"They are." The ass-kisser studied her device. "Everything is ready for your command, general."

"I'll escort you to your ship." Falke stood to walk the general out.

"Copy of the agreement is sent to both palaces," ass-kisser stated. She tapped her device against the holographic disk. "It's here as well."

Yevgen's face was replaced by a copy of the latest agreement.

"We'll take care of the prisoner and be on our way." Griggs pushed through the doors.

"What prisoner?" Payton asked.

"What prisoner?" Falke repeated, louder.

"The one responsible for the virus..." the general began.

"Cysgodian Nyle, bastard son of an unknown off-worlder and Diana," the ass-kisser supplied.

"No!" Payton ran to jump in front of them to keep them from leaving. "None of the Cysgodians are to be touched. He is Cysgodian."

"You said you didn't know the origin of the virus," Kirill countered.

"I said the medical team discovered nothing at that time of their search." Griggs gave an arrogant smile. "Nyle is not a resident of Shelter City, and the newspaper chip evidence we recovered offers proof of his involvement. Unlike you, we were completely within our rights to read everything transmitted over our secure communication lines."

"No," Payton repeated, flooded with fear and rage.

"I'm not surprised you feel that way. Captain Rita sent us the recording of your dalliance in the supply room. You're lucky we're not interested in holding you accountable for the death of her crewman," the general continued.

"You mean that mercenary who kidnapped us," Payton countered. "We had every right to escape when our lives were threatened."

"As per the agreement, the Federation must be able to act to preserve our good name as the primary rescuers and defenders of the Cysgodian people within the galaxies. The execution of the person responsible after decades of hunting those accountable and assurance of continued galactic wellbeing is just the symbol that we need to prove it was time to safely pass off our protection of the Cysgodians."

And there it was. The loophole in their simple agreement she had feared.

"You can't have him," Payton denied, feeling the rage build.

"Sit down, general. We will discuss the article," Falke stated, putting a hand on Payton's trembling shoulder as if he could hold her back if she decided to attack. "And I would like to point out that you had my daughter kidnapped by space mercenaries to get it."

"We already had the information. After we discovered the hidden documents in our supply log transmissions, we sent a team of contractors to collect the cyborg living within the borders of our city," the general corrected. "The Federation is not responsible for any alleged kidnapping that ensued at the hands of others. All we wanted was to take custody of the machine hacking into our private databases and stealing information. You are welcome to go after Captain Rita and her crew if you like, but I hardly see the need to waste resources on that matter."

"Alleged kidnapping?" Payton demanded. "Are you calling me a liar?"

"We did not agree to a prisoner transfer," Falke stated.

General Griggs looked to her minion, who in turn answered, "He's already been transferred. They're dispensing justice as we speak. After we finish our business here, we'll be ready to go on our way."

"Nyle is at the palace. Unless you attacked, there is no way they would hand him over," Payton denied. Fur sprouted over her cheeks and neck. Her voice became a low growl. "An attack on the palace is an act of war."

"Until a few moments ago, this was still our base," the general stated. "We sent a communication to your guards to have him delivered. If you have a problem with your guards following orders, I suggest you discipline them accordingly. This is not negotiable. We were always taking him. The man is responsible for genocide, and we have a duty to the universes to set things right—"

"No. Yeven Genetic Cyborgtronics used Nyle's organs. He didn't know what they were doing and would never have agreed to let them—" Payton argued.

"You might want to explain how the universes work to your daughter, Commander Falke. The Cysgodians deserve justice. This is a big win for the Federation, and for Qurilixen. We might not get what we want, but we both get what we need. Of course, if this man's life is that important to you, we can always try to stop the execution in return for a new agreement giving us complete access to the mines."

"We can't allow that," Kirill answered quietly. "I'm sorry, Payton."

His voice sounded far away. Execution? Payton felt like someone wrapped their hands around her throat as she struggled to breathe. This couldn't be happening.

"Did you know?" she asked her father. "Is that why I'm here and not at the palace?"

The commander's expression did not change. He grabbed her arm and leaned close to her ear. "We knew it was a possibility that the Federation saw the old newspaper chip. We did not agree to surrender Nyle, though when I spoke to him, he knew it was a possibility. He has accepted—"

"Where is he?" Payton yelled, fighting the tiger's need to take full control. She wanted to slash the superior, annoyed look off the general's face and rip the smug head off the ass-kisser. White fur spread down her arm to her clawed hand. Her fingers throbbed as they widened.

How they got here didn't matter now. All that mattered was that she needed to stop it.

"Get control of your daughter," the general ordered.

"Where?" Payton roared, ripping from her father's grasp as she fully shifted. She felt her delicate princess gown rip along the seams as she unleashed the tiger. If the commander had really wanted to hold her back, he could have forced her to stay next to him.

She lunged at the general, knocking the woman to the ground. Her paws pressed into the woman. The ass-kissing minion struck at her back. The blows barely registered in Payton's anger.

Payton roared, letting saliva drip out of her fanged mouth onto the general's face.

"He's being taken to a clearing outside the Var palace," the general cried out in fear.

Payton released the woman and charged out of the facility at full tilt.

"You're too late!" the minion yelled.

Adrenaline pumped through her veins, causing her legs to sprint harder than they ever had before.

She saw the land crafts but couldn't force herself to stop long enough to climb on board and start one. She kept running, driven to get to Nyle.

The scenery blurred until she couldn't see the trees lining the path. She heard a thundering noise following her but didn't stop to see who gave chase.

Payton had run this path many times. Normally her stress would blow away under the drumming of her paws, but now it only increased. Her heart pounded, and her breath rasped.

The forest had never felt so big or the path so long. She knew every inch, and those inches tormented her as she pushed her body harder than she ever had.

This couldn't be happening.

Not Nyle. Not Nyle. Not Nyle.

The thought hammered in time with her feet.

Not Nyle. Not Nyle. Not Nyle.

She leaped over the underbrush as she cut into the dense woods. A sharp slice cut along her hip as she darted too close to a branch, but she kept running. She used to pride herself on getting lost in the trees, outrunning the palace guards, and making it so they couldn't find her.

Now it was her turn to search.

A clearing by the palace? That could mean

numerous locations scattered about the forest. She knew them all and could easily draw the map of the landscape in her mind. The problem was that there were too many.

Payton broke into a small clearing in the forest. The field was empty, so she dug her claws into the dirt, sliding as she turned direction to keep running.

She should have stayed and made the general tell her where to go.

She should run faster.

She should have never left his side to begin with.

Not Nyle. Not Nyle. Not Nyle.

Low grunts escaped her each time her front paws landed. She vaulted up a thick tree and used the leverage of height to soar through an opening.

She landed in another empty clearing.

A frustrated roar erupted from her as she kept going. She saw a flash as her father appeared behind her in his tiger form. He jerked his head to let her know he was going another route. Roderic landed right behind the commander.

Payton charged back onto the main path and sprinted down it.

A small burst of flames drew her attention. Overhead she saw Grier in flight. The dragon swooped to glide over her. He kept pace for a few seconds before his large talons tapped her shoulders.

Payton reared back, retracting the full strength of the tiger as momentum propelled her upright, half shifted on two legs. Grier reached for her a second time, gripping her shoulders tight and not letting go. Her legs kept moving even as he picked her up from the ground. She gripped her clawed hands around his ankles.

Though she trusted her friend, Payton hated flying. Cats were not meant to be in the air.

The wind hit her fur-covered body as he sped her over the treetops toward the palace. From the vantage point, she could see more empty clearings. The Var palace jutted up from the forest in the distance. Grier carried her past it. He lifted higher, causing her to thrash as she held on tight.

Payton saw land crafts parked around a gathering of soldiers.

"Biosignatures match the information supplied by Captain Rita," a man said. "This is him."

Fire burst brightly beneath her feet, sending up billowing black smoke. A pained cry rang out. Grier instantly lowered her toward the ground only to drop her close to a lit funeral pyre. The soldiers scattered in fear of the dragon.

Payton watched a figure fall within the flames. The smell of cooking meat was unmistakable.

Nyle!

She roared as she landed, running toward the flames. Seeing a figure in the middle, she tried to jump into the fire to rescue him.

Wind blew her back mid-jump as Grier beat his wings to extinguish the fire. Payton rolled on the ground. Her body shifted back into full tiger form to protect itself.

A scream erupted inside her chest, releasing from her throat in a loud, agonizing roar. Pain, unlike anything she had ever known, filled her. A charred figure emerged in the heavy smoke and didn't move as the remains kneeled, head down.

She was too late. Nyle was dead.

Nothing mattered.

Payton's heart squeezed violently. Any second, the organ would implode, ending her torment. She stared into the smoke coming off the charred remains.

The sound of land crafts buzzed as the soldiers fled in fear. Grier spouted fire after them to chase them away.

Her tiger retreated deep inside like a wounded animal hiding in a cave, and Payton found herself crouching naked on the ground. Her limbs shook, barely able to support her as she tried to crawl toward the pyre. Rocks pressed into her knees and hands. Tears streamed down her face.

They should never have trusted the general.

Torn between wanting the pain to be over, and the sudden burning need to make every single member of the Federation pay for their crimes, Payton began to scream.

Her fingers dug against the ground.

She begged the gods to reverse time.

She begged them to kill her too.

She couldn't live without him.

Claws extended, and she reached toward her chest to rip out her own heart.

"Payton," Grier yelled, running toward her in his human form to stop her.

"I can't. I can't," she gasped between breaths.

Grier grabbed her wrists. "Look at me. Look at me."

She blinked, staring at him briefly in shock before turning her attention back to the pyre.

Grier jerked her hands and leaned to block her view. "Look at me."

"Grier?" She wanted him to tell her it wasn't true. "It can't be this. I need more time. We have to fix it."

His eyes teared, and all he managed to say was, "Just look at me, Payton."

The smoke had cleared. She used Grier's help to

push to her feet and tried to stumble past him toward Nyle. "I need to see him."

Grier kept hold of her, refusing to let go as he walked alongside her.

A strange gleam caught the light from beneath the ash. Stunned, she reached for it. Her touch dislodged the thick covering, and the metal frame of a leg appeared.

"It's not him," Payton whispered. Any relief she felt was short-lived. She knew those legs. "Yevgen."

Tears rolled down her cheeks for her friend.

"Why would they burn Yevgen?" Grier finally released her as she stopped trying to claw out her own heart. "Why not disable him?"

"We have to find Nyle," Payton said. "Fly up and see if you can—"

Grier leaped up from the ground, shifting into full dragon form before she could finish the request.

Shaking with emotion, Payton looked around the now empty clearing.

"Yevgen? Are you in there? Can you hear me?" She cleared the ash from the cyborg's metal frame, willing his eyes to flash with light. Scorched marks discolored the metal, and heat had charred the wires. He'd come back from the dead once on

Captain Rita's ship. He could do it again. "Yev? It's safe. You can turn back on."

Yevgen didn't react.

"Payton?"

She spun around at the sound.

Roderic emerged naked from the nearby trees, his fur retracting into flesh as he shifted back to his human form. His eyes darted behind her.

"Yevgen," she said.

"Why did they...?" Roderic frowned. "Was it because he hacked their database?"

"I don't know." Payton shook her head. She took a deep breath and looked frantically around. "I can't find Nyle. We must find him. Maybe they're taking him to the ship. We have to stop them."

"Payton, easy." Roderic held out his hands to his sides as if trying to calm a feral cat. "You're going to find him."

"How?" She turned in circles.

"Feel him," Roderic said. "He's your mate. Feel him."

"We're not married. Yev..." She gestured at the cyborg. He still hadn't turned back on. "None of this is right. This was not supposed to happen. They were safe at the palace."

"If things were not so dire at the moment, I'd

laugh at you for thinking your stubbornness was stronger than the will of the gods. I don't care what you call it, you love him. Nyle is connected to you. That's not something you can dictate. It just is. As real as the three suns. Now close your damned eyes and feel him."

Payton closed her eyes. All she felt was panic and sadness.

"Picture his face. Imagine calling out to him with your mind," Roderic said. "Which way is he?"

"I don't..." Payton felt a small tingle along her temple. She began walking before she opened her eyes. She followed the instinct, going into the trees.

Searching as she walked, she came across a cougar guard from the Var palace lying unconscious on the ground. She leaned down to touch his neck. He was alive.

Payton saw feet poking through the underbrush. She rushed around a bush to find Nyle on the ground. Payton gripped his arm tight and forced him to look at her. Tears still wet her face, and she couldn't stop shaking. "Nyle?"

He moaned. His legs moved restlessly as he fought to come awake. Seeing a mark, she pushed back the strands of his long black hair and found what looked to be a burn along the side of his neck.

Dark brown eyes opened to meet hers, and she released a grateful breath.

"I didn't think I'd get to see you again," he whispered.

"What happened?" Payton watched his mouth, wanting to kiss him even as she waited for an answer. Cupping his face with both hands, she stroked her thumbs over his cheeks. Warmth filled her fingers.

"I'm not sure." Nyle blinked several times, his eyes turning toward the trees overhead. His lids fell heavy, and he looked as if he might pass back out.

"Hey, stay with me." Payton moved his head to return his gaze to hers.

"I think you're a dream because I wished it so hard," he whispered. "Did I die today?"

"Try to think, Nyle," Payton insisted. "What happened to you? Why are you on the ground?"

"We were coming from the palace. Yevgen zapped the guard, and then..." Nyle moaned, reaching for his head. "You need to talk to him. He's letting his princely powers get out of control."

Roderic appeared next to the Var guard. He slapped the man's cheek. "Nap's over, Anwir."

Nyle blinked several times as if fighting for consciousness before wobbling to a sitting position.

"Anwir, get up," Roderic ordered.

"They burned Yevgen," Payton told Nyle, ignoring her cousin. "On a pyre. But you can fix him, right? It's Yevgen. He'll survive this. You just need to reboot his programming like when we were on Rita's ship."

"There isn't time." Nyle pushed up from the ground. He swayed as he reached his feet. "They're coming for me."

"No. We won't let them." Payton wrapped her arms around him, holding him close. "I thought they took you from me. I couldn't live through losing you. I thought I was strong. I thought I was making all the right, honorable choices, but I'm stupid. I should have told you the very moment I felt it. I love you."

"You told me." Nyle returned the embrace, stroking her hair. "I love you too. I was worried I wouldn't get to see you again before the end."

"We can't end. I want to be with you. I want to marry you. I want a forever."

"I want that too, Payton, but some choices are not ours to make." He sounded calm, resigned. "They need someone to pay for what happened on Cysgod. The guards received a communication from Shelter City. When Yevgen was processing the palace data he obtained, he told me what they said.

If my sacrifice will end the Federation's hold over Qurilixen and the Cysgodians, then that's what must happen."

Payton knew Nyle searched for redemption. She doubted he would ever fully forgive himself for the past. She hated his pain, even as she loved him for his honor.

"I'm happy I got to see you one last time—" he started to say.

Payton pressed her hand over his mouth, shutting him up. "I'm not letting them take you anywhere."

"Payton?" Grier shouted from the clearing. "The soldiers are coming back with reinforcements. I didn't see Nyle from the sky."

"I found him," Payton yelled.

Nyle looked down as if noticing her nakedness for the first time. His gaze lingered.

"I ran here from Shelter City," she explained.

"You have to let the Federation soldiers finish it," Nyle said. "They'll leave. You'll all be free. The Cysgodians deserve an end to this. Let me give that to them."

"You're my forever. If you climb on that fire, I'm climbing on with you. And that will be the end of it.

I die when you die. You're my mate. There is nothing you can do to change that."

"Payton, I—"

"I love you," she interrupted. "It's as simple as that. Those seconds when I thought it was you instead of Yevgen, it nearly destroyed me. All this talk of honor and duty. We've been stupid."

"Yevgen." Nyle frowned. "You said they burned him?"

"Are you confused? How hard did he zap you?" Payton tried to examine the burn on his neck.

"Is it because he hacked into their files?" Nyle asked, turning his head away from her attention. "I don't understand. It was supposed to be me."

"You're looking a little dazed. We need to get you into a medical booth." Payton studied his face.

"Pyres are meant to reduce organics to ash."

"I know. Yevgen's body doesn't look good, but his programming should still be in there, right?" Payton needed to believe that what she said was true. She needed her friend to be all right. Guilt filled her to know she'd been relieved when it wasn't Nyle in the fire. "We have to get him out of here before they come back. We'll take him to the palace. You can fix him after you get checked by a medical booth."

Payton pulled Nyle toward the clearing.

"Come on." Roderic helped the Var guard to his feet. He supported the man's weight. "This way, big guy."

"Yevgen was not constructed to withstand incineration," Nyle insisted.

They pushed through the underbrush. It scratched her exposed skin. When they came out the other side, Nyle tugged his hand from hers.

"Take my shirt." Nyle pulled the clothing over his head.

"I'm fine." Payton denied. If soldiers came for him, she would be fighting.

The soft sound of something falling drew her attention downward. An object had come from inside the shirt.

"What is that?" Payton asked.

Nyle picked it up, and his hand trembled. "An old recording disk. I haven't seen these since..."

"Since?" Payton prompted.

"Yevgen must have put it inside my shirt."

"So you can repair him with that?" Payton insisted.

"No." Nyle shook his head. "It's what we used on Cysgod in the labs for internal recordings. I'm not sure why he still has it. I figured he would have scavenged something better by now."

"Payton!" Grier yelled.

Payton wanted to say more, but they were out of time. The hum of land crafts approached.

"Grier, I need you," Payton answered as they came to the clearing. The dragon prince was there in seconds.

"Good, you found him." Grier nodded at Nyle. "We need to get him out of here before they come back. I can hide him in dragon territory where they'll never find him."

"I'm not running, or hiding," Nyle said. "Not when I can end this. Get Payton out of here. I'll stay and face—"

"He's confused," Payton interrupted. "Don't listen to him."

"If they know about Nyle, they know about the newspaper chip article." Roderic joined them. The palace guard remained inside the tree line leaning against a thick trunk. "They know where to look for the virus formula. Griggs said on record that they didn't find it when they first looked right after evacuations, but now..."

"They signed away all rights to the planet," Payton reasoned. "I'm betting Griggs will try to get someone there to look for it one last time before the Cysgodians can make arrangements to protect it. We can't let that happen. If those people didn't destroy the facility like they had planned, the virus could still be there. We can't let it get out."

All eyes turned to Nyle.

"Take Nyle to the west landing dock at the Var palace," Payton said. "Don't let him out of your sight until Roderic can join you."

Payton snatched the recording disk from Nyle before tucking it into his waistband for safekeeping.

"No, I—" Nyle began.

Grier instantly shifted into dragon form. Nyle stumbled back as the dragon hovered.

"He won't drop you. It's a short trip. Try not to look down," Payton advised as she pulled Nyle's arm toward the dragon. "I love you."

Grier wrapped his talons around Nyle's biceps.

Nyle kicked his legs in protest. His shirt fell to the ground as he automatically reached to hold on to Grier. "I can't..."

"Roderic, take Yevgen to safety. Hide him with Nyle on Rick's ship. Then tell Rick I need him." Payton gestured at her cousin to hurry.

Roderic half-shifted and gathered the metal pieces into his arms. He made a small noise of discomfort as he bounced them to indicate they were still hot before he ran into the forest.

Payton turned on the funeral pyre to let it burn. She grabbed the shirt from the ground and slipped it over her head. The cougar, Anwir, remained half shifted as he came from the trees to stand next to her. The man was a young guard, maybe only a decade out of his training. She knew him from the palace but had not spoken with him.

Two land crafts emerged from the trees. Armed soldiers leaped down before the vehicles came to a complete stop. The soldiers held blasters at the ready as they searched the sky for dragons.

As attention turned toward her, Payton said, "You've done your damage. You're no longer welcome on this planet. I suggest you leave."

One of the women motioned toward the pyre, giving a silent order to retrieve it. Her name tag read Robbie.

Payton moved to stand in front of the fire to stop them. She extended her claws. "We bury our own. Leave him."

Anwir growled in warning to offer his support.

"Gather the prisoner's remains," Robbie stated, again motioning her underlings to move. "Bio evidence needs to be logged."

The heat from the fire became uncomfortable, but Payton didn't move. She focused past the emotions churning inside of her. "They tested him before the execution. You don't need more."

"They'll test again. Protocol." Robbie jerked her hand harder than before to punctuate her orders to her men.

The cougar gave another growl of warning, causing the soldiers to hesitate.

"We have orders," Robbie stated. "You want us gone? We need that pyre. Create trouble, and we'll take it by force to fulfill our orders. Stop us, and more will come."

Payton took several deep breaths, staring them down. She slowly stepped aside.

The soldiers swarmed the pyre, switching off the flames. Breeze blew the remaining ash. One of the soldiers punched his finger at the controls without looking at his hands as if it were a task he'd done a million times before. A containment field appeared over the remains, stopping the ash leak, and the pyre lifted to hover over the ground for transport.

"Get it to the ship's medical team. They'll confirm," Robbie said, climbing back onto a transport.

Payton felt her eyes water as she watched them

push her friend away. She held on to the hope that they only took a shell, that Nyle would be able to revive Yevgen's mind, like rebooting a program. But what if everyone was right about the cyborg? People tried to tell her Yevgen was just a machine, that he couldn't love her.

Payton did not have answers to what it meant to be alive. A feeling was more than a recorded fact. It did not live in programming. But perhaps it did live in memories, and what were those if not a recording of the past?

Humanoid life could not be resurrected from ash. People did not get to come back from that kind of death. Was this the end of her friend? Would anything they found and put into a new body merely be a recording, an echo, of the past? Like a passage scrolled into a book or a holographic image?

Or would replacing his organs be like any alien being cured in a medical booth?

What did it mean to be alive?

Who decided, and by what right, what all this meant?

Payton watched the pyre hovering over the ground. Her thoughts swirled and bubbled like a ceffyl caught in a mud pit. The sound of the soldiers faded, and their bodies blurred until all she could see was that metal device. Her hands shook, and she wanted nothing more than to rewind time, to not have to see this or feel it.

Yevgen was a good man. He was her friend. She'd seen him watch over the people of Shelter City like a guardian. She saw him trying to understand love. And right now, she was mournful at the prospect that he was not coming back.

This was not the funeral a hero deserved.

"Princess?"

Payton jerked at the hand on her arm. The guard's touch drew her from her thoughts. The soldiers had gone, leaving only flattened plant life in the clearing and the horrible lingering smell from the pyre.

"We should leave," the cougar insisted. "I'll escort you back to the palace."

Payton wiped her eyes and nodded.

"I'm sorry about your grief over Prince Yevgen. Know there are those who support you."

Payton nodded and began walking toward the trees. It was the fastest route back. Suddenly, she stopped and frowned. "Why do you phrase it like that?"

The cougar hesitated.

"Speak freely, Anwir." Payton crossed her arms

over her chest and stared at him. "I am in no mood for cryptic messages."

"There are those who support your choice to return to the old ways." Anwir lowered his head as if keeping secrets from the trees. "We do not pretend to understand your choosing the cyborg as first husband, but perhaps it was a statement?"

Payton stared at him, not speaking.

"A way to make your family accept your decision to half mate. You'd have to marry another to have children. We all know Princess Samantha wishes for grandchildren."

Payton resumed walking through the forest. Still, she said nothing.

"There are those who would volunteer for the position," Anwir insisted, following her. "They would consider it an honor. I know I would."

Her father had been right. People often felt the need to fill the silence. She quickened her pace.

"Some—*not me*—feel that a cyborg should not have been named first, but I'm sure you have your reasons."

Payton didn't have time to listen to the ramblings of a Myrddinian follower.

"Do your brothers feel the same as you?"

Payton held up her hand. "Stop speaking freely."

"Yes, princess," Anwir stated, his tone clipped with disappointment.

"Report back to the palace. Don't speak about what happened." Payton didn't wait for him to answer as she leaped forward between two trees. She stretched her limbs, sailing through the air before hitting the ground on all four paws. Nyle's shirt ripped off her body, except for the sleeve that stayed around her wrist. She shook the paw violently between strides before finally snagging the material on a branch. It tore, freeing her as it stayed behind in the forest.

"ARE WE FIGHTING OR FLEEING, STARSHINE?" Rick said by way of a greeting as Payton leaped onto the auxiliary landing pad in her tiger form. They had him move his ship from the main landing dock with news of the Federation's arrival to keep it hidden from the sky. The pilot's half smile curled mischievously, and she knew the idea of an adventure, *any adventure*, would intrigue him.

Payton half shifted to keep her nudity hidden beneath her fur as she pushed up from the stone pad. "Neither. We're leaving."

"At the same time as the Federation?" Rick pointed upwards. "You do know the mothership is orbiting the planet as we speak. How about we go hide out in one of the guest suites until they leave?

I'll teach you a drinking game we play with the food simulator when the wives aren't on board."

"This can't wait," Payton denied. "We have to go now."

Rick grabbed her arm to stop her from going onboard. "Care to tell me what the crew is getting into?"

"Will it matter?" she asked.

He tilted his head. "Is it dangerous?"

Payton nodded, knowing that would entice the pirate in him.

"Does your mother know you're leaving?" he asked.

"I'll send her a transmission from the sky," Payton answered. "I need your help, Uncle Rick. Please. The Federation executed Yevgen, and they thought it was Nyle. We need to get them to safety before they realize the mistake."

"*Him* to safety?" Rick asked.

"*Them.*" Payton didn't feel like she had time to explain her scattered thoughts. All she knew was that she wanted them to run. "I want to take Yevgen somewhere he can be reanimated."

"Sam's going to be irate, but we'll leave your brother to pacify her," Rick said, as if angering Princess Samantha was their biggest concern.

"When Roderic told me they stashed Nyle on the ship, I figured it was best not to tell Ryland. He's not going to be happy, but I'll come and get him when we bring you back."

Payton didn't tell him she wasn't planning to return to Qurilixen. Nyle couldn't be here, so she didn't have a choice. That moment she thought he was dead lingered inside her, a fear forever changing her. Before, she would never have thought a being could survive such pain.

Something in her expression must have convinced him because he nodded. "All right, starshine. I don't understand the urgency when we can simply hide him, but all right. We'll get you into space."

"Thank you," she breathed in relief, nodding. "Thank you."

"He's in the medical booth. Strap yourself into the console seat."

"Don't tell anyone he's on the ship." Payton knew Grier and Roderic would only tell who was necessary. She could only hope Anwir kept his mouth shut until they were far enough away to disappear.

"This isn't the first time I've smuggled a fugitive. I'll show you the best places to hide on the ship once we're sailing the black." He jerked his thumb that she should go in without him. "I'll clear us for the skies."

"Thank you, Rick." Payton rushed into the ship. She found Roderic pacing outside the medical booth room.

"What are we doing?" Roderic asked. Seeing her naked from the shift, he took off his shirt and tossed it at her.

"Nyle?" Payton glanced at the door as she pulled the material over her head. She retracted the fur of her half shift. She never thought she'd be willingly stepping back onboard a spaceship, let alone planning to take a trip in one.

"He's in the booth." Roderic stopped her from going into the room. "He'll live. He was freezing from his shirtless ride with Grier. There is some brain swelling from where he must have hit his head after Yevgen stunned him. It also said he had residual drugs in his system. The booth recommended he be rendered unconscious because he kept trying to move around. The important thing is that he's safe. Tell me what's happening. What are we doing here?"

"Federation soldiers took the remains and left," she said. "I heard them detect Nyle's blood in

Yevgen before the fire, but I don't know what they'll find when they analyze the ash, or how much time we have until they do. They might come looking for Nyle. They can't find him."

"How did they get Nyle's bio profile?"

"I'm guessing it was in the laboratory records the Federation took from Cysgod. I have to wonder how much they've known from the beginning." Payton frowned. The details of all of this didn't matter. What's done was done. "I have to get Nyle and Yevgen to safety."

"And where is safety?"

She glanced upward.

"Payton, I looked at what was left of Yevgen. He's not... It's only a metal frame. I don't think you're going to find what you're looking for." Roderic glanced down the passageway as they heard the metal creak. "You have to prepare yourself for the possibility that you can't revive him."

"I have to believe there is a way to save him." Payton held back her emotions, trying to keep rigid control of them. "He can't end like this."

Roderic saw through her façade. He smiled sadly and patted her arm. "All Yevgen wanted was to belong."

"I don't love him the way he wants me to."

Payton stared at her cousin, unable to keep the tears back as they spilled down her cheeks. "I mean I *didn't* love him the way he *wanted* me to."

"He knew he wasn't your true mate. That's why he kept asking to be a half mate. Yevgen knew you loved him in your way. He wanted to be looked at like he was alive, to be part of a family, to be a prince and a hero. You gave him that."

"He took Nyle's place on that pyre." Roderic smiled sadly. "He chose to die a hero."

"Why would he do that? Those two aggravated each other. Always bickering." Payton ran her hands into her hair, pushing the length away from her face. "Maybe it just came down to his programming to protect the Cysgodians. I'm so angry at him."

Roderic gave her a hug. "Payton, you don't believe Yevgen was only programming. He did what any man of honor would do. He sacrificed himself for another's happiness. He saw what the rest of us do. That you're meant to be with Nyle."

Her hands shook, and she pulled away from him. "I don't know what to feel. I'm so mad at Yevgen for walking into danger and for not being here right now. I'm grateful for what he did in saving Nyle from execution. I couldn't have lived if Nyle had died. But I want my friend back. I need to believe that it's possible we can revive him. I have to at least try."

The sound of footsteps boarded the ship.

"Strap in!" Rick's yell carried through the passageway.

Roderic studied her face. He leaned his hand against the metal wall. "What are you planning?"

"Don't ask."

"You're flying to Cysgod to look for the virus formula, aren't you? And you think you can revive Yevgen while you're there." Roderic shook his head. "It's quarantined. You can't seriously think—"

She gave him a light shove. "Just get off this ship and go to your wife before Rick gets back. Justina will never forgive me if we kidnap you into space."

"If you do something stupid, *I'll* never forgive you."

"Thank you, for everything, Roderic." It was the closest she could come to goodbye. Anything more, and he would know she wasn't planning on returning home. "Now get off the ship."

Roderic started down the passageway, before turning to walk backward. He held his arms to the side. "Don't let Rick fly you into a star. We need you back here, safe. The planet isn't the same without you."

Roderic disappeared around a corner, and she listened to his steps as he left the ship.

"Goodbye," she mouthed, knowing he wouldn't hear her.

The ship began to creak and clang as it prepared for takeoff.

Payton placed her hand over the scanner to open the door. A shirtless Nyle slept inside the medical booth. Laser lights skated over him as the machine worked. She instantly went to him, leaning over to look between the bed and the lid to where he lay inside. She watched his chest rise in steady breaths.

The ship vibrated as engines rumbled to life.

"I wish you were awake." She reached into the booth to touch his cheek. The healing lasers tried to focus on her hand, and she pulled it away.

"Payton, strap in for takeoff," Rick ordered over the comms. "He's safe in the booth."

The medical booth gave a slight hissing noise as clamps appeared from underneath. They slithered around Nyle, locking him into place.

Payton strapped herself into the console's chair. The angle let her see the side of Nyle's arm along the edge of the closed booth.

"Going out quiet," Rick instructed.

Payton wasn't sure what that entailed. She

looked down to where the seat was bolted to the floor, wishing she could move it closer to Nyle.

An image on the console followed the path of the lasers, outlining his body. They seemed to concentrate on his neck and head.

She felt her seat vibrate, and lights flickered. The console darkened. The vibrations deepened, and she knew they were moving.

"Payton?" Nyle whispered. The lasers shut off. "Did they put you in the stars?"

The vibrations deepened, and they became cast into pitch black.

"I'm here," she said, narrowing her gaze to watch him through the darkness.

"Payton?" Nyle tried to sit and came up against the restraints. He began thrashing about, trying to break free. "What's happening? Let me out of here! They're trying to turn me into a cyborg, but I don't want metal blood."

Payton didn't think as she unlatched her straps and rushed across the room. She stumbled as the ship pitched. She reached for his hand. "Easy, I'm here. No one is going to hurt you."

"The organs," he insisted, trying to escape. "Is it in conscious thoughts? In actions? In free will? Some people don't think for themselves."

"Nyle, you're not making sense right now. Just try to relax. We're on a spaceship. You're safe." Payton's hand slipped out of his grasp as the ship jolted hard. Her feet slid from underneath her, and she caught the edge of the booth to keep from falling. Gravity lessened, and she felt her feet disengage.

"Some don't act when called upon. Others don't have the choice of free will. Yet, all of those people didn't live," he continued. "I lived. Why did I live?"

"Nyle, stop." She tried to reach in to pat his chest. "It's all right, my love, it's all ri—"

The ship tilted so that the floor became the wall. Momentum pulled her hard toward the console. Her hands ripped away from the booth as her body flung. Gravity reinstated, and she felt a sharp pain in her head as she crashed backward into the darkness.

28

"Concussion. Fractured wrist. Swollen eye. Fifty-seven cuts. Exhaustion. A myriad of other nonsense." Jackson's voice broke through Payton's darkness. "Doesn't say anything about stupidity."

"Hey!" Payton groaned, opening her eyes. She knew he was teasing her.

Dev stared at her from the outside of the medical booth. "We're not a medical ward, little one. We only have the one booth."

"Next time keep strapped in during takeoff, especially when Rick is flying," Jackson stated. She couldn't see him, but she heard him in the direction of the console. "That's like the second rule we taught you."

Payton gave a small laugh, coming more awake.

"Yeah, but if I remember correctly, the first rule is never to let Rick fly. Or have control of the food simulator. Or lure you into one of his games."

"Fair enough," Jackson acknowledged. "I stand by all of those."

"Where's Nyle?" She asked, pushing at the lid. "Let me out of here."

"Sleeping." Dev stood back.

The booth unlocked and released her.

"And we're safe?" Payton insisted as she pushed to her feet.

Dev and Jackson shared a look.

"What?" Payton held her head, feeling a little unsteady as she stood.

"Federation saw us leaving," Dev said.

"Did they engage?" Payton frowned.

"No, but we caught an encrypted communication. Thanks to Yevgen leaving a present in the form of an encryption program in the ship's computers for us, we were able to understand it. General Griggs has ordered someone to Cysgod." Jackson chuckled. "The cyborg erased some of Rick's recordings of Old Earth transmission waves to make room for his program. That in itself was a present."

"I knew she'd try something. Griggs is looking

for the virus." Payton frowned. "We have to get there first."

"Already on our way, starshine," Rick announced from the doorway. "It occurred to me that is where you were hinting at before takeoff. Yevgen's from Cysgod. Nyle built him there. That is where you hope to find the parts to reanimate your cyborg husband, isn't it?"

Payton nodded. "If you don't feel safe going, I can find—"

Jackson's and Rick's laughter cut her off.

"I'll unpack the old suits," Dev said. "It's been a while since we've gone into a quarantine area. I'll check them for holes."

"Did you tell the palace where we were going?" Payton asked.

"We couldn't be sure the transmission wouldn't be intercepted," Rick said. "But I'm sure Roderic will tell your mother for us when the time is right."

"Where's Nyle?" Payton asked.

Rick pointed his thumb down the passageway to answer her question, saying to Dev, "Dig out the containment canisters in case there's something to scavenge. The families are still waiting for us to return to Letame with the parts to repair the ship."

Payton walked down the passageway to the

same sleeping quarters her brother had locked her in. She opened the door and found the room was dark. Instantly she went to the bed where Nyle slept. Crawling next to him, she curled along his side and put her hand on his naked chest to feel him breathing.

"We did it," she whispered. "We told the Federation to take a flying tumble into the darkest black hole, and they're leaving Qurilixen. It's not over completely, but we can rest now."

He sighed in his sleep. It might have been her imagination, but she felt as if he breathed a little easier.

Payton closed her eyes and let the vibrations of the ship lull her to sleep.

She wasn't sure how much time had passed before she felt Nyle stroking her cheek.

"You're beautiful when you sleep," Nyle whispered.

"You can't see me." She gave a small chuckle. "The room is dark."

"I have been listening to you breathe, and I can see you perfectly in my mind." He snuggled her closer, holding her in his arms.

Payton felt his breath tickling her cheek. Their lips came together in a gentle kiss. The heat of his body curled through her. The darkness cocooned her, making her feel safe. Outside problems still stirred, but here, in his arms, none of that mattered. It was the emotions inside her, crashing around, that she couldn't escape. She loved him so much, and that fear of thinking he had died still haunted her. She also grieved for her friend. Relief for Nyle amplified the guilt she felt.

Their mouths parted.

"I'm sorry about Yevgen." Nyle reached along his waistband and pulled out the disk. His voice remained soft. "I have the recording he gave me when he zapped me."

"You sound less confused. Do you remember everything that happened?"

"It's a blur of moments, but I think I have the gist of what transpired." His grip around her tightened. "I'm not sure how we got on this ship, but it looks like Rick's. Unless you're telling me we never made it back to Qurilixen, and I just had one hell of a dream."

"It's no dream." Payton told him of the Federation agreement and their attempt to execute Nyle, trying to fill in any blanks in his memory. "They found the article with your picture. Griggs tried to dismiss the part about those patients they left behind going to find the virus in the laboratory. She said they'd already searched, but then Rick intercepted her sending orders to have someone go to Cysgod and check again."

"I have to get there first." Nyle tried to sit up.

Payton held him down. "We're flying there now. There is literally nothing to be done at the moment. We can't make the ship go faster."

"We need protective gear, medical equipment." He again tried to pull away.

Payton didn't let go. "We have gear."

"But..."

"There is nothing you can do right now," she insisted.

He settled next to her. "How did Rick intercept a Federation command?"

"Yevgen added a few software upgrades when he was connected to the ship. Doing it probably made him feel part pirate. He would have liked that. I know you think he was just a machine, but he was my friend." Payton felt the sadness bubble up inside her, causing her words to catch in her throat.

"Hey, come here." He held her tighter and stroked her back. "What do I know about anything? You lost someone close to you. Someone who sacrificed himself to save me, a person he seemed not to like all that much. Protecting me wasn't in his coding. Maybe I was wrong. Maybe he did evolve. You once told me that Yevgen wanted nothing more than to understand love, that yearning for it was enough to prove his humanity. That idea stuck with me. I have thought about it often."

Payton concentrated on the pressure of his body against hers. The world had always seemed so big to her, but now it felt small and fragile. She'd always pictured herself as a strong woman, but now she felt vulnerable and scared.

"I can't lose you, Nyle," Payton whispered. "My heart can't take it. I'll leave everything behind to be with you, but you have to promise me you'll fight for us. No more talk of surrendering to the Federation."

Nyle's hand found her thigh and swept up under the shirt along her hip. "I promise I will always fight for you."

"For us," she insisted.

"Yes, for us."

Nyle's lips met hers. She poured everything she had into that kiss as she clung to him. She felt the gentle hum of the ship. It didn't matter how much she hated space travel or the idea of the deep black surrounding them. As long as she was with him, she could live with those things.

His fingers moved around her back. Payton adjusted her position on the bed and pulled off the shirt. Nyle pushed his pants off his hips. Before he could work them completely off his legs, she had him fully on his back, straddling him beneath her.

Payton wanted him where she could see him, feel him. She leaned over to kiss him, the emotion exploding out of her as she devoured his lips with hers. His hands roamed her body, urging her closer as if he mirrored her desperation to join together.

She drew herself up and fitted his arousal along her sex, not stopping as need drove her onward. They made love in an aching frenzy of movements. Hands grasped. Lips pressed. Bodies strained. Even when the climax hit her like a rocket, it wasn't enough. She wanted more. She wanted them to last forever.

He pulled her down to his chest, holding her on top of him.

"I love you, Payton," Nyle whispered. "More than anything I have ever known and beyond all I could imagine. I don't know how I came to get you, and I know I will never deserve you, but I love you. I promise never to forget that or take it for granted. I promise to fight for us."

"I'm holding you to that," she answered just as

softly. "Because you're it for me, Nyle. My mate. My husband. My life."

He gave a soft moan of pleasure. "If you're asking, I'm accepting."

"It's already done. It's been done. I just didn't realize it before." Even with the slickness covering their bodies and the heat of the exertion, she didn't move off him. "I'm never letting you go."

TIME HAD LITTLE MEANING IN SPACE. THEY took their meals with Dev, Jackson, and Rick. All of their conversations willfully avoided what they flew to do. Every moment he could, Nyle gravitated toward Payton. And, if he couldn't reach her, he wanted to look at her. He hated the moments they were apart.

Nyle saw the guilt in her eyes. He recognized the emotion easily because he also carried it. He couldn't help but think that the more she loved him the guiltier she felt about Yevgen.

Dev and Jackson formed a quiet contrast against Rick's boisterous stories. Jackson cracked smiles and nodded, but Dev merely watched. Having a large Belvon demonic creature staring at him was a little unnerving, and Nyle did his best not to make eye contact.

Days were marked by the artificial lifting and dimming of lights. There were minutes when he first opened his eyes that Nyle could convince himself they were in some kind of vortex with no beginning or end, a time where he could pretend that these moments with Payton were forever.

It was all he ever wanted, more than he dared hope for, and sure as Bravon's hellfire more than he deserved.

This morning was different. He felt it even before the lighting changed. It stirred a fear inside him as if some beacon called him home.

Cysgod.

The planet loomed on the viewing screen of the cockpit. They stood crowded around the pilot's chair as Rick flew. The light blue and white appeared so innocent and welcoming, nothing that would hint at the deadly virus waiting beneath the clouds.

Well, nothing but the alarm triggered by the warning beacon the Federation had left behind. Red lights flashed on the ship's panel as urgent words moved over the screen in multiple alien languages.

"Where's this laboratory?" Rick asked.

Nyle went toward the screen and pointed along the edge. "The city should be over here."

"Everyone, get to a seat and buckle up," Rick ordered with a pointed look at Payton. "Nyle, you sit in here with me so we can find a place to land close to where we need to be. I don't want to expose ourselves longer than necessary. Dev, check the seals on the medical hatch."

"Already done," Dev answered.

Nyle sat where he was told, unable to take his eyes away from the viewing screen.

"Do it again," Rick said. "We have precious cargo onboard."

"That's the sweetest thing anyone's ever called me," Payton teased.

"Who said anything about you?" Rick grinned, leaning back in his chair to look at her. "I meant me."

Payton squeezed Nyle's shoulder before leaning to kiss his cheek. "It might not seem like it, but they know what they're doing."

It didn't take a genius to see that the crew used playful humor to deflect all other emotions, especially the pilot. As if to prove the point, Rick winked at Nyle and grinned.

Nyle reached to touch Payton's cheek as she pulled back, lightly caressing her.

He listened to her walk away as he strapped himself into the chair. His eyes remained on Cysgod's surface. He had thought it was etched in his memory, but found he'd forgotten the planet's exact shade of blue. When he thought of the surface, he remembered the funeral smoke and ash snowing down over the streets.

Rick began singing softly to himself as he leaned forward in his chair, punching buttons on the console. *"Our birth was a hard one, or so we've been told, our mothers were harlots, our fathers out cold. The doctor was drunk, lads, the bartender did pour, as we shot out with the thunder and came with a roar."*

Nyle kept his eyes on the planet, ignoring the pilot. He stared at the edge where the dark sky met the sphere. His hands shook, and he pressed the palms flat against his thighs. With each second, the orb grew larger on the screen.

*"And we sail the high skies, looking for gold, looking for treasures that never grow old. The wind in our sails, lads, the stars at our feet, as we plunder for—*what in the cursed black holes is this nonsense?" Rick swore as he reached for the comms.

"On the ready, we have company."

"Who is it?" Nyle asked.

"If I had to guess, I'd say Griggs sent Captain Rita to check out the planet. Ship matches the *World Traveler*. Looks like they beat us here." Rick frowned as he magnified the image of the ship. "They must be preparing to land."

Rick started humming his song as the ship gained speed, changing course to arc around the other spacecraft. Nyle's gaze shifted between the *World Traveler* and the planet. "Why would anyone want that virus? Why can't they just let it die?"

"You're smart enough not to need me to answer that," Rick said, the music leaving his tone. "The universes are full of bad beings and the greedy slargnots willing to sell them the goods."

Nyle continued to stare.

"Can I ask you something?" Rick continued to watch the screen.

"What?"

"If you're immune, why didn't they use your blood to do that science-y stuff to find an antidote?"

Nyle shook his head. "There was no time to try. Those who knew the truth kept the origin a secret. By the time I found out, everyone was sick. The damage had been done. It wouldn't have worked anyway. They grew the virus on my clones, but who knows what alien splices they pieced together to make it resistant. I looked, but someone tried to hide what they had done and deleted the information."

"Hm." Rick nodded. His hands moved over the controls like a musician with an instrument. Under his breath, he whisper-sang, "*And we sail the high skies, looking for gold, looking for treasures that never grow old.*"

"It's dangerous down there," Nyle said. This wasn't a game, and he didn't want Rick treating it like one.

"Never is down there," Rick answered. "*The wind in our sails, lads, the stars at our feet, as we plunder for women, thick brown, and good mead.*"

A beep sounded.

"There we are." Rick cleared his throat and opened communications with the other ship. His tone changed to mockingly formal. "Greetings, *World Traveler*. I hope your quarantine protocols are ESC-89 standard if you're thinking of landing in that hotbed of virus activity."

Rick paused, waiting for a response.

"What is ESC-89?" Nyle asked.

"Whatever I want it to be," Rick answered, before hailing the ship. "*World Traveler*, please respond with your ESC-89 quarantine plan, including your three-year supply list and quarantine docking location."

Finally, Captain Rita's voice answered, "Who is this? Why are you on the Federation's channel? Your credentials are coming in scrambled."

Rick smirked but kept his voice even. "*World Traveler,* this is the Federation Health Protocol ship *Cysgod Guardian.* Please respond with your ESC-89 quarantine plan, including your three-year supply list and quarantine docking location confirmation."

There was a long pause before Rita answered, "We're here on Federation orders."

"*World Traveler,* we do not have you cleared for biohazard landing. Check your planetary advisory channel. This is an active virus location. I repeat, active level one virus location. We have orders to contain any universal threat for the greater good of all aliens. No one is allowed to leave the planetary atmosphere without an ESC-89 quarantine plan. Trespassers will be blasted from the sky in accordance with MAPH, ESC, HIA, and Federation joint protocols."

Rick didn't slow their speed as they neared the other ship.

"We're here on Federation orders," Rita repeated, "from General Griggs."

"*World Traveler*, you are not authorized. Turn your ship around immediately. This is your last warning. If you proceed to Cysgod, you will not leave it. This is a level one virus containment with a one hundred percent infection to death rate."

Rick switched communication off.

"What are they thinking?" Nyle grumbled.

"Dev, get ready to divert power to the shields," Rick said over the ship's comms. "Jackson, going to need you on weapons. Payton, get your strap back on and stay put, or I'm locking you in a room for the rest of the trip."

"They had a child on the ship when we were with them," Nyle said. "We can't shoot them down."

Rick stiffened. "Jackson, they might have a kid with them, so if it comes to it, disable, don't destroy."

"Who in all the stars brings a child to a place like this?" Jackson answered.

Nyle stared at Rita's ship, willing them to leave. There was no love lost when it came to the mercenary crew, but that boy...

He took a deep breath. No one wanted to be in a spaceship battle in the middle of the deep black. There was no telling which, if either, ship would fly away from it. An instant explosive death would be better than being stranded and drifting, hoping a benevolent rescuer would not only answer a distress call but would stop to help.

"*World Traveler,* we're going to need your response. A Federation elimination fleet has been dispatched to your location," Rick warned, lifting his hand as if to silence Nyle before he spoke.

Nyle held his breath.

Seconds ticked by.

"Rick, are we a go?" Jackson asked.

Rick motioned his hand to wait even though Jackson couldn't see the gesture.

"Our mistake, *Cysgod Guardian,*" Rita finally answered. "We have the wrong coordinates."

Nyle released his breath. Rick clenched a fist and pounded it up into the air in celebration.

Rita's ship began to move away from the planet.

"Stand down," Rick ordered. "We're good."

"Remind me never to play poker with you." Nyle leaned back in his chair. "That was one hell of a bluff."

"It's easier when the other side knows they're doing something they shouldn't. They know they're expendable to Griggs, just as they know they're in it for the space credits. Being trapped on a planet with a deadly virus isn't worth the risk." Rick grabbed the controls and realigned them toward the planet. They kept an eye on the ship, making sure it left the airspace.

"We're lucky we got here in time to stop them," he said.

"Half the galaxy is built on luck," Rick answered, sounding distracted as he manned the controls.

As the *World Traveler* disappeared, Nyle focused on the planet. Though glad to see the mercenaries go, he did not feel relieved. It had been so long, but he could picture the cityscape in his mind. There were two images that warred within him—that of his youth full of light and shine, and that of his leaving filled with smoke and char. What would time have made of it? All those endless days and nights passing without disturbance from the Cysgodians. He imagined nature had reclaimed its territory like the citizens had never been there.

The planet became magnified on the viewer.

"There?" Rick asked as the lines of a city emerged.

Nyle nodded. "That's it. East side is the laboratory. There was an old landing dock that should fit us, but I don't know what condition it will be in now."

The ship shook as they entered the planet's atmosphere. A feeling of dread clenched Nyle's stomach. Payton should not be here. He'd told her that several times, and each time she refused to hear it.

When the turbulence calmed, the land below came into focus. From the sky the line between city and nature was easy to see, but as they closed in the buildings blocked the long view. The tall buildings that had reflected like wet glass were streaked as if cleaning droids had circled them without fresh cleaner. As if to prove his assumption, he watched as a small unit passed around a structure's center mass. It hung from a long cable attached to the top of the building.

Nyle felt a hand on his shoulder and glanced up to see Payton next to him.

"You're supposed to be buckled in, starshine," Rick said. Payton ignored him.

"It's so..." Payton whispered to Nyle.

The ship turned through a wide street. The empty roads were clear.

"Is that the hospital?" Payton pointed toward the building.

Nyle nodded.

Her grip on him tightened as if she sensed his inner turmoil and wished to comfort him. "It's not what I was expecting. The soldiers must have cleaned up when they were evacuating."

"No. They didn't." Nyle put his hand over hers, keeping her against him. He detected a slight discoloration on the street where the pyres had burned, but the bodies were gone. "Maybe they came back? Griggs said they searched here."

"All right, lady and gentlemen, we're inside the hot zone," Rick announced to the crew. "Suits and boots. Best behavior."

30

PAYTON HAD SEEN THE PICTURES OF CYSGOD after its fall. The city looked nothing like the images in her mind, but she could match them to their locations. The photographs flashed from her memory as she looked around. There had been people pressed against the now-empty glass doors of the hospital. The streets had been aflame with large bonfires. An abandoned doorway had held a screaming woman. The echoes of the past were like ghosts in her thoughts.

"Shields holding," Dev's voice announced.

"I didn't expect the apocalypse to look so tidy," Rick said.

Rick flew slowly through the deserted streets. He angled the ship to navigate around obstacles.

Payton held on to the back of Nyle's chair. The metropolis appeared to be waiting for a populace to take it back. Scarred buildings were shells. Rubble from any damage had been cleared. Roads were clean.

Thank the gods the roads were clean. It was one thing to see pictures of dead bodies and another to see the actual bodies still piled after decades. She didn't want that memory for Nyle. The ones he carried were bad enough.

"We've got movement," Rick said.

A tiny street sweeper robot emerged from a dim nook and moved forward. It passed under the ship.

"They didn't turn off the robots," Nyle said, as if clearing his confusion. "That's how the city looks like this. The units kept working as if nothing had changed. They cleaned up our mess."

Payton saw a broken-down unit tucked inside an archway. "It's not your mess, Nyle. You didn't do this."

She hoped he believed her and doubted he ever fully would.

"There." Nyle pointed into the distance. "The labs are there."

They flew toward a large complex. A hole had been blown into the brick wall surrounding the laboratories, but the rubble was swept away. The damage seemed to tell the story of an attack. A secondary gate had been cut open. A flickering holographic sign on the front lawn read, *Yeven Genetic Cyborgtronics Laboratories.*

"It's like the news chip said. The Cysgodians must have tried to storm the facility to destroy the virus." Payton stepped around the chair to get closer to the viewing screen. A door was bashed in. "Do you think they succeeded?"

"No," Nyle stated. "Even if they knew where it was, I doubt any of them had access to get inside. Security was tight. With the scientists gone, the defense droids would have been left activated to protect the labs."

"Shields holding," Dev repeated over the comms.

"It seems strange that they would have just left something so dangerous inside that building where anyone could go after the virus. I thought it would look more secure. Hidden. Underground. Something." Payton glanced at Rick. "I would think pirates would be crawling all over this place."

"Only fools would step out on this surface," Rick answered. The words were hardly comforting. "Flying in, the planetary warning system advised of faces melting off and insides coming through to the outside in animations I really didn't need a visual for."

"That's not how the illness presents," Nyle denied.

"The fear served its purpose. The Federation isn't averse to lying to the rest of us, or to each other, or to themselves," Rick answered. "Besides, everyone knows that a planet killer is here. It was all over the universes when it happened. Pirates and scavengers tend to enjoy being alive. Not many people will risk having something like that hanging around on their ship."

Nyle gripped the arm of his seat. "We're not taking the virus with us. We're making sure it's destroyed."

"Obviously," Rick quipped. "Not much space credit to be made if everyone dies in the transaction."

"Destroying the threat is the only reason we're here," Payton said to soften Rick's reaction. She was sensitive to the fact that sometimes her uncle's devil-may-care nature could come off as callousness to those who didn't know him.

They hovered over a landing dock. The markers on the surface were faded, but the wide-open space left plenty of room. A broken column from an old communications tower jutted from the docks like a broken claw pointing upward. The top half had fallen over the side, too big for the robots to haul away.

"Suit up," Rick said. "I'll land and meet you in the airlock."

Payton waited for Nyle to join her as they walked through the ship's corridors.

"I still don't want you out there," Nyle said when they were alone. "It's too dangerous. I don't even like you on-world right now. I'm immune, but you—"

"Are going wherever you go," Payton finished for him. This wasn't the first time they'd had this conversation. "You're my life, Nyle. You and me. That's everything. You're here, I'm here."

They found Dev and Jackson waiting in white biohazard suits with ESC insignia on the chest. The ship jerked and settled as Rick landed.

Dev handed her a similar black suit with a Federation Military logo. "This should fit. No claws on the inside."

Jackson gave Nyle a white suit that matched theirs.

"ESC?" Nyle questioned.

"Found them in an abandoned container on a scavenging trip," Jackson said. "Never used. Seemed a shame to let them go to waste."

Payton didn't ask him if that container was in a locked storage crate at the time.

"Payton, you can't use your claws," Jackson said.

She sighed and glanced sideways at them as she dressed. "No holes. Got it."

"Did you remind Payton not to make claws?" Rick asked, joining them.

Payton turned on the three men and growled. "I'm not going to—"

Their laughter stopped her.

Rick pointed at her hand, where her claws were extended.

Payton retracted the claws. "Point taken."

"Have you ever walked in a quarantine suit before?" Nyle asked her. He pulled on his suit and began sealing it as if he'd done it thousands of times.

"It was one of the lessons our parents had us take when we were space training," Payton answered. She remembered hating the confines but didn't tell him that much. Being put outside the ship in deep space had been worse. It had been like being caged inside a beautiful infinity, unable to touch, smell, or hear, only to see through a small window in her helmet. She'd been able to move, but barely as she floundered around. At least on the surface, they'd have gravity.

"And did you claw open your suit?" he insisted, glancing at Dev, Jackson, and Rick.

"When I was a child, whenever I got emotional, or nervous, or mad, or whatever, my claws came out like an involuntary reaction," Payton said. "They like to tease me about it."

"She ripped several of her fancy princess gowns before big dignitary presentations," Rick stated, pulling on his suit. "Our little kitten would be gripping her puffy skirts and poking long holes in them. Sam would get so irritated."

"You were adorable in fluffy pink," Dev added, his stoic expression remaining intact.

Payton arched a brow. "I could say the same about you."

Nyle kneeled next to her and began checking her suit's connections. She felt the material tighten up her calf. The grip reminded her of the compression shirt Captain Rita had trapped her in. A rope of green light flashed up her leg, and Nyle moved to the other side.

Silence fell over them as they finished getting dressed. Nyle checked and rechecked her suit. He would have done it a third time, but she stopped him by grabbing his hands. She could barely feel him through her gloves except for the pressure of his fingers moving against her.

"I love you," he whispered.

She smiled at him, doing her best not to appear nervous. "Attach my helmet?"

He slid a helmet over her head. Payton watched his face as he fastened it and checked the connections.

"Can everyone hear me?" Jackson's voice sounded like it came from behind her head.

"Clear," Dev and Rick answered.

Payton touched her wrist to activate her microphone and said, "Yeah."

She looked at Nyle, who nodded. "I hear you."

They fell back into silence as they went through the process of leaving the ship through the small airlock. As she finally stepped out on the dock, her legs shook. She caught herself holding her breath, watching the lights on their suits for changes that would indicate a contamination breach.

"We're good," Rick said, attaching a containment canister to Payton's waist for her to carry. "Let's do this, my little twinkle lights. Keep an eye on your fresh air, and don't run it to empty. No one goes off on their own."

Nyle held up the small recording disk Yevgen had left them to show her before tucking it into a fold in his suit front. Rick gestured at Nyle to lead the way.

The landing dock doors had been pried apart and left with a broken lock. When Nyle pulled it open, it made a horrible screech that echoed in the surrounding silence.

A small robot activated as they entered. It made a grinding noise as it moved to sweep the floor. It bumped into Dev's foot.

"We'll stand watch," Jackson said. He and Dev remained by the doors. "We won't find parts here. I don't see any ships to scavenge."

"I wouldn't want to take them if we did" Dev answered.

Rick followed Payton and Nyle as they went through the hallways. The light from outside helped, but the path was dim. Payton's eyes shifted so she could better see inside the shadows.

Payton tried to reach out to Nyle with her feelings to comfort him. Through their deep connection, she knew this wasn't easy. He worried about her being there. His mind relived the past. His guilt and sadness over it simmered. She wanted to talk to him but knew their conversation wouldn't be private.

Nyle stopped at a door and pushed his way inside a dark room. A light activated on his chest. He pointed at a wall. "Hold down the red button."

Rick moved past Payton and did as instructed.

Nyle pumped a lever up and down, grunting with each stroke. A generator tried to start. Payton reached out to help. The stiff lever resisted their efforts, but they finally managed. Lights came on overhead.

"We have power," Dev's voice came through the helmet.

"We have about an hour of power in this sector before this thing dies," Nyle said, reading the controls. His chest light shut off.

"Let's move," Rick ordered.

They went back into the hall, walking faster than before now that they could see better.

Cysgod had loomed over her thoughts like a dark cloud, in those pictures of the end. But seeing the planet firsthand, she could imagine beyond those last moments. The laboratory was not the big scary monster of nightmares. It wasn't an evil lair. It was just a building, like so many buildings she'd seen with sterile walls and precise lines. The rooms looked as if they had only been recently abandoned. There were a few scattered devices and empty workstations, as if the scientists would suddenly come back to resume their work.

What frightened her were the things she couldn't see. It was the air around them, stopped only by a suit. It was an intangible fear, like ghosts echoing the hallways.

Suddenly, Nyle stopped at a glass door encasing a steel one offset into the wall. Score marks scratched the glass as if it had been struck but had not shattered.

"I've never seen security like this," Rick said.

Nyle held up his hands and pressed them to the glass. He began to lean forward.

She heard a soft tapping on the other side of the door.

"Something is in there moving around," Payton said, reaching to stop him.

"It's probably another cleaning droid," Rick said.

"There shouldn't be cleaning droids in there," Nyle denied. He kept his hands on the door and pressed his helmet against the glass. He rocked his head back and forth, triggering light to scan the three points of contact. It must have recognized him because the door shimmered and disappeared. A panel opened in the center of the steel.

The tapping turned into thumps. It didn't sound like the other robots.

"Be careful," Payton whispered. She felt her claws starting to extend and had to forcibly keep them retracted.

Nyle's gloved hand hovered over the screen as he hesitated. He hummed a tune and then punched the keyboard symbols to repeat the sounds of the security code. The door groaned as it slid open to let them pass.

A high whiz sounded, and Payton jumped toward Nyle to shove him aside. A laser blast passed between their bodies. Rick pressed against the wall next to the door and instantly drew a weapon.

"Status?" Dev demanded.

Rick quickly leaned into the open doorframe and fired before hiding against the wall once more. Electricity zapped.

Nyle pushed Payton's back to the wall and began running his hands over her to check her suit. Their lights were still showing they were good, but he kept checking.

"Status!" Dev yelled.

"Rick one, security nub zero," Rick stated.

"Don't you dare get yourself killed, space cadet," Dev warned. "I'm not going to be the one to tell Harper you're not coming back to her."

Rick quickly swayed several times in front of the door, but no other shots were fired.

Another soft clank sounded.

"What is that noise?" Payton asked.

Keeping his weapon drawn, Rick went inside. "Clear."

A destroyed security nub smoked in a ceiling corner. A robotic arm attached to a bench worked analyzing samples from a long cabinet.

"It's still working," Payton said.

Nyle went to shut the arm off and pulled up information on the table terminal. "It's still attempting to grow organs. They never shut it off when they left."

"Check your air," Jackson reminded them through the comms.

They automatically looked down at the monitors on their arms.

"Good," Payton said as the other two nodded at her. They couldn't linger too long, but they were fine for the moment.

"Where did they keep the virus formula?" Rick asked.

"I'm checking the system now. Give me a minute. It's been a while since I used this kind of interface." Nyle pulled a chair to the table and leaned over next to the arm to read the screen on the top. Soft musical tones sounded as he typed.

"It's just like flying a ship," Rick said. "It'll come back to you."

Payton walked around the lab for clues, not that she would understand much of the Cysgodian scientific writing. She touched the strange symbols and then the small containment canister at her waist. "Should we maybe copy some of the literary works and send them back to Qurilixen? It might be nice for the elders to teach the children. Maybe picture archives?"

They'd been so focused on the virus that no one had stopped to consider what else they should take.

"Priority has to be the virus," Rick said. "We'll see what air we have left after that, but I'm not staying on-world to browse a library."

"I was right. They deleted any information about the virus out of the system," Nyle said, standing. "They tried to hide the fact they were responsible."

They.

He said *they* were responsible, not *we*.

Payton took a deep breath at the tiny admission. Maybe Nyle could someday forgive himself.

He searched the lab before putting a recording disk that looked like a larger version the one Yevgen had left behind on top of the table. Lights began flashing.

"What are you doing?" Rick asked.

Nyle watched the lights. "Copying the system. The only thing people know about my homeworld is the Cysgodian virus, but there is so much more. This database contains everything my people worked on. Grafting advancements for cyborgtronic limbs. Medicines. Technology. You talk about a library; this is my people's library. This is what we strived for, what we wrote about."

"We need to hurry this along," Rick insisted. "We'll circle back for it if there's time."

The lights stopped. Nyle took the recording disk and turned toward Payton. "I know no one more honorable than my wife to entrust this to for safe-keeping."

He put the disk into her containment canister. Payton wrapped her hand protectively around it. "We'll need a way to access the data."

"Virus," Rick prompted.

"Storage facility," Nyle answered.

Payton glanced down at her air gauge to check it. "Wait, play Yevgen's disk."

Nyle started to reach for it.

"Virus," Rick stated louder. "Priorities."

"Storage is this way," Nyle said. To Payton, he added, "We'll try to find a handheld player to take with us."

Nyle hoped the others didn't see his hands shake as he moved around his old workplace. He had thought himself prepared for the rush of emotions he felt being on-world again, but it was more than he could have imagined. Everywhere he looked he saw something from his past.

Outside, it had been childhood walks with his mother down the busy streets or educational trips to the various buildings. He remembered waiting in line for a lecture and giving up because it was too cold.

Inside the facility, it was Valn reciting inappropriate jokes but never getting into trouble because she had a charming smile. Or the time Ward and Darryn had a cart race through the halls and crashed into a week's worth of food crates. Or when a small lab accident killed a scientist in Sector B that he'd never met.

Nyle had prepared himself for the big memory but not these small ones. This wasn't his assigned laboratory, but it looked close to the same. Touching the tabletop console, hearing the soft musical notes of his fingers on the keys, it brought him back to those workdays that ran together in an endless stream. So many tiny things he'd forgotten to remember—the sound of muffled voices moving along the hallway past his lab, the clomp of feet as cyborg frames learned to walk.

"Storage?"

Rick's voice was urgent as he broke into Nyle's thoughts. He couldn't blame the pilot for not wanting to hang around a virus-infested lab.

Nyle went to a wall and ran his hand over a small seam in the white-coated metal. After several attempts to open it, he sighed. "This is the most secure room in the facility. It can't read my biorhythms through the suit."

"You're not taking it off," Payton said. "Rick shook the wall."

"No, hold on," Nyle lifted his hands to stop the man. "Just wait."

Nyle returned to the robotic arm and rolled its table to wave the metal in front of the seam. A click sounded, and the wall popped open enough for him to push it aside.

The storage facility lights activated, which he expected. But there shouldn't have been a steady hum of storage units. There would have been no reason to leave them all on. A narrow walkway was flanked on each side by metal storage containers and shelves. The room was the largest in the building.

Seeing a handheld reader, he handed it to Payton before giving her Yevgen's disk. "Try this while I check the storage logs."

Payton glanced around and then set it on the floor. She placed the recording disk on top. And stood back to watch. The holographic image of Yevgen's head in a crown fluttered, and the sound of his voice warbled as the message started.

"Greetings. You are watching this in honor of me, a fallen hero, having courageously sacrificed myself on the pyre of destiny. You have ventured to the land of the dead to hear my royal message. Henceforth, the day of my sacrifice will be known as Prince Yevgen Day, a day where all must sacrifice in honor of my greatness." His tone lowered, adding, "A yearly ball at the Var palace would be in order where all the cyborgs in the land are invited. All except a cyborg named Harriman from the Vortexian District. If he shows up, turn him away from the planet. His transmissions are subpar."

Yevgen's image paused. Other devices on the storage rack and down the walkway picked up the signal of his recording, creating several holographic Yevgen heads. The privacy glitch in the device would have been an issue with a full lab, but now it hardly mattered.

"Are there more cyborgs on Qurilixen?" Rick asked.

"A few Shelter City sweeper borgs left over from the Federation's rule. They're powered down," Payton answered.

"Is that all?" Nyle asked, nudging the player with his toe.

"To my beautiful wife, my forever princess," Yevgen continued as images of Payton appeared with a mild delay to all the linked devices. The cyborg's voice sounded like an echo as the other players repeated him. "I am sure you have received my many messages by now—"

The message stopped.

"What is he talking about? Messages?" Payton frowned.

"Maybe he left them at the palace?" Nyle suggested. "He was in the palace system."

Payton lightly tapped the device with her foot.

"—and know what you must do," Yevgen continued. "Now please take a moment of silence to honor my sacrifice."

Regal music played as images of Yevgen and Shelter City showed on the holograms.

A soft laugh sounded through the comms, only to grow louder as Payton leaned over. Her shoulders shook, and he wasn't sure if she was laughing, crying, or both. "His important message was to establish Prince Yevgen Day. That is so like him."

Rick motioned at his air monitor and then toward Nyle to keep working.

Nyle tried to draw up the storage areas for the corresponding lab, looking for samples whose reference numbers had been deleted. The problem was that there were too many of them.

"This doesn't make sense," Nyle whispered, trying to reboot the log.

"What?"

"The files are corrupted. It has designated too many samples to that lab." He watched the screen reboot only to show the same information.

Yevgen's show continued to play. Nyle ignored it.

"Or maybe there are more samples than you thought?" Rick surmised.

"Suit check," Jackson reminded them, his voice crackling.

"We're good," Rick answered, not bothering to look at his controls.

"Comms are breaking up," Dev said.

"Stay put. We won't be long," Rick answered.

"This way." Nyle led them deeper into the storage area. "We'll just have to destroy all of them."

The sound of Yevgen's music continued. He glanced back to see Payton carrying the handheld. The devices stopped playing, and she put the disk into her canister along with the handheld to take it with them.

The mechanical hums increased as they neared rows of vertical stasis pods large enough to hold a person or a rack of organs.

"They must be running off solar power," Nyle said, going to a pod to see specimen containers of his cloned organs. "When everyone left, no one shut off the system, so it just kept growing organs."

"Like the arm in the lab," Payton said.

Nyle nodded. "I'm not sure how it's still going.

It doesn't make sense that it would continue this long. These stasis pods were not assigned to that lab."

"The system adapted to its protocols," Payton said. "Just like Yevgen grew and bettered himself in Shelter City without the help of scientists to monitor his programming."

Rick went to look inside one of the pods. He swiped his glove over the window. "What in the blazing star trails? There's a child in here."

Payton rushed to look for herself.

"What's happening?" Dev's voice came over the static.

"They got kids in stasis pods," Rick answered, rushing to look inside another. "There's a boy in this one."

"We're on our way," Dev stated.

"No, don't," Nyle interrupted. He went next to Payton to look inside at the figure of a young girl. A shapeless cloth gown hung on her thin frame. "They're not children. They're cyborg shells."

"There are adults, too," Rick said, going from pod to pod. "Blasted! This one's a freaking giant."

Payton and Nyle went to look at the boy.

"What do we do?" Payton asked.

"Kill the virus," Nyle said. "They could all be

carriers. Yes, with it looking the way it does makes it more difficult, but they aren't sentient beings. They're shells waiting for programming."

Payton placed her hand against the pod as if lightly stroking what was inside. "But can't you feel it? They're made from you. Just like Yevgen was. They feel like him."

"Just because I am immune and not a carrier doesn't mean these shells grown in this environment won't be infected," he reasoned.

"Congratulations, Daddy," Rick muttered, still staring in at the giant. "It's a virus army."

"We can't kill..." Payton turned to stare at him, not finishing her sentence as if the idea warred inside of her.

Nyle knew his wife was attached to Yevgen, but these shells were not him.

"I would have thought clones would have been like versions of you," Rick said, tapping on the small window before moving to look inside another.

"They took multiple samples from me," Nyle explained, gesturing at his waist to indicate his sperm. "Looks like the robots found a use for all of them."

"So what do we—? Payton began.

A light tapping came from inside the girl's pod.

Payton gasped and jumped a little as they all turned to look toward the sound. The tap came again, like fingers drumming against the metal interior.

They slowly moved to peer inside.

Nyle found a version of his genetics looking back at him from the round face of the girl.

"Greetings," the girl said, giving the awkward smile of a cyborg new to its programming. "You are watching this in honor of me, a fallen hero, having courageously sacrificed myself on—"

"Yevgen?" Payton whispered to the child. "Is that you? Are you back?"

"—the pyre of destiny. You have ventured to the land of the dead to hear my…"

The girl stopped talking, but her eyes remained open and unwavering as another voice picked up the recording.

They instantly moved toward the boy.

"…royal message. Henceforth, the day of my sacrifice will be known as Prince Yevgen Day, a day where all must sacrifice in honor of my greatness," the boy said, his head twitching as he kept talking.

"What's going on?" Payton asked as she and Rick both stared at him for answers.

"I don't…" Nyle glanced at the canister Payton

carried. "They must have picked up the signal and loaded it."

The boy stopped talking and didn't move. Overhead a digitalized voice continued over the facility's comms system. "...Vortexian District. If he shows up, turn him away from the planet."

"Did you guys hear that?" Jackson asked.

"We're on it," Rick said, turning in circles. His hand strayed to the gun at his waist. "Stay where you are."

"His transmissions are subpar." Suddenly a deep voice picked up the message, and they all hesitated before going toward the giant. The creature was crammed into the pod in what looked to be an uncomfortable position. The voice stopped.

"Is that it?" Rick asked when it didn't resume. "A signal blip?"

The giant's stasis pod began to shake. The large shell jerked violently and punched his fist at the door, cratering the metal from within.

They jumped back as the stasis pod flew open.

"To my beautiful wife, my forever princess," the giant continued Yevgen's message as he climbed out of the pod. He stretched to his full height to tower over them. Except for his mechanical eyes and abnormal size, the cyborg looked Cysgodian down to his temple markings. Material covered his midsection. The top edge was torn as if it had ripped as he grew.

"Yevgen?" Payton asked.

The sound of Yevgen's musical moment of silence played softly, and the giant's eyes flashed as if he loaded the images from the recording disk.

Nyle felt his stomach tighten as he went to stand possessively next to Payton. On the one hand, he should be happy that Yevgen's programming was not lost because that would make his wife happy. On the other, he did not want to share his wife with her first half mate back from the dead.

Nyle knew enough about cloning to know that the giant cyborg shell had been a misstep in the laboratory. A scientist would have eliminated the sample the moment the anomaly was discovered during screening. Robots and computers would have only known if it was viable or unviable.

The giant's eyes flashed with different colors as it looked at each of them before settling on blue. He turned his attention to Payton.

"Yevgen?" Payton asked, her voice shaky.

"You received my messages." Yevgen nodded, his deep voice not sounding like they remembered. "How many years have I been offline?"

"Days, not years," Nyle said. "We left Qurilixen the day of your fire and came here to destroy all traces of the virus's source so it could not be spread."

"The first Prince Yevgen Day," Yevgen stated. "I am heartened that you missed me."

The cyborg completely ignored the fact that they came to destroy the virus, not look for his replacement body.

"I thought I lost you." Payton moved to hug the giant. "Don't you ever do that to me again."

Yevgen's arms were awkward when he patted her back as if his programming was still settling into his motor controls. "There, there, princess."

"How did you manage to fit all of yourself onto a single recording disk?" Nyle asked, wondering how much the cyborg could actually remember of his past.

"I'm a better programmer than you." Yevgen gave a cocky grin over Payton's head as she continued to hug him.

Nyle felt his irritation surface. Yep. Same Yevgen, different giant-sized body.

"What were you thinking pulling that sacrificial stunt?" Payton demanded, pushing out of his arms. "You should have fought, not jumped into the flames!"

"Self-preservation?" Yevgen chuckled as he shook his head in denial. "Nice try, my love, but you have shown me the royal path by example. A prince must live honorably and do his duty above all else. He must sacrifice all that he is for his people and his family. You would have jumped onto the fire."

"Yev..." Payton sighed as she looked at Nyle. He saw the torment in her expression. He knew she loved him, felt it, believed it with all his heart.

Nyle did not want to share his wife. The very idea burned inside of him like the plague. But worse was the notion of not having her at all. Yevgen was right. Payton would always do the honorable thing by others. She would not abandon the cyborg any more than she could stop from being a princess. She talked of staying with Nyle in the skies, but he could not let her do that. She loved the wilds of Qurilixen. She loved her family and her life. He would be taking her home.

"I had to place myself on the funeral pyre," Yevgen reasoned as he looked at Nyle. "I was following my new program directive. I am to take care of Princess Payton and consider her safety and happiness as my primary function. My death freed you to fully mate to a man you love more than me, and it saved the man you love from death. I have fulfilled my honorable mission."

"But you are alive," Payton said.

"I was dead." Yevgen gave her a pat on the head. "I will always love you, princess, but I cannot marry you in this life. Logic says you will have life mated to Cysgodian Nyle, bastard son of an unknown off-worlder and Diana. A full mate cannot take a half mate. The mating math does not add up. You must learn to go on without me, my love. I will always be here to protect you, just as I protect the Cysgodian people."

The pressure on Nyle's chest lightened as relief flooded him.

"I don't mean to interrupt this—*whatever it is*—but virus formula?" Rick prompted, tapping his monitor. "We're on limited time. We must head back to the ship."

"Over here." Nyle moved past the stasis pods. "Yevgen, can you interface with the facility?"

"Of course." Yevgen's heavy footfall followed him.

Nyle activated the disposal fires and began pushing buttons to storage containers. "Are the fires at operational temperature?"

"Yes," Yevgen answered.

Nyle purged the first row of containers, not knowing what exactly was in them. "Help me get rid of these."

"Which one?" Yevgen asked.

"All of them. The logs were corrupted. We don't know which one had the contaminated formula." Nyle kept pushing buttons when suddenly they all became selected. He drew his hand back, and they purged on their own.

"All formulas have been disposed of," Yevgen said. "Fires are set to burn the requisite three days."

"Make it ten," Nyle said.

"Is that it?" Rick asked. "We done?"

Payton glanced around the storage facility before settling her gaze on the pods. He knew what she was thinking, felt the thought as if it were his own.

"You can't stay like that, Yevgen." Nyle gestured at the cyborg's new body. It would be cramped in the air lock and could carry the virus.

Yevgen stepped back. "Your obsession with removing my legs is disconcerting."

Payton lifted her hand toward the cyborg. "He means we can't take you home in this body."

"We have to destroy the shells," Nyle explained. "That means all the clones. They could be carriers. There was no oversight when they were grown, and we don't have the months to test them."

Yevgen rushed to put himself between the stasis pods and Nyle. His chest puffed up, and his arms lifted as if ready to fight. "You will not touch them."

"They're shells," Nyle insisted.

"I have a directive to protect the Cysgodian people," Yevgen stated.

"They're all on Qurilixen waiting for you." Payton showed him the canister. "We have your memories right here. I promise we'll figure out a new body for you."

"I have a directive to protect the Cysgodian people," Yevgen repeated.

"You can, from the Var palace," Payton insisted. "I promise, I won't stop until—"

"He means these Cysgodian people," Rick interrupted, motioning his hand at the pods.

"Yes, I have a directive to protect the Cysgodian people." Yevgen kept himself defensively in front of the shells. "I will protect my brethren. You will not destroy them."

"They're not—" Nyle started to say they weren't alive, but a knock sounded in the little girl's pod followed by the boy. Soon more noise filled the storage facility, reaching deep into where the lights did not shine.

"All right, space cadets, it's time to get moving," Rick ordered. "Nyle's children are waking up and I, for one, don't want to face your cyborg prince's virus army."

"They're not my children," Nyle said, leaning to see into a nearby window. A cyborg adult moved, lifting his arms like a baby discovering his limbs for the first time.

"They're my children. As Prince Yevgen of Cysgod, I must protect them," Yevgen stated.

"Fair enough, your highness," Rick said. "Yevgen, buddy, good to see you, but we have to fly."

Rick walked quickly to leave the room, and they could hear his voice calling to connect with Dev and Jackson who had gone quiet.

Nyle looked at his monitor. The air supply had gotten low.

"You're not coming?" Payton asked softly, moving toward her friend. "Is this really goodbye?"

"Never, my love. We will establish communications between Cysgod and Qurilixen. My brethren and I will monitor for the day when the virus is no longer a threat and the old Cysgodians can rejoin the new."

The sound of opening pod doors clanked in the distance.

"You should go now," Yevgen said. "I must help my subjects."

"I love you, Yev." Payton hugged him. "Thank you for your friendship. Thank you for saving Nyle."

The lights on her suit turned yellow.

"Payton," Nyle said. "Our air. We have to leave now."

"Nyle, take care of her," Yevgen stated. "That is your primary directive."

Nyle nodded. "Thank you, Yevgen. For everything."

The sound of heavy footsteps began filling the storage room. Nyle gently placed his hand on Payton's back to guide her back into the lab so they could leave. She hesitated as if she wasn't ready to say a final goodbye.

The children stepped out of their pods and looked up at him. Their eyes flashed with colors.

Nyle nudged Payton harder, urging her to walk ahead of him. Once they started moving, they didn't stop. They passed through the hidden door in the lab's wall and then past the workstations. There was no more time for him to reminisce.

The yellow on Payton's suit deepened to brown. Nyle glanced down and saw he was still green.

"Payton, check your monitors," he said.

She grabbed her controls and said, "I'm almost out of air. How am I almost out?"

Nyle turned on his chest light and checked her suit while pushing her to keep walking. "Did you snag it on something?"

"No, I..."

"Claws?" he asked.

"No, I've been careful," she insisted, sounding panicked.

He found a small fray over the oxygen filter. "We have to get you back on the ship."

"What's going on?" Dev demanded, his voice coming in clearer than before.

"Get the hatch ready," Nyle ordered. "The security blast skimmed Payton's suit. Her filter isn't working."

"You heard him, go," Rick ordered.

Payton's indicator lights turned red and flashed. She weaved a little as she walked. He heard her breathing rasp through the comms when she tried to speak.

Nyle swept her into his arms and began carrying her toward the ship. He ran as fast as he could. The loud clomp of Yevgen's giant feet sounded behind him, but he ignored it.

Her rasping became lighter.

"She can't breathe," Nyle yelled.

Rick held the facility door open. Dev and Jackson waited near the ship. Seeing him, Dev darted forward to take Payton out of Nyle's arms. Jackson climbed inside and helped Dev lift Payton into the airlock.

Dev latched the hatch shut, taking Payton from Nyle's view. He heard Jackson's voice begging Payton to open her eyes.

Nyle fell to his knees, breathing hard. "Don't let her be sick. Please, let her be all right."

Yevgen appeared in the doorway to stare out at the ship. The cyborg girl tried to follow him.

"Get back inside with the others, little Payton," Yevgen told the girl. "I can tell you're going to be an adventurous handful just like your namesake."

Nyle ignored them, choosing to stare at the hatch as he listened for signs of what was happening inside the ship.

32

Payton opened her eyes and felt the warmth of lasers moving over her body. The familiar sensation of the medical booth automatically told her she was back on the ship. Soft vibrations indicated that the ship was in flight.

"What happened?" she asked.

"There you are," Nyle appeared next to her. "You're all right. We ran all the tests. You're not infected."

"Infected?" Payton pushed at the lid, trying to get out of the booth. It didn't open. "The last thing I remember is talking to Yevgen and then trying to leave."

"Your suit was damaged when you jumped in front of the laser blast to save me." Nyle stared at her. The utter relief was evident in his expression as he reached in to cup her cheek. "I thought I had lost you. I could not have survived if I had lost you."

"I know exactly how you feel." Peyton smiled at him. "Now get me out of this damned thing."

"Just a minute more. It is almost finished with the latest scan." Nyle withdrew his hand as the lasers came close to her face.

"How many scans have I had?" she asked.

"Twelve," he answered. "We wanted to make sure you were unharmed."

"Let me out," she insisted.

Instead, Nyle went to the control console to use the comms. "She's awake."

"About time, starshine," Rick said.

"Patching through the palace now," Jackson added.

"Welcome back," Dev said.

"Palace?" Payton leaned to look at Nyle.

"Your mother has been waiting in the Var control tower for news," Nyle said.

"Payton?" Her mother's voice practically screamed from the comms on top of the booth. "Are you there?"

"Hey, I'm all right," Payton soothed. "The booth has cleared me multiple times. We're all good."

"Bless the stars. You have got to stop scaring us like this," Samantha scolded. "What's this nonsense about you not coming home?"

"Is that Payton? Ask her if she knows what's up with the computers," her uncle Quinn's voice sounded farther away. "All the dignitary meetings have been wiped out of the system for something called Prince Yevgen Day."

"That's not all," King Kirill added, "messages with inappropriate limericks have been popping up for you."

"Not now," Samantha scolded before shooing the men away. "I'm talking to my daughter."

"I can't come home," Payton tried to explain. "Nyle..."

The booth beeped, and the lid lifted to let her out.

"Yes," Samantha stated. "Rick filled us in. The Federation accidentally executed a Var prince. We've already been in contact with them over it. Trust me. They're not coming back for Nyle. They're not coming back for a long time. They'll be lucky to get that blasted ore shipment they want so badly."

Payton slipped out of the booth. Nyle was instantly next to her, holding her in his arms. She dropped her head against his shoulder and sighed in relief.

"So it's really over?" Payton insisted, hardly able to believe it.

Nyle nodded.

"It's over," her mother said.

"Tell her we're coming home," Nyle said.

Payton looked at him and mouthed, "Are you sure?"

He nodded.

"Mother, I'll talk to you when we get home," Payton said. "And tell everyone to get ready to celebrate. I'm officially going to introduce you to my life mate, Prince Nyle."

"Full mate?" Samantha queried.

"Yes, full mate." Payton leaned up to kiss him. She heard more voices speaking as the crew answered Samantha's questions about their travel itinerary.

Payton led Nyle from the medical booth toward their private quarters.

"You didn't tell her goodbye," he said.

"She'll get the hint when I stop answering." Payton kissed him again before moving to study his handsome face. She could gaze into his eyes for the rest of her life and be completely content. "Are you sure you're all right living on Qurilixen? We don't have to. As long as I am with you, I am happy."

"I'm tired of living in the stars," Nyle said. "I want a home. With you. And you're happiest with your family. Besides, the parasite ship thing has been bothering me. I want to update the planetary security. It shouldn't be as easy as it is to sneak on-world."

"I'm happiest with you, Nyle," she corrected. "I love you, my husband. You are all I ever want. This is all I ever need."

She ran her fingers into his hair, feeling the soft texture of it against her skin as she pulled his mouth to hers, intent on never letting go.

The soft vibrations of the ship were nothing compared to the steady beat of his heart. The road to this moment was far from perfect. She had made a lot of mistakes but none of that mattered. He was her husband. She was his wife. And they were forever.

The End

MEET PAYTON'S PARENTS

Keep Reading!
Find out about Payton's Parents

Lords of the Var®: The Bound Prince

Nominated for the Romantic Times
Reviewers' Choice Award!

While completing an intergalactic scavenger hunt with her crew, Captain Samantha Dorsey finishes up the list by capturing a wild beast. But she doesn't realize that the cat she just snagged is actually Falke, a sexy warrior prince...

"Fun, emotional, and full of wonderful characters" (*RT Book Reviews*).

Cat shifter Prince Falke commands the royal armies, so it's a little embarrassing when a beautiful female space captain captures him in his shifter form. Since they left his home planet and no one would know where to send a rescue party, it's up to him to use all his training and powers of persuasion to find his way back home.

Captain Samantha Dorsey and her space crew are on a mission to complete a intergalactic scavenger hunt and claim the prize money. Drunk and feeling like some fun, they snag the last thing on their list–a primitive wild beast. The next morning she realizes that they got more than they bargained for... a sexy warrior prince. And he doesn't look pleased.

ABOUT MICHELLE M. PILLOW

New York Times & *USA TODAY*
Bestselling Author

Michelle loves to travel and try new things, whether it's a paranormal investigation of an old Vaudeville Theatre or climbing Mayan temples in Belize. She believes life is an adventure fueled by copious amounts of coffee.

Newly relocated to the American South, Michelle is involved in various film and documentary projects with her talented director husband. She is mom to a fantastic artist. And she's managed by a dog and cat who make sure she's meeting her deadlines.

For the most part she can be found wearing pajama pants and working in her office. There may or may not be dancing. It's all part of the creative process.

Come say hello! Michelle loves talking with readers on social media!

www.MichellePillow.com

facebook.com/AuthorMichellePillow

x.com/michellepillow

instagram.com/michellempillow

bookbub.com/authors/michelle-m-pillow

goodreads.com/Michelle_Pillow

amazon.com/author/michellepillow

youtube.com/michellepillow

pinterest.com/michellepillow

5 stars! "I love how they treat their women."

Cat-shifting King Kirill knows he must do his royal duty by his people. When his father unexpectedly dies, it's his destiny to take the throne and all of the responsibility that entails. What he hadn't prepared for is the troublesome female prisoner he inherited.

Undercover Agent Ulyssa is no man's captive. Trapped in a primitive alien forest awaiting pickup, she's going to make the best out of a bad situation… which doesn't include falling for the seductions of an alpha male king.